The Good Life

The Good Life

Dorian Sykes

www.urbanbooks.net

Urban Books, LLC
300 Farmingdale Road, NY-Route 109
Farmingdale, NY 11735

ISBN 13: 978-1-64556-169-9
ISBN 10: 1-64556-169-0

First Mass Market Printing March 2021
First Trade Paperback Printing July 2020
Printed in the United States of America

10 9 8 7 6 5 4 3 2 1

Distributed by Kensington Publishing Corp.
Submit Orders to:
Customer Service
400 Hahn Road
Westminster, MD 21157-4627
Phone: 1-800-733-3000
Fax: 1-800-659-2436

Acknowledgments

Family

First, my loving **Mother**. You're my heart, and you know it. Always on time, and always sending God my way when I need it the most. My **Auntie Janice,** who's been my angel since coming home. I'm grateful God put us together. When the chips were down, you put 'em up! Nothing but love for believing in me. **Aunt Karen**, my heart. **Nephew**, so happy to be home. I'm taking your advice, doing the right thing. Unc **(Gene)** for always giving it to me straight, even when I didn't wanna hear it. You've been like a father to me my entire life. Both my cousins, **Justin** and **E.T.**, y'all were down with me, and I trust y'all will stay down.

Industry

Richard Jeanty, respect a million times over for mentoring me and continuously pushing me in the right direction. **Kevin Chiles,** for being a solid guy about the struggle.

Ms. Michel Moore, special thanks for not hesitating to embrace me as I chase down these dreams. You had a hand in making this happen, and I'm forever grateful. Last but not least, my devoted readers. Here's another one! Thanks for the continued support and helping my dreams become reality!

Prologue

June 1988

Just like every other major city back in '88, Detroit fought hard to be crowned the murder capital of the world as the crack epidemic spread like wildfire, taking a strong hold of the city and a vast number of its residents. Bodies were dropping in numbers, as up-and-coming drug dealers went to war over territory. Drive-by shootings had become the norm, and innocent people were caught in the crossfire, often being killed. It was just a total disaster and a setback for the once-striving, predominately black city. Almost overnight, Detroit went from being ole Motown, the home of Motown Records and the birth of the auto industry, to a widespread battlefield. It was a prison for the still law-abiding citizens who remained.

The rise of crack and its availability not only sprung the murder rate, but also the level of theft and robberies. These crimes were often committed by crackheads against people who had nothing to do with the life of the underworld that engulfed them. Detroit had become known as Murder City instead of Motown. All sorts of government programs, such as Ronald Reagan's "Just Say No" War on Drugs campaign sprang into action, but to no avail. Crack was everywhere, and there to stay for a long time.

Within this mayhem, Wink plotted how he would get into the drug game and take it over. He had grand plans and aspirations, but one problem existed—he didn't know a single thing about selling crack. He didn't know where it came from, how to make it, or who was supplying it. He'd seen the empty, tiny-size packets, which once contained rocks of cocaine, scattered on the sidewalks and curbs of his neighborhood, but he'd never seen an actual rock. It was crazy because something called "crack" was taking over his city, and yet he had never even laid eyes on it.

Wink was seventeen and fresh out of high school. He'd graduated by the hair on his face, which was slim to none. He was a baby-faced, light brown–skinned, tall and lanky nigga. He wore a high-top fade and cuts in his eyebrows. His mom worked at GM, and as the only child, he pretty much got whatever he wanted. The problem was he wanted it all, which was why, when he saw all the drug dealers with their expensive cars and clothes, Wink knew he had to get in on the game.

School was out, and so was all the fun stuff he and his crew used to do prior to the crack era. All the things they enjoyed coming up—roller skating, break dancing, house parties—ceased to exist when crack hit the scene. Niggas went from being B-Boys to D-Boys. All the B-Boy crews were now full-fledged drug crews, each trying to reinvent themselves as gangsters. Niggas were funny like that, though. One day they were standing on the corner in a circle, breakdancing with the boom box on; the next day, they were on that same corner with fully automatic Uzis, selling crack.

"Oh, you still breakin'! That's some li'l boy shit," dudes would say of the ones not yet in the game. Pretty soon, all the youngin's were standing out there, trying to establish a reputation as a crew. It wasn't even about the money, for real, because money was coming in hand over fist. It was about power.

Wink's crew was the last crew to get on board, and he felt behind. He went to the barber shop and cut that goofy-ass high-top fade, let his eyebrows grow back, while he plotted and watched. The first thing he had to learn about the game was who was supplying the crack, or *work*, as niggas started calling it. His first mission didn't take long. All he had to do was observe everybody. For a week straight, all he did was sit on the porch and watch the traffic come and leave. Niggas serving crackheads, police chasing niggas down the block, the raid van jumping out in the middle of the block: all these were mental notes for Wink when he finally got in the game. College hadn't crossed his mind. Despite his mom's protest, he told her not to waste her money because he wasn't going to college. Wink's mind was set on the streets. Cars, money, women, and clothes were all he could dream about.

Everything Wink wanted and dreamed of having, J-Bo already had times ten. J-Bo had to be the first nigga in Detroit to start selling crack. He was getting down in '85 and '86, when the Chambler brothers came up from Arkansas. He wasn't personally fucking with them or even necessarily getting on through them, but he was around and on deck, making noise. Everybody and they mamma knew who J-Bo was. He had seven Porsches, same exact car, but different colors. Minks, gators, Rolex . . .

you name it, J-Bo had it. He was probably the first one you'd ever seen with the shit on.

Wink had never personally met J-Bo. Two words were never exchanged between them. But growing up as a shorty, you idolize certain niggas in the game, and Wink idolized J-Bo. He wanted everything he had, starting with the fire engine red Porsche he'd just hit the block in. When J-Bo hit the block, everything stopped so that niggas and bitches could give him his props. But that's not only why J-Bo came down Charest every day. He came to personally collect his ends from all the workers. That way, it would never be a discrepancy on the strength of the money touching too many hands.

It was evident who was supplying the work. Now all Wink had to do was figure out a way to cut into ole J-Bo.

"Wayne, you comin' to eat?" asked Hope as she stepped out onto the front porch.

"I'll be in later," said Wink. His mom was the only one who called him by his real name.

"You out here watching these bums sell that shit. I know one thing. If ya ass thinking about trying to join them, you won't be living under this damn roof," snapped Hope.

"Ma . . ."

"Don't *Ma* me. If you ain't goin' to school, ya ass need to find a job until you figure out what you doin' with ya life." Hope had no idea that her one and only son had already figured out what he'd major in: selling crack. And there was nothing she could say or do to stop him.

Wink had blocked his mother's bitchin' out. His idol was barking orders, and niggas were listening. J-Bo climbed back in his new Porsche and started its turbo engine. He shifted the gears, peeling away from the curb.

Wink's head followed the red blur down the street until J-Bo made a right on Emory.

I gotta get in the game, thought Wink. He could see himself pushing a Porsche of his own, with diamond rings on each finger, on his way down to Belle Isle to show it all off.

"You hear me talkin' to you, Wayne?" Hope said as she slapped the back of Wink's head.

"Ah, what?"

"I said to get in the house. These niggas aren't looking right. I can tell something's about to happen, and I'm not catching somebody else's bullet."

"I'm okay, Ma. I'm seventeen. I can handle myself."

"Wayne, I said to get in the house. I don't want to see anything happen to you." Hope held the door open as Wink reluctantly got up.

He knew his mom didn't mean any harm. She loved him to death and would do anything for him. But Wink was set on being the next big thing to come out of Detroit since Cadillac, and crack was going to get him there.

Chapter One

Trey pulled up in his mom's new Honda Civic, blasting EPMD's "Strictly Business." He hit the horn twice, then jumped out, leaving the car running. Wink turned in his seat on the sofa and pulled back the blinds. He stood up and met Trey at the front door.

"What up, doe," said Trey, extending his hand for a pound. His high yellow face was pulled back into a smile, obviously happy about something.

"Chillin'. Fuck you smilin' so hard for, and why you all dressed up?" asked Wink as he walked back into the living room and took a seat on the sofa.

"Don't tell me you forgot," said Trey as he patted his flat top in the mirror mounted above the fireplace.

"Today's the senior picnic. I thought I told you," he said, turning to face Wink.

"You probably did. But I'm not going."

"Why not? Do you know how many chicks is gon' be on the Rock, all ready to do whatever?"

"That shit ain't going nowhere. It's all gon' be there."

"What's up with you lately? First you cut your fade off, now you talkin' 'bout it's gon' be there. What's gon' be there?"

Wink lifted a magazine from the coffee table, revealing ten dime rocks packaged in plastic packs.

"You're still on that shit?" asked Trey as to say he wasn't impressed. "Where'd you get that from?"

"That's not important. What's important is that it's going to make us rich."

"Wink, what do you know about what you holding? It's more to it than what you think."

"You're right, and that's why I'm gon' learn all there is to know. This right here is just an experiment to get our feet wet."

"You keep saying *we* like I agreed to this. Tell me this, where you plan on sellin' that shit at?"

"Right here. We're from this block."

"And you think J-Bo's gon' go for that?"

Wink smiled. "We'll cross that bridge when we get there." That was his whole plan. He hoped J-Bo would say something to him about being on the block. He would use that conversation when it took place as his means to cut into J-Bo.

"I wish you'd leave that shit alone and come to the picnic with me."

"Then what? When we get back, then what?"

"What you mean?"

"What are we gonna do for the rest of the summer, ride around faking? Going to the same clubs, breakdancin'? Trey, we ain't kids no more. It's time to get this money, and this is the best thing going," said Wink as he raised one of the crack packs up like it was gold.

"So, you're not going to the picnic?"

"Fuck that picnic. If you had any sense, you'd say fuck it too and put your money with mine's and get on."

"I'm straight."

There was a pound at the front door. Wink covered the rocks with the magazine, then stood up. Before he could get the door, Krazy walked right in with Willie on his heels.

"What I tell you about walkin' in my crib like that, huh?" asked Wink.

"I ain't try'na hear that shit. What's up? Y'all niggas ready to hit the rock?" asked Krazy, walking around Wink.

You could look in Krazy's eyes and see where he got his nickname. He tried to live up to his name every chance he got. He was always down for everything.

"Why you not dressed, Wink?" asked Willie.

"He says he's not going," informed Trey.

"What? Why not?" asked Willie.

"He wants to be the next Butch Jones," Trey said, hitting up on the magazine.

"Now, this what we 'pose to be doing," said Krazy. He picked up one of the rocks. He was all too familiar with the sky-blue clear pack. He had found a thousand empty ones just like it lying around his house. His moms was strung out on crack.

"Not you too," said Trey.

"You know how much money these niggas is out there making? All the other crews gettin' money except us. We the only ones still runnin' around doing the same shit we was doing last summer," said Wink.

"You ain't gotta tell me, my nigga. I already know the business," said Krazy.

"Can we kick it about this later after we come from the picnic?" asked Trey.

"Y'all go 'head. I gotta take care of something," said Wink.

"Yo, Wink, I'm with you, my nigga. Make sure you put me down," said Krazy.

"Me too," said Willie, always one to follow along. There were leaders and followers. Willie belonged to the latter group.

"What about you?" Wink asked Trey.

"I'ma see what's up," Trey said, not wanting to seem soft in front of the crew.

Wink walked them to the door and gave them all pounds. "Tomorrow, come through and we gon' chop it up on how we gon' get this money."

"Stay up, my nigga," they all said.

Wink watched as they piled into Trey's mom's Civic and peeled off. He hoped Trey would eventually come around once he saw how easy it was to make the money. Trey was his best friend, and Wink wanted him by his side, making money too. They were both spoiled rotten by their moms. Only difference was Wink had more heart. He was willing to try his hand at new things, while Trey just wanted to continue being spoiled and ride around flossing in his mom's car. But Wink felt it was time to grow up and start holding they own nuts. So, in order to get them up and running, he'd have to be the one to show his crew the ropes. The only problem was he had to learn the game himself.

Wink looked across the street at Ms. Bowers' house. All her grandkids were drug dealers out there pumpin' for J-Bo, and in return, J-Bo would hit Ms. Bowers off with a cut of the money made. Her crib sat in the center of the block, directly across the street from Wink's house. Ms. Bowers' crib was the central office of all the drug activities. Her grandchildren would stand in the drive-way, making sales as customers pulled up. They stashed their dope sacks on the sides of houses in empty potato chip bags or under any other garbage, so if the raid team pulled up, nobody would be found with drugs in their possession.

Wink was catching on quick. It was time to test his hand at pitching. He went inside the house to grab the ten dime rocks he'd bought from Ms. Bowers' grandson, Cedd, the night before. Wink was trying to buy some weight, but nobody would sell him any. They knew he was green to the game, so Cedd made him pay like he owed the game. He charged Wink one hundred dollars for ten dime rocks, no deal, no nothin'. Straight up dollar for dollar. Wink couldn't argue because he didn't even know what type of deal he wanted, and all he had was a little over a hundred dollars to his name. For real, Wink didn't care about making a profit. He just wanted the experience of being out there on the block, pitching. The money would come later, he told himself.

Hope, Wink's mom, was at work and would be until midnight, so he had all day to scratch the block. He locked up the house and started down the stairs. Crackheads were pulling up on the block left and right, copping and going. Cedd and his brother, Small-man, had the block on lock. Cedd would line the cars up like it was a fast food joint. He'd wave each car forward, taking the money first, then hand signaling Small-man their order. They had the shit moving like an assembly line out that mothafucka.

Wink already knew posting up in front of Ms. Bowers' crib was out of the question. He had to find his own spot to set up shop. Wink walked up the block while watching the constant traffic. The majority of the customers were white people coming all the way down from the suburbs to get those little white-and-yellow rocks that everybody was going crazy over. Wink wondered exactly how much money each one of them crackers was spending.

For them to drive a country mile, he knew they weren't spending no ten or twenty dollars.

At the corner of 7 Mile and Charest sat an old automotive shop. Out of all the years Wink had been living on Charest, he had never once seen the shop open, so he figured it would be the best place to set up shop. He dug inside his pocket and pulled out the quarter-size bag of ranch Ruffles where he had the ten rocks. He scanned the side of the shop for a stash spot, then put the bag inside the aged mailbox and walked up to the bus stop. After watching the traffic for a few days, Wink knew every customer by face and car, so it wouldn't be hard to spot them when they drove past.

A matter of seconds passed before he recognized a battered burgundy pickup. Wink flagged the white man down before he could turn the corner.

"Woo, I got you right here. What you need, my man?" asked Wink.

"Since when y'all start doing things up here?" asked the older white man as he suspiciously looked Wink over a few times.

"Things change every day. You coppin' or what?" Wink shot back at the man while leaning inside the passenger-side window.

The man unfolded a fifty-dollar bill and said, "I don't want no funny business."

"You gonna get the same stuff you been getting. Just pull over in the alley right there." He raced over to the mailbox and poured five rocks into the palm of his hand. He tossed the bag back inside the box and rushed around to the back of the shop.

"Here you go," he said, handing the man his order.

"Looks the same. A'ight, see you later," the man said, pulling away.

Wink was so geeked that he had to take another look at the fifty-dollar bill. His first sale in the game, and it was for fifty dollars. He thought about having it framed 'cause he knew there'd be plenty more where that came from.

Two more cars turned the corner. Wink let the first car pass and flagged the blue Fiesta down.

"Pull in the alley," Wink said, waving his hand.

"In the alley? You bet' not be try'na rob me, 'cause I'ma fight 'bout mine's," the no-teeth, nappy-neck woman said before she buzzed into the alleyway.

"What you got, baby girl?" Wink asked, leaning into the driver-side window.

"Twenty. Make sure they're two nice ones," she said, handing Wink a sweaty twenty.

He looked at the faded bill on his way to the mailbox and wondered how many hands that same bill went through already. He tucked the money in his pimp pocket on his Guess jeans and then raised the lid on the box. He hadn't seen J-Bo approaching the block, coming from Gallagher Street. Wink closed the mailbox and walked around back to the alley.

"Thank you, baby," said the woman. She didn't waste no time packing her pipe and taking a hit right there in the alley.

Wink watched the woman's reactions like a first grader at the zoo. Her eyes bucked the size of silver dollars, as she held the smoke in for as long as she could before blowing out a stank cloud of crack smog. The smell made Wink's stomach turn over. He backed away from the car with his hand over his face.

"Damn," he said, fanning the stench.

The woman finally buzzed off down the alley. When Wink turned around, there sat J-Bo in his yellow 924 Porsche, just sitting there, staring dead at him. Wink got to the end of the alley and tried not making direct eye contact with J-Bo, but he hit his horn.

"Com'ere, young dawg," Ordered J-Bo with a wave.

The moment Wink had been waiting on had arrived sooner than he thought. He played it cool and walked over to the driver's side.

"What you doin' out here?" asked J-Bo.

"The same thing everybody else is out here doing, Try'na eat," answered Wink.

J-Bo sorta liked the young nigga's answer because he didn't lie, but he didn't like the fact that the young nigga didn't show any signs of fear.

"You know who I am?" asked J-Bo.

"I've heard of you here and there. Why? What's up?" asked Wink.

"Then you know this my block. This whole hood is mine's, and everything in it."

Again, Wink showed no sign of fear. This made J-Bo angry because he had put so much work in to keep every nigga in line, and now some youngin' wasn't recognizing his authority. The last thing he needed was for a renegade to sprout up. Next thing you know, everybody would be on renegade time, bucking J-Bo's system to getting money.

J-Bo pulled over and got out. "I think we got off on the wrong foot," he started, extending his hand for Wink's. "What's ya name?"

"Wink."

"I'm J-Bo, as you may know. Don't you stay down the street?"

"Yeah, across from Ms. Bowers."

"I thought you looked familiar. Anyway, check this out, young dawg. I saw what you were doin', and that shit can't happen again."

"What, me try'na get some money, or me sellin' in the alley?"

"Both. Come on. Let's walk down to the corner," said J-Bo. They started walking, and he continued speaking. "You can't be out here, especially not in the alley. That's a sure way to bring the cops around here. There's a reason why I got things centered in the middle of the block. What I just saw you doing is called short-stoppin', and it can get you killed out here."

"By who?"

J-Bo laughed, then stopped to face Wink. "Young dawg, when somebody kills you, the last thing you're going to be worried about is who. Hopefully we understand each other that I won't see you back out here on my block again."

"J-Bo, with all due respect, I grew up on this block. Born and raised. How can you or any other nigga tell me I can't get money out here?"

"I'm not tellin' you. I'm warning you. Young dawg, I don't know what you think this shit is out here, but it ain't a game. What, you woke up this morning and just decided that you were going to sell drugs? It don't work like that."

"Then how does it work? Why don't you teach me, because I'm gon' get some of this money."

J-Bo had to laugh. He held a smile while he looked Wink over. He reminded him so much of himself, thirsty and eager to learn the game. But just as fast as the smile appeared, it vanished. "You have to first learn the game before anything. Then once you do that, you have to stack yo' own money. Then find you a spot you can call your own and get your own clientele. You see," J-Bo said, raising his hands and spinning around in a circle. "You see, this is mine's, and I will do what's necessary to protect it. If you ever make it this far in the game, you'll feel the same way, and only then will you understand."

Wink soaked up every word. He'd never listened to any of his teachers at school as intently as he was listening to J-Bo. He couldn't believe that he was actually standing there, having a face-to-face talk about the game with his idol.

"Let me see what you're out here workin'," said J-Bo.

Wink raced to the mailbox and came back with the last three rocks. He poured them into J-Bo's palm for him to inspect.

"Where'd you get these from? They look like some of mine's."

"That's like tellin', ain't it?" asked Wink.

"Sho' is. I was just testin' to see if you'd tell something. That's the first rule of the game, No snitchin'."

Wink nodded at this. He waited for further instructions, anything. As long as it was coming from his idol, it was good as gold.

"Come on and take a ride with me. I'ma take you up under my wing," said J-Bo.

Wink damn near shouted; he was so excited. To be in J-Bo's presence was enough, but to ride shotgun in his

Porsche was some other shit. Every head on the block turned as J-Bo blew past with Wink shotgun.

"We'll go downtown and cruise Belle Isle," said J-Bo.

"That's cool," said Wink. He was hoping they'd bump into his crew so they could see him doing it big with J-Bo. Wink told himself that he could get used to this, and he was ready to put in whatever work he had to.

Chapter Two

Wink didn't sleep the whole night. He stayed up thinking about all the fancy cars he would buy, all the pretty girls who'd throw themselves at his feet, and all the money, fame, and jewelry he'd have. J-Bo rode him around the night before, schooling him to little things, giving up the basics of the game, but nothing too serious. He told Wink he'd have to work, earn, and learn what all he wanted to know. It was called paying dues. He told him that the game was there, you just had to pay attention.

J-Bo had no plans on making things easy for Wink. He wanted to show him that it was more to the game than just fast cars and fast money. To be successful in the game, you had to be a thinker. The ability to think on your toes would be the deciding factor of whether you were going to be a boss or worker. You had to be a people person first and foremost because, you were going to be dealing with people from all walks of life. J-Bo told him just because a person smoked crack didn't mean they were less of a man or woman. It just meant that they liked the high. You still had to treat them with respect.

He also said you had to be respected. Niggas had to know without a shadow of a doubt that you'd bust they wig if they played with you or your money. J-Bo told him the importance of growth, saving his money, and having lawyers' fees put to the side. He gave him what he needed to know in order to survive, but Wink would have to earn the tools he needed in order to become the infamous drug lord he dreamed of.

He sat on the living room sofa, watching the hand of the clock mounted on the wall. Time wasn't moving fast enough, and neither was his crew. He had called Trey, Willie, and Krazy over an hour ago, and still no show. Had he made mention about having some hood rats over, they would have flown their asses over like they did about the picnic.

Fuck it, though, Wink thought as he stood up. He wasn't about to let nothing or no one stop him from getting what was his. J-Bo said he'd be by to pick him up so they could go check out one of his new crack houses on the Westside. He wanted Wink to help him open it.

"Where are you going this early on a Saturday?" Hope caught Wink on his way out the front door.

"Uh . . ."

"Don't you lie to me, Wayne. I know it's not no damn job interview, which is where you need to be carrying yo'self to."

"I love you too, Ma," Wink said, kissing his mom on the cheek. "I'll be back. I'ma walk around to Trey's."

"I need you to help me around the house later, moving this furniture, so don't stand me up," said Hope, following Wink out on to the porch. She stood at the landing and watched her son walk down the street. She wasn't no fool, and her intuition alone told her Wayne was up to something, but what?

Wink heard the sounds of McBreed blasting. It was J-Bo bending the block in his triple-white 500 SEC Benz. Wink looked over his shoulder and thanked God his mother was already gone in the house.

J-Bo slowed down and pulled over to the curb. As always, he was looking like a cool million. He had the top missing on the Benz, the chrome deep dish hammers were blinding in the sun, and the cocaine white interior set J-Bo's black skin off like the moon at night. He gripped the wheel with one hand and let the other drape out the window with his 18-karat gold Rolex gleaming.

"You ready?" asked J-Bo.

"Yeah," said Wink. His stomach was in a nervous knot as he prayed that his Ma Dukes wasn't looking out the window.

"Yo, Wink!" Krazy yelled from the end of the block. He broke into a sprint, trying to catch up.

"Who's that?" asked J-Bo.

"One of my guys I was tellin' you about yesterday. I don't know where the other two are at."

Krazy caught up to the Benz before J-Bo pulled off. "What up, doe," he said, a little out of breath. He broke down, putting his hands on his knees.

"You rollin'?" asked J-Bo.

"Yeah, just let me catch my breath."

"Let's go, youngin'. Time is my money," said J-Bo.

Wink leaned his seat forward, letting Krazy climb in the back seat. He was so tall and built that he had to sit sideways.

"J-Bo, this my man Krazy," said Wink.

J-Bo met eyes with Krazy in the rearview mirror, and they nodded. He put the car in drive and pulled away from the curb. Wink kept his head turned until they passed his house. He could hear his mom's loud-ass voice in his head, calling after the car, ordering him to get out. They made it down the street without Hope embarrassing Wink.

J-Bo didn't say two words the entire drive. He was done talking. School was in session, and the only way to learn was through experience. All heads turned, and the frivolous conversations ceased as J-Bo cruised down Linwood Ave. People stopped and waved. Crackheads tried flagging the legend down to plead their individual cases as to why they needed some credit and that they were good for it.

J-Bo was known and respected all over Detroit, and as a result, he could go anywhere and would be welcomed with open arms. As he told Wink, he was a people person. Everybody loved J-Bo. He had an aura larger than life, and everybody wanted to latch on to something great. That was the secret behind his success. Success brought more success.

They pulled up in front of this nearby condemned two-family flat on Linwood and Arlington. It sat on the corner right across the street from an old penny candy store called Mr. Kennedy's. Wink looked up at the brick castle and hoped this wasn't the new spot J-Bo told him about yesterday. Two women with faded silk scarves wrapped around their 'do's leaned out two upstairs windows, while old musty-lookin' black men lined the front porch, all staring down at the Benz.

"Come on," J-Bo said, pulling on the door handle.

"Fuck we at, South Africa 'round this mothafucka?" Krazy joked as they climbed out the car.

"I know, right?" agreed Wink. He and Krazy fell two steps behind J-Bo.

It sounded like the floor on Wall Street going up the steps to the porch. All the crackheads went crazy, trying to put their bids in. Some were tussling over who'd hold the door open for J-Bo. It was like the return of Jesus.

J-Bo stopped and asked, "Where's Gator?"

"Should be around here somewhere," answered one of the crackheads in hopes that his information might get him off crap and J-Bo would throw him a bone. There was no such thing as free with J-Bo. You had to spend some money first, and lots of it, before he even thought about blessing you with a lookout.

"If you see him, send him upstairs," said J-Bo.

He led the way inside the muggy house and up the staircase leading to the upstairs unit. Surprisingly, the unit was nothing like the downstairs or the exterior. Fresh paint could be smelled as soon as they hit the door. Brand new but cheap furniture filled the place. There was a huge 52-inch flat screen in the living room. On top sat a brand-new Nintendo game system with a bunch of cartridges. A stereo system sat over in the corner. All the latest tapes filled its shelves.

"This shit almost looks as good as my house," said Wink, walking over to the chess board, which was perched on the coffee table.

"And that's the way it's 'pose to be," said J-Bo.

He watched Wink and Krazy as they both got comfortable. Krazy did everything except take his shoes off. He was going through the many cassette tapes, while Wink pretended to be knowing what he was doing on the glass chessboard. Nice and comfortable, that's how J-Bo wanted them. He had learned over the years that the best way to get somebody to sit in a crack house and stay put, they first had to want to stay put. So, J-Bo made the necessary investments to make his crack spots as comfortable as possible. His workers would be glued to the houses, all the while making him filthy rich!

"What you know about what you're sitting in front of?" asked J-Bo as he took a seat across from Wink.

"I know I'd beat you," Wink said with as much confidence he could muster.

So eager to learn, thought J-Bo. He pulled back a closed smile, then waved his hand across the board. "Your move."

Wink pushed his center pawn up two squares, only to me matched by J-Bo's. J-Bo matched Wink's every move, until all his pieces were scattered out across the board.

"I wouldn't make that move," advised J-Bo.

Wink shifted his hand from the knight he was about to move over to his rook.

"I wouldn't make that move either," warned J-Bo.

Wink made a frivolous move, pushing his queen next to J-Bo's. J-Bo moved in for the kill, bypassing Wink's queen and taking his bishop instead.

"You see what I see? That's checkmate," said J-Bo.

Wink looked the board over in complete disbelief.

"Don't worry yourself about that. You lost before you even made your first move," said J-Bo.

"Run it back," said Wink. He turned the board around and hurriedly went to setting up the pieces, but J-Bo stopped him.

J-Bo just smiled. "You don't get it, do you?"

"Get what?" asked Wink.

"Look at the board." J-Bo waited a few moments, then continued. "You see how all your pieces are scattered out? Your king was left vulnerable. You see, young dawg, in this game we play, every man has to be his own king, and we gotta learn to use everything and everybody around us to get to where we trying to go, and that's to the top. Everybody around me is like a piece on this board, and some less, including you. You got the basics down, how the pieces move, but now you've gotta learn how to use them to protect you."

Wink nodded in agreement while looking down at the chess board.

"You see, I'm not no chess wizard, but I know how to play the game. I know the rules and each piece's purpose. What you just did is sat down and jumped into a game head first, not knowing how to win the game. And the same goes for this street game you just jumped into. You gotta learn the game. Don't be so eager to play. Watch and learn. I'ma ask you one last thing, then we can get down to business. What piece do you think you are on the board?"

"Right now, I'd say a pawn," said Wink.

"Not quite, but at least you didn't say a king. I'd let you know when you're a pawn," said J-Bo. He turned to face Krazy, who was standing in front of the stereo system violently rocking back and forth to the new Dayton Family LP.

"What's his name?"

"Krazy," said Wink.

"Yo, Krazy, turn that down and take a seat."

J-Bo stood up and started pacing the floor in front of the coffee table. He occasionally looked Wink and Krazy in the eye as he explained the breakdown. "Under no circumstances are you to give anyone credit. I don't give a fuck if Jesus Christ co-sign the shit. Don't do it. All shorts come out of y'all pay, not mine. No company. This is a place of business, not a chill house or hangout. If they're not coppin', no stoppin'." J-Bo continued to pace while he jogged his brain. He wanted to make sure he covered everything, so there would be no excuses.

"Oh, yeah. Always separate mine's from yours. I'm putting the work in your hand, Wink, and you're responsible for it. I'ma pay y'all a thousand a week starting off, and the more we sell, the more you'll start making. It's on y'all how you split the grand up."

"What about the police?" asked Wink.

"There's a hole right here," J-Bo said, walking over to the fireplace. He lifted the wooden panel and stepped aside for Wink and Krazy to see.

"If there's a raid, just throw everything down this hole. All the money and dope. I'll have Gator dig it out the chimney later."

"What about if a nigga tries to rob us?" asked Krazy. "We need some heat."

"Ain't a nigga in his right mind gon' rob none of my spots. Just remember, separate mine's from yours. When one of y'all leave for the store or something, don't be carrying mine's with you.

"Nah," said Wink. He and Krazy were too busy looking over their first sack.

"J-Bo, you up here?" asked Gator as he hit the door twice, then stepped inside.

J-Bo hid the sack behind one of the throw pillows on the sofa, then met Gator in the kitchen.

"I got some youngin's I want you to meet," said J-Bo as he walked Gator into the living room.

"This is Wink and Krazy. Y'all, this is Gator."

"A'ight," said Wink and Krazy. From one glance, they could tell how the old, dusty, skinny man standing before them got his handle. He had a mean overbite, which made it impossible to close his mouth. His side teeth hung over his bottom lip just like a real-life gator.

"Gator is going to be bringing a lot of customers through here. He's my man, and this is his house, so respect him. But the no credit thing applies to him as well, no matter what he says," said J-Bo.

"I'm not going to work the youngin's," Gator spat as he lied through gapped teeth.

"Yeah, that's what you said about the last workers. Come on and walk me to my car. I got something for you." J-Bo stopped and looked at Wink and Krazy.

"Y'all need anything? Y'all straight?" he asked.

"We good," Wink answered for them both.

"A'ight, Gator got my number. Call me if something comes up. And remember everything I said."

Wink and Krazy nodded and watched as J-Bo led Gator downstairs. Wink reached behind the pillow and poured the rocks onto the coffee table. He looked up at Krazy, then extended his hand with a smile.

"We on, my nigga." He gave Krazy some dap then grabbed the house phone off the receiver. He couldn't wait to call Trey and let him know J-Bo had put them down.

Chapter Three

Six days had passed since J-Bo put Wink and Krazy up in the spot. In that short time, money was coming in hand over fist. Gator was bringing all kinds of crack-heads through the spot—white, black, whatever. Long as they had that green, Gator was bringing them.

Wink couldn't believe that some of the people who were coming through the spot were really crackheads. A lot of them had recently been turned out by the likes of slick-talkin' niggas like Gator. A lot of the turn-outs were young white women from the suburbs. Gator would gladly assist them in spending their checks, then smoking half of their shit with them. After they ran out of money, he'd figure something else out for them to do. Gator had the women turning tricks for ten or twenty dollars, enough so they could continue their crack binge. Wink and Krazy had become the women's number one customers. Gator had tried every line in the book on them, trying to get some credit, but Wink wasn't falling for it. But the power of pussy still ruled the nation. Gator sicced the women on the two youngin's every chance he got, which had become the norm.

"Where you find her at?" asked Krazy as he leaned his head back against the back of the sofa. He was referring to the fine young white thang lying across his lap, giving him the best head job of his life.

Gator stood in front of the coffee table with this dumb grin pulled back across his face. He looked from right to left at Krazy, then Wink, who were both getting their little dicks sucked by two turn-outs, courtesy of Gator.

"That's right, baby. Turn they young asses out," said Gator. He turned toward the TV and picked up his pipe. He packed it with one of the dime rocks Wink just gave him for the head job, then sparked his lighter.

"That's enough," Wink said, lifting the white girl's face from his lap. He couldn't even bust a nut because the smell of burning crack made his stomach do a back flip. Wink got up and buckled his pants, all the while watching Gator beam up.

"Why you always smokin' that shit in the living room? That shit stank," Wink said as he walked around the table and stood next to Gator.

Gator was on cloud nine. He hadn't heard a single word Wink said. His eyes were bugged like a bullfrog, and his jaws were puffed out as he tried to contain the crack smog as long as possible.

"Let me hit it, baby," said Amy, the girl who'd been sucking Wink's dick. She took the pipe from Gator's death grip, then sparked the lighter.

Wink shook his head as he watched her join Gator on cloud nine. Wink grabbed Amy's car keys off the coffee table and set two more dime rocks on the table.

"I'ma shoot to the crib and take a shower. You need me to grab you anything?" Wink asked Krazy.

"Nah, I'm good," said Krazy. He was too lost in Kristy's mouthpiece.

"A'ight, well, you got the sack. I'll be back in about an hour." Wink grabbed EPMD's "Strictly Business" LP off the stereo and was out the door. He stepped outside into the beaming summer sun. Those six days of sitting in the spot felt like six days of being on lockdown. He hadn't washed his ass, brushed his teeth, or changed his clothes. To say the least, Wink was musty as a mothafucka.

He power-walked across the street to Amy's white Escort. In the six days he and Krazy had been over on Linwood, every crackhead within a ten-mile radius knew Wink's name. It made him smile as all the fiends shouted his name on the way to the car. They were all putting in bids for a lookout rock or some credit.

"Look out for me, baby boy," said Dennis as he stopped Wink at the car door. "Come on, baby boy. You know my word is good. I'll have yo' money by the time you get back," Dennis said, running his game down.

But Wink wasn't going for it. Instead, he spun Dennis. "Tell Krazy I said to hook you up. He's upstairs," said Wink. He hurried up and climbed behind the wheel and started the engine before Betty could cross the street. She was always begging but ain't never spent no money.

Wink skirted away from the curb, damn near blowing the clutch, as he was late coming out of first gear. The no-credit thing was about the only thing Wink had listened to from J-Bo's lecture on the game. He and Krazy had tricked off a bunch of money fucking with them crackhead bitches, and Wink wasn't doing like J-Bo said by separating his money from theirs. He wasn't even supposed to be leaving the spot unless it was to get something to eat. Even then, J-Bo felt like that's what Gator was there for.

But Wink not only wanted to go home so he could wash up; he wanted to ride down on Trey and Willie. Wink turned down Charest Street and leaned his seat back, trying to look cool. Nobody paid him any attention, though. Wink attributed that to him being in an Escort.

Just wait until I pull up in a Porsche, he thought.

Wink was glad to see his driveway empty. His mom's Pontiac Lemans wasn't in its spot, so he knew she wasn't home. The last thing Wink wanted to hear was his mother's bitching about where he'd been for the past six days.

He parked across the street and got out. Wink stood on the front porch, fiddling with his house keys when the front door swung open. He looked up like a deer caught in headlights. It was his mom, and she had her murda mask on.

"Ma, I thought you were—"

"What, that I was at work? Nah, I knew if I parked in the garage, ya ass would turn up!" snapped Hope.

Wink opened the screen and tried to walk inside the house, but his mom stood firm, blocking his path.

"You not gon' let me in?" asked Wink.

"Ya ass don't live here no more," said Hope, folding her arms.

"Ma, why are you trippin'?"

"I'm not the one trippin'. You stay gone for six days and don't even have the decency to call and say 'I'm okay. I'm alive.' You can go live with what's-his-name, J-Bo."

Wink's eyes got wide.

"Don't try and tell me no lies, boy. I already know he's got you selling that shit all these fools running around here losing their minds over. But ya ass won't be selling it under my roof."

Wink could hear the hurt in his mom's voice. Her eyes were glossy as if tears were just a blink away. Wink felt sorry for hurting his mom. All she wanted was the best for him.

"Can we talk about this inside?" asked Wink.

Hope pushed two trash bags in front of her with her foot. Wink looked down at the bags and knew it was real. His mom was really kicking him out. He looked up at Hope, and she had tears streaming down both cheeks.

"I can't watch you destroy yourself, Wayne. You don't want to get a job or go to school. All you want is what you see. Nothing," said Hope.

Wink was about to say something to try to calm his mom's nerves, but the figure standing behind her made his blood boil. It was Gary's dusty ass, Hope's on-and-off-again boyfriend. Wink hated Gary with all his might. Gary was a bum nigga who didn't work, hustle, or nothing. All he did was live off Hope, and Wink hated him for it. He felt like the nigga was using his mom.

"Yeah, Wayne. You gonna get yourself jammed up in some serious trouble messin' around out here in these streets," said Gary.

"Ain't nobody ask you nothin'," said Wink.

"You show him his respect," snapped Hope.

"Nigga ain't my daddy. You tellin' me to get a job when you need to be on his ass 'bout gettin' one."

Hope slapped the shit out of Wink. "You don't tell me what I should be doing. This is my house, and my man!" yelled Hope.

Wink staggered back, holding the side of his face. He pulled back a smile and stared at his mom. "And y'all two deserve each other," he said, then turned and headed down the stairs.

"Let him go," Wink heard Gary say, as he crossed the street.

Hope cried her eyes out into Gary's shoulder. She didn't really want to let Wink go because he was all she had.

Wink grimed Gary hard as he shifted the stick into first. The Escort jerked violently, then skirted away from the curb. Wink was furious that his mom would side with Gary. She always did, and Wink hated it because he felt like Gary was coming between them. Wink's hate for Gary only fueled his thirst to become the man in the game.

"Fuck that nigga. If she wants to be with him, then fuck it. I'ma do me," Wink said, trying to shake the thought of what just took place.

EPMD rattled loudly from the cheap factory speakers in the Escort. Wink crossed Outer Drive onto Gallagher Street. He could see Trey and Willie leaning against Trey's momma's Honda, talking to some hood rats. Wink parked across the street. He thought to himself that the first thing he'd buy would be a car. That was the second time he had pulled up and no one noticed him.

"What up, doe," Wink said, jumping out of the Escort. He crossed the street and gave Willie and Trey some dap.

"Ain't shit. Where that fool Krazy, and when can we get down?" asked Willie.

"Soon, my nigga. And Krazy's still at the spot," said Wink.

"I don't know why y'all keep talkin' this *we* shit. What we need to do is get our own shit," said Trey.

"Fuck what he talkin' 'bout. Put me in the game," said Willie.

"I got you."

"Hey, Wink," Cynthia and Martina said in unison.

"That's your car?" asked Martina.

"Nah, a rental."

"You gon' take me for a ride later?"

"We can do that," said Wink. He put his arm around Trey and pulled him away from the bunch. "Let me holla at you."

"Damn, you musty," said Trey, pulling Wink's arm from around his shoulder.

"That's what I need to holla at you about," Wink said, walking up Trey's sidewalk to the side door.

"What's up?" Trey asked, opening the door. He led the way down into the basement.

"My mom done found out I'm fuckin' with J-Bo."

"So, what she say?"

"She put me out."

"Word?"

"Yeah, she 'round there with that bitch-made nigga Gary. He all in my business," Wink said, pacing the floor.

"What you need me to do?"

"I need some clothes. I left all my shit over there. I don't want her to think I need shit."

"Why don't you just try to talk to yo' mom. You know she ain't gon' kick you to the curb for real."

"I don't know, my nigga. I ain't never seen my mom cry before. I think she's dead-ass serious."

"I got you, my nigga. You know where everything's at." Trey nodded to his dresser and closet.

"I don't need but two outfits. I'ma hit the mall up tomorrow when J-Bo pays us."

"Y'all making money like that over there?"

Wink stopped digging through the drawers and dug in both his pockets. He tossed Trey two bricks of money that had rubber bands wrapped around them. Trey caught one of the stacks. The other one hit the floor like a brick. Wink pretended to be focusing strictly on the clothes, but he couldn't help but see the amazement on Trey's face as he looked the stacks over. Trey fanned through the bills, seeing mostly twenties and some tens.

"You ready now?" asked Wink.

Trey tossed the stacks back to Wink and tried to play it off. He wanted to know how much it was. "I told you, Wink. I'm with it, but I'm not with workin' for no nigga. We can do our own thing."

"I feel you. But we need money to buy the coke. That shit ain't free. And we gotta have some-for-where to sell it. All I'm doin' right now is learning and stackin'. I'm not 'bout to be workin' for J-Bo for no long time, but I need you on my side. We can get this money together," Wink said, raising the two bricks of money.

"When?" asked Trey.

Wink pulled back a wide smile. He was happy that his best friend would be joining him.

"I'ma holla at J-Bo and see what's up."

"Just until we can get our own shit."

"We gon' be on top in no time," Wink said, extending his hand for Trey's. He pulled him in for an embrace.

"A'ight, now go wash yo' ass. You smell like hot baby shit," Trey snapped, ending their half-hug embrace.

"You got jokes, huh?" laughed Wink. He grabbed up the clean clothes and headed for the bathroom. He purposely left the stacks of money on Trey's dresser for him to finger-fuck and drool over. All Wink wanted for his crew was to be in the game and getting money. Now that Trey was down, it was officially on. They were about to come up!

Chapter Four

Wink finished showering and changed into some fresh clothes. He found Willie and Trey outside, still entertaining Cynthia and Martina.

"I'ma get up with y'all tomorrow," Wink said, giving Willie and Trey a pound.

"Don't forget to holla at ole boy for us. I'm try'na get down as soon as shit's ready," said Willie.

"I'ma say something to him. Tomorrow," said Trey.

"You still gon' take me for that ride?" asked Martina's hood-rat ass.

"Maybe later. I gotta handle something," said Wink as he crossed the street and jumped behind the wheel of the Escort.

He pumped up the sounds, then peeled away from the curb. Things were looking good in Wink's eyes. Tomorrow, he and Krazy would split a thousand dollars after grinding one long week out in the spot. Wink was already making plans for his half. He was gon' hit the mall up and cop the new Jordans, and the rest he was gon' save so he could buy his own work when the time came.

Wink's pleasant thoughts vanished as he crossed Outer Drive back onto his street. Hate and some more shit ran through his veins as he passed by his mom's house.

"I'ma show they ass," he said, shifting the stick into third gear. Within minutes, Wink was coming up on the

Chrysler Expressway on Linwood. He rode past the spot, and everything seemed to be normal, so he kept going. He knew it would be a long day and night in the spot, so he thought it best to get as much air as possible before going in.

He pulled into the parking lot of Hank's liquor store on Grand River and parked beside a fresh-to-death IROC Camaro. Four niggas, each sporting Jehri curls and thick gold rope chains, decorated the hood of the IROC. They were drinking forty-ounce Old English and just shootin' the shit when Wink got out the car.

Wink kind of nodded to the men on his way inside Hank's. The men didn't seem to be paying Wink any mind. He walked to the back cooler and grabbed a two-liter Pepsi, two bags of Flamin' Hot Cheetos, and some Snickers bars. He knew he and Krazy would have the munchies after smoking the leftover weed they had back at the spot.

There were four chicks standing at the counter, directing one of Hank's Arab brothers as to which slices of pizza they wanted. Two of them were bucketheads, cool for the late night. But Wink was caught up on the two yellowbones. They looked as if they were sisters or cousins.

Damn, thought Wink as he allowed his eyes to travel up both girls' gleaming thick legs, resting on their onions.

"You gon' go?" a guy behind Wink asked.

"What?" asked Wink, snapping out of his trance. "Oh, my bad," he said, setting the chips and Pepsi on the counter.

"You J-Bo's li'l man, ain't you?" asked the man as he watched Wink dig out one of the stacks of money.

"Yeah, that's my nigga," said Wink. He wasn't paying ole boy behind him no never mind. He was too busy flaunting the bankroll, hoping the girls would catch a glimpse of it.

"Yeah, and let me get a pack of Zig-Zags," he said to ole Hank.

Wink caught the eye of one of the girls. He motioned her over, using the bankroll as bait.

The man who had been standing behind Wink in line was Keon, one of J-Bo's cohorts. He slipped out of the store and walked over to the pay phone. He put a quarter into the slot and dialed seven quick digits, then turned to face the entrance of the store.

"Come on, pick up," he said as he tapped his foot a thousand miles per second.

"Hello," answered J-Bo.

"Bo, it's me, Keon."

"What's the business?"

"I'm up here at Hank's, and ya worker is up here flossin' with all yo' money on him."

"Word," said J-Bo. He became furious.

"Yeah, what you want me to do?"

"The only thing to do. Teach his ass a lesson. But don't hurt him," ordered J-Bo.

"I got you. Here he comes now." *Click.*

Wink came walking out the store with the four girls in tow. Zeta, the one he pulled, was on his side. She was all smiles as she jotted her number down on a lottery ticket.

"When you gon' call me?" asked Zeta as the group stopped in front of the parking lot. Her sister and two butt-ugly friends were standing a few feet back, snickering like little schoolgirls.

"I'ma hit you up tonight. We can set something up for tomorrow," said Wink.

"Okay," gushed Zeta. She turned on her heels and purposely threw her thick ass as she walked away.

Wink was already making plans on how he'd get up in that young pussy, then maybe her sister, too, if he was lucky. Wink daydreamed on his way through the parking lot. That was the kind of respect he knew he deserved and was worthy of receiving.

"It's all about the money," he told himself.

Wink set the bag of munchies on the roof of the car, then opened the door. Before he could reach for the bag and get in, an empty forty-ounce of Old English shattered across the back of his head, sending him straight to the ground. He was dazed but came to when he felt hands probing his body.

"Get the fuck off me!" yelled Wink. He lay on his back with his feet propped up, ready to kick the two men like a wild horse if necessary.

"You wanna kick, huh?" asked Keon. He pulled out a chrome .45 with a pearl-white handle. He pointed it down at Wink's face. "You ready to die, young nigga?" he asked.

"Nah, man," Wink answered. He lowered his legs in defeat. His throat was dry, and his lips became instantly chapped. "Don't kill me, man. Please."

"Get that up off him," Keon ordered his cohort.

This cock-diesel, shitty-black nigga bent down and snatched both stacks of money and handed them to Keon.

"Now close your eyes," ordered Keon.

"Please don't kill me," pleaded Wink. He was so scared he nearly shitted himself.

"Nigga, close your eyes!" yelled Keon as he cocked the hammer back on his .45.

Wink closed his eyes and sparked a conversation with God. He hadn't called on the Lord all his life, never went to church, now all of a sudden, some nigga standing over him about to cancel Christmas, and he wanted to call on God.

That day, God must have been listening, because when Wink opened his eyes, he was still alive. He scanned the parking lot, and it was empty. He hurriedly rolled onto his knees and stood up. Pain shot through his entire body, starting at his head where the bottle had struck him. He patted the back of his head, then looked at his hand, covered with blood.

Just like a nigga, Wink forgot to thank God, the one who saved his life. He jumped in the Escort and spun out the lot. He shifted gears like he was part of the Daytona 500 and made two sharp turns, reaching Linwood Ave. Wink pulled up at the spot and jumped out of the car, leaving the engine running. He climbed the porch four steps at a time, ignoring the begging crackheads. Wink busted through the door of the spot, startling Krazy from what he was doing. He was butt-ass naked on the floor with Amy and her friend. Krazy was in mid-stroke, fucking Amy from the back while she ate her best friend's pussy. And that's exactly what the spot smelled like—beat-up pussy.

"Fuck happen to you?" asked Krazy as he slid out of Amy's pussy. He stood up and put his boxers on, then walked over to the fireplace mirror, where Wink stood nursing his wound and picking glass out of his scalp. "What happened, my nigga?" asked Krazy.

"Some niggas just got out on me up at the liquor store. They took all the money too," said Wink, turning to face Krazy.

"What?" yelled Krazy. He quickly got dressed, all the while talking shit. This was what Krazy lived for—drama.

"Where them bitch niggas at? We gon' go through there and lay all they ass down."

"They're long gone. Forget that, Krazy."

"Forget about it? Fuck that! We can't let that shit ride. It's the principle. We gon' go find them pussies and give 'em the business," said Krazy.

"We don't even have a gun, Krazy. They do. A big chrome gun."

"Shit, we can ride to the hood, and I'll snatch my grandfather's twelve-gauge."

"We'll see them again. I need to worry about how I'ma explain this shit to J-Bo."

As soon as Wink said that, J-Bo came walking through the door. Wink's stomach dropped, and his heart started beating a hundred miles per second.

"What the hell is that smell?" asked J-Bo as he bent the corner into the living room. "It smells like booty, dick, and pussy up in here." J-Bo stopped dead in his tracks at the sight of Amy and her friend, lying across the carpet, ass naked and smoking crack.

"What's this?" J-Bo waved his hand at the two snow bunnies while looking at Wink.

"They, uh . . ." stuttered Wink.

"They spending some money, or are y'all up in here trickin' off?" asked J-Bo. From the strong stench of pussy, he already knew the answer. He handed the two women their clothes and politely sent them on their way.

"J-Bo, I can explain, man," Wink said as the two women left.

"Ain't no need to explain. Let's just not let it happen again. I keep tellin' y'all this is a place of business, not a chill spot. Now, let's count that money." J-Bo walked into the living room and took a seat on the sofa.

Krazy handed J-Bo the seven hundred dollars he had made while Wink was gone.

"Okay, where's the rest of it?" asked J-Bo.

Wink took a deep breath, then looked up at the ceiling.

"Just tell 'im," said Krazy.

"Tell me what?" asked J-Bo.

Wink gulped, then told J-Bo what had happened in the parking lot. Silence lingered between them for a few moments. Wink couldn't tell whether J-Bo was mad, because his face showed nothing.

"What does that have to do with my ends? I'm sure that I told you to always separate mine's from yours. So, what you tellin' me? You had mine's with yours?" asked J-Bo.

"I went home to change clothes and forgot that I had the money on me," said Wink.

"But that's not what I told you. Now you sittin' here givin' me a sob story about how some niggas robbed you."

Wink just stood there with the shit face while J-Bo continued to scold his ass. "You's a spot worker. You don't do shit like that. You was probably flashin' all my money in the store, and some niggas laid on you."

"The dude did say he knew you," said Wink.

"That could be anybody. The whole city knows who I am. But that's not my concern. I'm concerned with my ends. Ole boy didn't rob me. He robbed you."

"J-Bo, man, I'll make it up. Just give me another chance," pleaded Wink.

"You damn right you gon' make it up, and it can never happen again, 'cause then I'ma feel like you playing on me."

"It won't happen again. I'll die first before I get caught slipppin' again."

"You owe me thirty-three hundred still. I'ma deduct the grand you would have been gettin' tomorrow, so you owe me twenty-three hundred," said J-Bo.

"What?" snapped Krazy. "Some niggas robbed my man, and you want us to work that shit?"

"I keep tellin' y'all this is a business. I gave y'all clear instructions. You didn't follow them, so now you owe up. It's the game," said J-Bo.

"Just say when," said Wink.

"I'll be through tomorrow around two. Be ready." J-Bo stood up and walked around the table into the kitchen.

Wink was at his heels. He held the door open for J-Bo. "I was gon' ask you if I could bring my other niggas with me," said Wink.

"The more, the better. But I'm holding you responsible for any losses," said J-Bo. "A'int gon' be no more losses." J-Bo pulled back a smile, then said, "Young dawg, in this game, there's always gon' be losses. You just gotta hope your losses don't outweigh your wins. Tomorrow," He said, then turned to leave.

Wink watched as J-Bo's head got small. That was his first lesson of the game. Many more were sure to follow.

Chapter Five

"This like some gay shit for real. I don't think I can do it," said Trey. He set the cucumber-size baggie on the bathroom sink. He and Wink were locked in the bathroom at the spot.

"Y'all hurry up in there! We gotta be hittin' the road!" yelled Gator.

"My nigga, they all waitin' on us. It ain't no gay shit. It's some money shit," said Wink as he pulled the shower curtain back and stepped out the tub. He stepped over to the sink and washed the lotion off his hands.

"It didn't hurt?" asked Trey. He was talking about the four and a half ounces of cocaine Wink had just boofed up his asshole.

"Nah, that's what the lotion is for. It just feels like you gotta shit, that's all. Hurry up and get that shit missin' so we can be out," said Wink.

Trey picked up the log of cocaine and smeared lotion all over it. "Here goes," he said, climbing into the shower.

"I'll be out front," said Wink as he opened the bathroom door and stepped out into the living room, where Willie, Gator, and Krazy sat.

"You get it up all right?" asked Gator.

"Yeah, but I don't know how long it's going to stay put," said Wink.

"What about what's-his-face?" asked Gator.

Trey came walking in the living room, looking like he just got off a bull. Krazy and Willie were in tears, laughing.

"Fuck both you niggas. Next go 'round it's y'all turn," said Trey. His asshole and manhood felt a little violated. But to Wink, it was all about the come up. J-Bo always had his workers boof the coke when hitting the highway. A police dog can't sniff the inside of a man's ass, was J-Bo's logic, and so far, it had been working.

J-Bo had rented a conversion van for the trip, and he paid Gator a nice little something in crack to make the trip. He had been working with J-Bo for a few years now and knew just what to expect at every turn. J-Bo was a real calculated nigga, always plotting and thinking. He made it to the level in the game that he was on because he understood that most niggas, you have to think for them as well. Otherwise, they'd grow a brain and fuck everything up in the process.

Today was no different. J-Bo had everything already mapped out. He was the coach, drawing all the plays. All Wink and the rest of them had to do was follow the play.

"Man, we been drivin' for hours. Where the fuck is we going, and when is we gon' get there?" Krazy asked from the back seat of the van.

"J-Bo told me not to tell y'all. He says it's not important," Gator answered, looking in the rearview for a second. He gripped the wheel with both hands and sat up in his seat with his back arched perfectly.

Wink rode shotgun, despite Gator's instructions to sit in the back with the rest of them. Wink was watching the signs on the highway. He wanted to know exactly where they were headed. He leaned forward in his seat as he squinted at the sign ahead.

WELCOME TO DAVENPORT, the sign read.

Gator reached across the seat and put his arm on Wink's chest. "Sit back," he said, then nodded at two state troopers sitting in the cut just yards ahead.

Gator looked in his side mirror as soon as he passed the two cruisers, and sure enough, they pulled behind him.

"Listen up!" Gator announced as he turned off the radio. "Don't look back for nothin' in the world, but we got two Ohio state troopers tailing us. If they flick us, everybody knows what to say. Don't add nothin', and don't take nothin'."

No sooner than Gator had finished his spiel, both squad cars hit their lights. One of the crackers got on the intercom "Pull it over!" he ordered.

Gator eased the van over to the shoulder. One cruiser boxed them in at the front, while the other one sealed off the back.

"Whatever y'all do, don't panic," whispered Gator as he looked in his side mirrors. The troopers were approaching on both sides.

Gator cracked his window a smidge and tried speaking in his white voice. "What seems to be the problem, officer?"

"License and registration," said the trooper standing on the driver's side. His tone said it all: *What are you niggers doing in Davenport?*

"Here you go," said Gator as he passed his credentials out the window.

Wink was nervous as shit. His stomach was tossing and turning, and the brick of coke packed in his ass wasn't helping matters any. The second trooper stood at the passenger-side window at an angle, with his hands on his pistol. He peered into the van at Wink, then at Krazy, Willie, and Trey in the back seat. The trooper kept a watchful eye on the group while his partner went back to his cruiser to run Gator's information.

"We going to jail," whispered Willie.

"Ain't nobody going nowhere long as we play it cool," Gator said through clenched teeth. His grill was so fucked up, it was hard to tell if he was talking or not. He looked in the side mirror at the trooper as he walked back up to the van.

"Where are you headed?" asked the trooper as he passed Gator his information back through the window.

"Cedar Point Amusement Park," said Gator.

"And who are these men you got with you?"

"They're not men. This here's my son." Gator pointed at Wink. "And those are his friends in the back."

"You know we don't take kindly to you people coming through Davenport. There's been a lot of you runnin' drugs in and out."

"Well, I'm sorry to hear that, but that's not why we're out here," said Gator. He looked in his side mirror only to spot what he'd already suspected. The trooper had stalled him out long enough for a K-9 unit to arrive.

"You mind if we take a look around?" asked the first trooper.

Gator was a seasoned vet in the game. He knew that it was all a play on words. When the trooper asked if he minded, that meant consent—and Gator wasn't about to consent to anything.

"Yeah, I mind. What's the cause?"

"You runnin' drugs."

"Am I under arrest?" asked Gator.

"Not yet. But when—"

"You're not going to find anything, because I'm not moving anything. Unless I'm under arrest, I am going to be on my way," snapped Gator.

The K-9 unit officer had walked his dog around the van three times as slowly as he could. He stopped in front of the van and made eye contact with the trooper who had been talking to Gator. He shook his head no. The trooper turned beet red because he had to let them go when his gut told him they were drug runners.

"I suggest you get going, boy. And I don't want to see your smart ass out here drivin' these roads again." The trooper slapped the hood of the van.

Gator had already started the engine. He pulled the shift down to drive and peeled away from the shoulder, kicking up a dust cloud in those honkies' faces.

Wink had to crack the window to let out the smell of his nervous fart. He just knew they were on their way to jail. Trey was in the back seat, thinking the same exact thing, and *Why did I let this nigga talk me into this shit?*

Willie turned around and peeked out the back-window curtain to see the distance between them and the troopers. "You handled they cracker-dog asses, O.G," he said, turning back in his seat.

"Yeah, I thought we was gon' have to beat they ass and get little on foot," said Krazy.

Gator looked in the mirror at the bunch and decided to give them all some game, for they had earned it by not panicking. He said, "See, the first thing you gotta know when you ridin' dirty is what these pigs can and can't do. If all your paperwork is legit and you're not smoking or drinkin', then they can't search you unless you let them. So, always have your shit together. And no matter what they say, never get out the car. Make 'em drag you out if they want to search that bad. That way, even if they do find something, you'll beat the charge on illegal search and seizure."

Wink was the only one soaking up the game ole Gator was spittin'. The rest of them, that shit went in one ear and out the other.

Gator pulled in the parking lot of the Regency Motel off Clifford Ave. He parked the van and told the gang to come on. They all looked around at the motel like, *Where the fuck we at?* They reluctantly climbed out the van into the sweltering heat and stood near the rear of the van while Gator knocked on one of the motel doors.

Wink looked down Clifford Ave., which was nothing but a dirt road. The only thing he could see was heat-waves bouncing off the road in the distance. When J-Bo said they'd be going out of town, he imagined maybe another city, but this was some hillbilly hick town.

"Man, that nigga J-Bo know he wrong as shit. Got us way in Mayberry some fuckin' where," said Krazy.

"I know I won't be going out at night. These crackers won't hang my black ass," said Willie.

"Ain't nobody gon' hang us, so chill," Wink said. He was trying to calm everybody's nerves.

"Nigga, stop fakin'," said Trey. "You just as scared as all the rest of us."

They all busted out laughing but ceased when the door to the room opened and Gator waved for them to come on. They all fell behind Wink as he led the way inside the room. On the bed sat J-Bo. He stood up as Gator closed the door behind them.

"Y'all enjoy the trip?" asked J-Bo.

"Hell nah," said Krazy. "The whole way here, ole Gator-grill here wouldn't even tell us where the fuck we was going. Then we gets flicked."

"I told him not to tell you where y'all was going," said J-Bo.

"Why?" asked Trey.

"You see how y'all got pulled over? Now, let's say they would have made y'all get out, or if they would've asked all y'all where it was y'all were going. Somebody would've gave a different answer, and that would let them know y'all lying. It's just best not to know," said J-Bo.

That was part of the reason. The other half was just in case any of them had snitch in their blood, they wouldn't be able to lead the police to their destination.

"What's out here, though?" asked Wink.

"Money, and lots of it. I know y'all seen the dirt roads and barns on the way up, but trust me when I tell you these pink mothafuckas holding," said J-Bo.

"Bo, I need to get out the street, baby," Gator said. He was pacing the floor, geeking like shit.

"Let me get that so I can get this nigga something before he paces a hole through the floor," said J-Bo.

Wink nodded at Trey, then toward the bathroom. Willie and Krazy snickered and hit each other as Trey bull-walked for the bathroom.

"You two niggas is silly. What y'all laughing at?" asked J-Bo, pulling back a wide grin.

"You got them two niggas stuffed like a turkey." Krazy laughed.

"You'll get your turn," said J-Bo.

Willie and Krazy's smiles disappeared at the thought of having to suitcase some dope. A few minutes later,

Trey and Wink came walking out the bathroom with their packages.

"That shit on one thousand," Willie said of the smell coming from the two shitty packages.

J-Bo took a deep breath, then said, "Ahh . . . that's the smell of money." He strapped on some latex gloves and took the packages from Trey and Wink.

"Gator, why don't you take them to get something to eat while I put this together," said J-Bo from the small makeshift kitchen where he stood, unwrapping the coke.

"Y'all heard him. Let's go," ordered Gator. He was getting agitated because he hadn't had a hit all day.

Wink was standing over J-Bo's shoulder at the stove, watching him like a hawk as he emptied the coke into a Pyrex jar. J-Bo turned around and saw Wink and stopped what he was doing.

"Why don't you go with them to grab something to eat?" he said.

"Nah, I want to watch you," said Wink.

J-Bo smiled, then wrapped his arm around Wink's neck, all the while leading him out of the kitchen. "This game cost me ten grand to learn. When you get ten grand, come holla at me and I'll show you all you need to know."

J-Bo opened the door and patted Wink on his back. "But I tell you what. Grab a couple boxes of baggies, and when you get back, I'll let you help me bag up."

Wink was thirsty for any game J-Bo was willing to sprinkle him with. His brief disappointment was replaced by a huge Kool-Aid smile. He turned to hurry up and catch Gator before he pulled off.

Chapter Six

When Wink got back to the motel, J-Bo was waiting on him in the kitchen.

"Come on. Time is money," shot J-Bo.

Wink rushed over to the counter, setting the two boxes of baggies down. He waited like an eager third grader preparing for a science project.

"A'ight, here's what we're doing. You listening?"

"Yeah."

"A'ight. We got two scales here. I want you to weigh out exactly .50 grams, a half of gram. Not a pinch more or less. Use this razor blade to cut it. Once you get .50, put 'em into a baggie and tie 'em in a knot."

"That's it?" asked Wink.

"That's it," said J-Bo. He cut a chunk out of the crack cookie and showed Wink an example.

"Once you bag it up and put it back on the scale, it's gon' weigh a little more. We could use the weight of the bag to get over, but these crackers is paying so good, ain't no sense in beatin' 'em over the head anymore."

Gator promptly got his boulder from J-Bo, then disappeared into the bathroom. Trey, Willie, and Krazy were all in the front room, smashing their White Castle burgers. Wink was the only one focused on learning.

The shit was easy. Just cut and weigh. A first grader could do the shit, thought Wink.

Every so often, J-Bo would put one of Wink's rocks on the scale. He nodded and said, "You got it."

Now all Wink had to do was learn how to cook. Ten thousand was a lot of money, though, to be learning how to cook crack, he thought.

"How much one of these go for out here?" Wink asked, holding one of the packaged rocks.

"A hun'd dollars," said J-Bo.

"For this? This is like, what? Two, three at the most dimes back in Detroit."

"Yeah, but we ain't in Detroit. You'll see there's a big difference in outta town hustlin'. It's spots like this that'll put a nigga on his feet."

Wink looked at all the rocks before him and the chunks of crack yet to be weighed. That was a whole lot of hundreds.

"How long it's gon' take us to move this?"

"No more than a week. It's gon' move itself."

Everything was on a need-to-know basis with J-Bo. He never just gave you his whole plan. He'd give it to you in pieces once you got to that point.

"Here's the deal," he said, stepping in front of the TV.

Wink, Krazy, Trey, and Willie all sat up at attention for J-Bo.

"Y'all gon' be out here for a week. I already got everything set up. All y'all gotta do is sell the work. My man Jason is gon' be runnin' all the clientele through. He's in a red pickup truck. You'll know him when you see him. He's an old white dude with a long, dirty white beard. Each one of these is a hun'd dollars, not a dollar less," J-Bo said, holding up one of the rocks.

"So, we 'pose to just sit in here for a whole week?" asked Trey.

"Yeah. But I got another room right on top of this one. That's where the money and all the work will be kept. Come on and follow me." J-Bo led them into the small bathroom. He stood on the toilet seat with his hands reached up to the ceiling.

"Y'all see this?" he asked as he pushed up one of the drop ceiling boards. There was a large enough hole in the floor upstairs for a hand to fit through.

"Wink, you'll be upstairs with all the work. You and whoever else you pick. It'll be two of y'all down here. When a custo comes through, bring the money back here and send it upstairs. In exchange, Wink gon' pass down the order. Make sure y'all close the door, though. We don't want nobody knowing where we keeping everything at," said J-Bo. He closed the ceiling and jumped down from the toilet.

They all walked back into the living room, where J-Bo continued to run down the operation. "It's real easy. Everybody stick to the script, and in seven days, we'll be back home breaking bread," he said. This, of course, brought smiles to all their faces.

Willie's funny-lookin' ass was rubbing his fat, greedy fingers together. "How much we gon' get?" he asked, his beady little black eyes peering over at J-Bo.

"Ten grand, minus what was lost the other day," said J-Bo. He could see dollar signs light up in Willie's and Krazy's eyes.

Trey wasn't impressed. He was only doing it because Wink kept pressing the issue. Soon as they had enough of their own money, he was cutting J-Bo off. Trey wasn't even sure if he really liked J-Bo neither. Something just wasn't right about him.

"Have you decided who you want upstairs with you, Wink?" asked J-Bo.

Wink looked at his crew. His first thought was to pick Trey because that was his best friend, but he looked at Willie and Krazy and knew it'd be a disaster if he left them two together.

"Yeah, I'ma take Willie. Trey, you and Krazy post up down here," said Wink.

J-Bo nodded his approval. He put his arm around Wink's neck and they excused themselves from the room.

"Help me carry this stuff up," J-Bo said as he grabbed up one of the grocery bags full of rocks. "I'ma clean up on this residue before I leave."

"Leave? Where you gon' be at?" Wink asked as he followed behind J-Bo with both hands full of grocery bags.

"I'ma be in the city. As long as y'all stick to the script, everything is gon' be straight."

The thought of J-Bo leaving them out of town had Wink a little nervous, but he wouldn't show it. He had to show J-Bo that he could handle it and that the last fuck-up was a fluke.

The room upstairs was identical to the one below. In the living room sat a small table, sofa, two stiff wooden chairs, twenty-inch Zenith television, and a queen-size bed. Wink made mental notes of all this as J-Bo led him through the room back into the bathroom.

"Com'ere, I want to show you something." J-Bo pushed open the bathroom door and walked over to the window. Tied around the base of the toilet was a rope.

"You see that rope?" J-Bo nodded.

"Yeah."

"Well, just in case the police hit the downstairs room, I want you to pack everything up and use that rope to climb down. Look, there's an alley right through there." J-Bo moved to the side so Wink could see. "There's a Denny's about a square mile down. If something happens, just call me from the Denny's and I'll have you scooped up."

"A'ight." Wink's lips said one thing, but his mind was filled with all kinds of scary questions. He hadn't planned on no raid popping off. He'd seen them in action almost every week growing up, watching niggas on his block book down the street with police on their heels. It was funny to watch, but the thought of it being him made his stomach turn.

"One more thing." J-Bo stopped in the living room and dug in his pocket. He handed Wink a business card with some woman's name and address on it.

"There's a MoneyGram inside the motel lobby. Every three thousand that you make, I want you to wire the money to that name A.S.A.P. And don't worry. The little redhead working at the desk knows the business.

Wink stared down at the card. "I got it." He tucked the card into the pimp pocket of his Guess jeans, and then followed J-Bo to the front door.

"One week and you'll be home countin' ten grand," said J-Bo as he stopped on the balcony just outside the room.

Wink pulled back a smile, and for a second, the butterflies disappeared. He couldn't believe that he was actually out of town on a mission with J-Bo, not to mention J-Bo leaving him in charge.

"One week," J-Bo said again, then walked down the two flights of stairs.

Wink watched as Gator backed away from the motel with J-Bo riding in the back seat. The van turned into a speck on the dirt road, then disappeared into the horizon. He stepped back inside the room and closed the door, leaning against it.

Suddenly, the butterflies were back as Wink looked at all the crack sitting out on the bed. "One week," he told himself, then pushed off the door and over to the phone. He flopped down on the bed and called downstairs. Trey answered the phone.

"Y'all ready to get this money?" asked Wink.

Trey's eyes bucked at the sight of all that money—and off of just one sale! "I'll be right back," he said, then shot to the bathroom. He climbed up on the toilet and pushed the ceiling aside.

"What he want?" asked Wink. He was already on point.

"Five hundred. Here." Trey passed Wink the bills and waited for the order.

A few seconds later, Wink passed the five little rocks down and said, "Y'all niggas stay on point."

"A'ight." Trey closed up the ceiling, then rushed back into the front room. He handed the work to Jason and awaited his approval.

Jason didn't even look at the rocks. He already knew J-Bo kept some good stuff, so he just stuffed them inside his old, stained, no-name jeans pocket and turned for the door.

"Like I said, my name's Jason. I've been knowing J-Bo for a long time. If y'all need me to make a food run or something, just give me a holla. It's not a problem."

"A'ight, that's a bet," Trey said, walking Jason out to the parking lot.

"See y'all in a bit." Jason climbed in his truck and handed the young blonde riding shotgun one of the rocks. Trey watched as the woman packed her pipe and set fire to it. Jason backed away.

Before the night was out, Jason had made at least thirty runs, and each time, he was spending no less than five hundred dollars. Word had gotten out that J-Bo's good crack was back in town, and that was all the reason for every redneck in a twenty-mile radius to hit up the bank and make a withdrawal. As they made withdrawals, Wink was making wire transfers through MoneyGram.

Chapter Seven

Five minutes after Gator and J-Bo left, Jason pulled up in his beat-up Ford pickup. He climbed out the truck exactly how J-Bo pegged him—dingy-ass mothafucka with a long, white dirty beard. Jason tapped on the door with his keys a few times. Trey and Krazy both looked at each other like, *It's on*, but still, neither really wanted to budge from their spots on the sofa. They were kicked back, watching a special on the Greek mafia.

"Why don't you get it, my nigga? I'll get the next one," said Trey.

Krazy reluctantly popped up and walked over to the door. "Who is it?" he yelled.

"Um, Jason."

Krazy undid the chain, then the locks. He cracked the door, peeking out at the old white man.

"J-Bo sent me."

"A'ight," Krazy said as he backed away, allowing Jason to enter the room.

"How's it going?" Jason asked, sounding country and friendly as hell. He rocked back on his heels while fiddling with a roll of money in his hands.

"We chillin'. What can we do for you?" asked Trey.

"Whatever you can for five hundred." Jason unfolded the dirty bills and handed them to Trey.

Sleep was impossible for all of them. They tried working in shifts, one sleeping while the other served, but it was just too much traffic, to the point where they were all scared to close their eyes. Money was changing hands too fast, and none of them were used to seeing that much money in their life.

Willie would be standing in front of the bed, counting and recounting the money, pretending it was all his. "What we gon' buy once we start gettin' our own money like this?" he asked.

"Shit, the first thing I'ma buy is some game. I want to learn everything, so we can have niggas sittin' in a motel somewhere. Feel me?" asked Wink.

Willie hadn't thought that far ahead, but he nodded as he daydreamed and envisioned everything Wink had said. "Yeah, I feel you, my nigga."

"I was thinking, too. When we do get straight, maybe we can shoot down to Mississippi and set up shop. I know they probably paying just as much as these crackers since it's the South. You know y'all niggas slow as shit down there," Wink teased.

"Fuck you." Willie laughed. "I'll see what's up," he said. Willie was originally from Mississippi, but he moved to Detroit when he was ten to live with his moms. But every once in a while, he would go back down south to visit his grams.

"Yeah, right now we just stackin' and learning. Pretty soon we gon' have all this shit, and some," Wink confidently said as he waved his hand at the crack and money sprawled out across the bed.

Downstairs, Trey and Krazy were making short-term plans on how they were going to run a train on the white chick Jason kept pulling up with. The only problem was she never got out the truck.

"Let me holla at him," said Krazy as he stood up to let Jason in for the fortieth time.

"Here's eight hundred," said Jason.

Trey took the money, while Krazy stayed out front, rapping with Jason about pink toes.

"Who is she?" asked Krazy.

"She's a buddy of mine's old lady. He'd flip his wig if he knew I had her do something like that," said Jason.

"I mean, he ain't gotta know. And I'ma make it worth both y'all while. I ain't gonna lie. I'ma try'na see her," Krazy said, peeking from behind the curtain out into the truck. He flicked his tongue seductively at the woman as they met eyes. She broke into a smile and shook her head.

"See, she's with it," said Krazy as he let the curtain close.

"I tell you what. Let me talk to her, and if she's okay with it, I'll send her up. But it won't be tonight, 'cause her old man's at my house partying."

"A'ight, just set it up for whenever," said Krazy. He was lost and turned out ever since Gator sicced those white broads on him at the spot. Lately, all he wanted was some pink toes.

Trey stepped back in the room and handed Jason his eight stones.

"Don't forget me," said Krazy as he opened the door for Jason. He flicked his tongue again at the woman, to which she covered her face to conceal her blushing.

"I'm tellin' you, my nigga. We got that bitch," said Krazy as he locked the door.

"What he say? He gon' hook it up?" asked Trey.

"Yeah. I'm tellin' you. You ain't had no head until you get some dome from one of these snow bunnies while they high off that shit. It's like they be in another world, just them and yo' dick."

"I ain't fuckin' with you." Trey laughed.

"She look like she got that lockjaw, too," said Krazy as he continued to fantasize about ole girl. He flopped down on the sofa and flicked through the channels, looking for something good to watch.

"Leave it right there," Trey said.

"You see how them Mexican mothafuckas gettin' money. That's how we should be doin' it," said Krazy. It was a documentary about the Mexican Mafia out in California.

"Word," Trey agreed as he pretended he was standing right next to the short, fat Mexican who seemed to be running shit.

"That can be us," said Krazy.

They rolled up two joints and kicked back, each lost in la-la land, fantasizing about a life of luxury. Krazy thought about all the pink toes he could afford with that kind of money, while Trey plotted on a new Beamer. Slowly but surely, Trey was falling in love with the game. J-Bo knew a week of seeing that out of town money would have all they young asses turned out. It's what the game did to him.

Chapter Eight

Four days had gone by since Jason told Krazy he'd hook him up with pink toes. Every time Jason would come cop, Krazy would be pressing the shit out of him about ole girl. Finally, he just chalked up that she wasn't gon' show. He kept quoting some old pimp line he heard back in Detroit to Trey, who was tired of hearing it.

"I know, I know. Ain't but two things you never seen before: a UFO and a hoe that won't go." Trey took the words out of Krazy's mouth.

"You damn right," said Krazy as he got up and started pacing the floor. The small-ass room was closing in on him. The shit was boring as a mothafucka, and a nigga with as much energy as Krazy needed some type of action. Selling crack to crackers all day didn't constitute action for him.

"Who is it?" he shouted as someone knocked on the door.

"Mandy," a soft white woman's voice said.

Krazy rushed over to the door and snatched it open. It was ole girl who he'd been sweating the hell out of Jason about.

"Aren't you going to let me in?" asked Mandy.

"My bad. Yeah, come on in." Krazy snapped out of his brief daze. He was lost in the young woman's curves. She wore next to nothing. Her outfit consisted of a wife-beater, Daisy-Duke shorts, and some thong flip-flops.

"Yeah, come on in," Krazy said with a bit of rhythm. He quickly locked up the door, then joined pink toes on the sofa.

"What you say your name was?" asked Krazy.

"Mandy."

"Well, I'm Krazy, and this is my boy, Trey."

Krazy was all up close and personal with Mandy. He stretched his arm around her back and leaned toward her so he could get a full view of her perfect titties. His eyes traveled down to somewhere between her thighs.

"So, um," Krazy began. He concentrated on Mandy's camel toe between her legs. "What's up? Did Jason holla at you?"

"Yeah. I would have came days ago, but my old man took a few days off work. But here I am."

"Yes, you are," said Krazy.

Trey pulled beside Mandy, and together he and Krazy took turns getting her ready.

"So, I'm sayin'. You gon' do that for me, or what?" Trey whispered into her ear.

"I guess so. But can I have something to get me started? I'm a lot better when I'm rolling," said Mandy.

Hearing her talk like that made both Krazy's and Trey's dicks hard. Krazy leaped from the sofa and ran inside the bathroom. He tapped on the toilet pipe, then slid the ceiling back.

"What's up?" asked Willie as he bent down next to the hole.

"I need one," said Krazy.

"A'ight. Where's the money?"

"Nigga, just give me one. We got this little freak bitch down here. Me and Trey 'bout to bust her head."

"I'm on my way down," said Willie.

"Nah, you gon' fuck the move up. Plus, I don't want Wink ass to know, 'cause he gon' be trippin' 'bout the money. Just give me the stone."

"A'ight, but tomorrow we switchin' out. I'm tired of sittin' up here all day," said Willie. He passed Krazy a rock, then closed the hole up.

"Who was that?" Wink asked from the bathroom door.

"Krazy. He wanted to know if he could do a deal for eighty. I told him no shorts, no losses."

"How much more work we gotta sell?" asked Willie as he followed Wink back into the living room.

"By the looks of it, we should be finished by tomorrow morning. So, we'll be done a day early. Unless J-Bo shoots us down some more work."

Back downstairs, Krazy and Trey had Mandy's thick white ass in the buck. She had hit her pipe and was on cloud nine. She sucked Trey's dick like a porn star would. She had her eyes closed and held it delicately with two fingers. She would deep throat his entire dick, then pull it out and lick around the head. All the while, Krazy's freaky-zeaky ass was drilling her from the back. He was the only one ass naked. He took everything off except his long white tube socks, the ones with the green stripes at the top.

Suddenly, there was a loud pound on the door. The pounding grew louder with each thrust. Whoever it was sure wasn't leaving. The noise was messing up both Krazy's and Trey's concentration.

"Man, who is it?" yelled Krazy as he slid out of the pussy.

"Mandy, get your cunt out here now! You little whore, I know you're in there."

Mandy snapped out of her crack state of mind. She held Trey's stiff dick in her hand while looking back from the sofa at the door.

"That's my husband," she whispered.

"I don't give a fuck if he was yo' daddy. His ass betta stop pounding on the door," said Krazy as he slid into his boxers.

"Yeah, he's making shit hot," said Trey.

"Mandy, I know you hear me. Get your ass out here now!" The man's shadow could be seen from behind the curtain as he tried to peek inside the room.

"He'll leave. But please don't open the door," said Mandy. She was in fear of an ultimate beat down.

"Go hide in the bathroom while I get rid of him," said Krazy. He waited as Mandy scooped her clothes up and scurried toward the bathroom.

Trey decided he would finish getting his dick sucked in the meantime. He grabbed up his clothes, then followed Mandy in the bathroom.

Krazy snatched the door open wildly. He was standing face to face with a huge, thick-neck cracker who weighed every bit of three hundred pounds. He looked up at the muscle-faced cracker and put his murda mask on, even despite only wearing his boxers, tube socks, and Nike Cortez.

"Where is she?" asked the man as he looked over Krazy's shoulder in attempt to scan the room.

"Where's who?" asked Krazy.

"Mandy, my fuckin' wife!"

"Listen, ole boy, I don't know who the hell you're talkin' about, but ain't no Mandy here."

"Oh, no? Then why are her panties on the sofa?" asked the man.

Before Krazy could turn to look, the cock-strong cracker lowered his head and bull-rushed him back into the room. The blow of the man's head knocked the wind out of Krazy. He stumbled backward and crashed into the center of the coffee table.

"Mandy, you bitch! Get your ass out here now. I know you in here, 'cause I can smell ya!" shouted the man.

Krazy came to his senses. He groaned as he rolled off the shattered table.

"Robert, I can explain," Mandy pleaded, as she inched her way out of the bathroom, half naked.

"Oh, you bet your ass you got some explaining to do. You can tell the good Lord all about it when you see him, 'cause I'm about to kill your ass." Robert spread his arms wide as he closed in on Mandy, cornering her in the front room.

"Please, Robert," pleaded Mandy as she closed her eyes and braced herself for the impact of Robert's bear claw.

Boom! Boom!

Robert's heavy frame crashed forward, hitting the floor hard. He grunted and squirmed in pain from the two back shots. Trey and Mandy looked up at Krazy, who had his gun pointed at Robert's head.

"Ahh!" screamed Mandy at the top of her lungs. She knelt down to tend to Robert.

"You didn't have to shoot him!" she yelled while cradling Robert in her arms. "Baby, I am so sorry. Please get up. Please," she begged her husband. All Robert could do was groan in agony from the two .25 shells lodged in his spine.

Trey's eyes were bucked with fear. He hurriedly rushed over to Krazy and grabbed his arm, lowering the gun to his side.

"Dawg, what you trippin' off of?" asked Trey.

The phone started ringing. Trey grabbed the gun from Krazy, then rushed over to the phone. He snatched the receiver up to his ear. "What up?"

"That's y'all down there?" asked Wink.

"You need to get down here, like now," said Trey.

Wink jumped from the sofa and slid into his shoes. Willie was awaiting the news.

"So, what happened?" asked Willie, his eyes bucked with fear and anticipation.

"I don't know, but we 'bouts to find out," said Wink. He stood up and snatched the room door open. As he stepped out onto the landing, he saw a Davenport police car pulling into the motel's parking lot. Wink pushed Willie back inside the room, backstepping all the while, not taking his eyes off the police.

Wink peeked from behind the curtain. Two white officers were standing outside their squad car, talking to some old white woman. She talked with her hands and pointed in the direction of the room. The two officers looked directly at the room, then thanked the woman.

"What they doing?" whispered Willie.

One of the cops spoke into his shoulder radio.

"I think they just called for backup," said Wink. He raced over to the phone and called downstairs. "Don't look out the window, but there's two police outside," Wink told Trey.

"Four. Two more just pulled up," advised Willie as he took Wink's place at the curtain.

"What the fuck happened down there?" demanded Wink.

"Hold on. They're pounding on the door. What should we do?" asked Trey. His heart was racing a million miles per hour.

Just when he thought things couldn't get any worse, Mandy screamed at the top of her lungs. "Help! He shot my husband!"

Wink could hear the ruckus downstairs as the front door crashed in. "Police! Get down on the ground!" was the last thing Wink heard before he dropped the phone.

"Grab the work and let's go," ordered Wink as he snatched up all the money off the bed. "Let's go!" he yelled, running for the bathroom.

He didn't have to tell Willie. He was so scared that he almost beat him there. Wink slid back the stained window next to the shower and looked down into the alley. He didn't see any cop cars or anything out of the norm, so he tossed the rope down.

"You get everything?" he asked.

"Yeah," answered Willie in a nervous tone.

Wink gripped the rope around his hands, then climbed out the window. He scaled down to the alley, then shouted up for Willie. "Come on, Will." Wink looked from right to left at both ends of the alley, then back up at Willie, who was struggling to climb down. Wink could hear the crackling of police radios coming from inside Trey and Krazy's room.

"You 'bout halfway. Jump, my nigga," said Wink.

More police sirens could be heard in the nearing distance, as well as an ambulance.

"Jump," ordered Wink.

Willie closed his eyes and let go of the rope. He met the pavement hard, almost twisting his ankle. But Wink didn't give him time enough to complain about the pain.

He grabbed Willie by the arm and dragged him down the alley.

"Can we slow down?" asked Willie. He was gassed out and ready to collapse.

"We're almost there," said Wink, not letting Willie's feet stop moving. "Come on, my nigga. You can make it."

Wink slowed down just a little bit after looking over his shoulder and saw that no one was chasing them. They crossed the alley, reaching the Denny's J-Bo had told him about. Wink raced for the phone booth, sitting dead center of the parking lot.

Willie held himself up on the glass, trying to catch his breath, while Wink slid inside the booth. Wink's stomach sank to his ass when J-Bo answered the phone. He had to tell him that he had failed once again.

"Bo, it's me, Wink."

"You callin' me. I hope everything straight out there," said J-Bo.

"Nah, it's not. Something happened downstairs, and the police just ran down on Trey and Krazy."

"So, where are you at?"

"I'm at the Denny's, me and Willie."

"You get everything?" asked J-Bo. That was his only concern.

"Yeah. So, what you want us to do?" Wink asked as he looked around the parking lot.

"Stay at Denny's. I'm sending Gator to get y'all," said J-Bo, then hung up.

Wink looked at the phone, then placed it on the hook and stepped out of the booth.

"What he say?" asked Willie.

"He said to wait here, that he's sending Gator to get us." Wink looked around and felt out of place. "Come on. Let's go inside and get something to eat while we wait."

"What about Krazy and Trey?" asked Willie as he followed behind Wink.

"We got away and they didn't. They just gotta sit tight until we can figure something out."

Chapter Nine

J-Bo was waiting at the spot on Linwood when Wink and Willie got back. He stood at the top step with his short arms folded, disgust written all over his face. Wink regretted each step up. All he could do when he reached J-Bo at the landing was drop his head.

"Don't put the puppy-pound faces on now. That shit's spilled milk, but y'all gon' clean it up. Come on in here," ordered J-Bo. He walked them into the living room, then gave Gator his crack for making the trip.

Wink and Willie sat on the sofa with their eyes glued to the floor. Both their hearts were thumping and ready to burst out their chests. J-Bo locked the door behind Gator, then returned to the living room. His demeanor seemed to change at the sight of the crack and money set out on the table. J-Bo had been in the game so long that he could eyeball a stack of money and tell if it was short. Judging from the crack and the money, he could tell that wasn't much missing. But he still wasn't going to let them off easily.

"I sent y'all outta town so y'all could get a taste of some real money. Introduce y'all to some new thangs, and what do you do? Fuck it up," said J-Bo.

"All the money's there. We only had a little work left over," said Wink.

"That's beside the point. Y'all fucked that cake bake up. I been going out to Davenport since '85, and I ain't never been ran down on. Y'all wasn't even out there a week and got the town hot as a pistol. Now it's gon' be a minute before I can send some work up there again." J-Bo picked up the money and began separating his from theirs.

"I told y'all I was gon' kick ten grand down, minus the twenty-three hundred you already owe. But seeing as though y'all left two days early and fucked my cake bake up, I'ma tax that ass."

J-Bo handed Wink three thousand dollars, all hundreds. He folded the rest and put it in his pocket. "And you might wanna take that three grand and see about ya guys. They down in Davenport County Jail," said J-Bo.

"For what?" asked Wink.

"Attempted murder. I had my lawyer do some calling around, and he says that they shot some white dude in the back. Something about his wife."

"What's their bond?" asked Willie.

"They ain't seen a judge yet, but I can tell you it won't be no three grand."

"'Bout how much?" asked Wink.

"At least a hundred grand. In a little town like Davenport, they're going to want two houses, a cat, and a dog."

"So, what are you going to do?" asked Willie.

"I'ma do what I been doing. That's on y'all to figure out. I didn't tell them niggas to shoot nobody. Shit, I didn't even know y'all had a gun."

Wink thought, *Me neither.*

"So, you're just going to leave 'em in jail and not do nothin' for em'? snapped Willie.

"Not one of them niggas is worth a hundred thousand to me. So far, y'all ain't did nothin' except fuck up. When you play the game, you gotta have shit in order. Lawyer money, bail money, and more money for when you get out so you can bounce back and get on your feet. I'm not about to go all in for them two niggas," said J-Bo. He wasn't holding no cut cards. He was just keeping it real.

"Y'all wanted to play this game, remember? Question is, are you done, or are you gon' dust yaself off and get back in the game?" J-Bo knew that they were in too deep to quit. Plus, he knew Wink was just like him when he first came into the game—hungry and hardheaded.

"What about a lawyer?" asked Wink.

"What about one?"

"Can't you at least send your lawyer to see them?"

"That's my lawyer. But I'm sure he'll accept a retainer. Give me that three grand back, and I'll have him go down and see what he can do."

Wink reluctantly passed J-Bo the money—the very money he and his crew were supposed to be laughing over and high-fiving as they broke bread.

"It's gon' cost way more than this once they start going to court, so I suggest y'all two get nice and comfortable," said J-Bo as he nodded at the leftover crack on the table.

"That should hold y'all for a couple of hours. I'll be back to re-up y'all. I should know something by then," said J-Bo.

Wink stood up and followed J-Bo to the door. "Bo, man, my bad. I don't know what happened down there," said Wink.

"It's all good. You live and you learn. The first one was on you. This one's on your boys. But you're paying for both. You just gotta tighten up, that's all."

Wink nodded at these wise words, but they didn't seem to stop the hurt of knowing he was still on ground zero. In fact, he was in the hole once they found out how much it would cost to spring Krazy and Trey. Wink watched as J-Bo disappeared down the stairs and out the front door.

Willie was standing at the window, looking down at J-Bo as he climbed in his yellow Porsche. "We should rob his little bitch ass," said Willie as he watched J-Bo skirt off.

"And what's that gonna solve? We'd still be broke, and Trey and Krazy would still be in jail," Wink said, flopping down on the sofa.

"That bitch mothafucka sat up here and talked all that shit. He don't give no fuck about us!" yelled Willie. "Trey and Krazy could get sent upstate, and all he care about is his money."

"You don't think I know this? But for real, he's right. It's our fault."

"How you gon' defend his ass when our boys is somewhere sittin' in jail?"

"I'm not defending him. I just said that he's right, and he is. How the fuck them niggas even get a gun, and where from? We was 'pose to be out there gettin' money."

Willie got quiet and turned back toward the window.

"You knew, didn't you?" asked Wink.

"I ain't know they had a gun," said Willie.

"But you knew they were down there trickin'. Don't lie to me!" snapped Wink.

"Yeah, Krazy told me not to tell you."

"That's some bullshit, and you did it. I already know it was Krazy who had the gun. Trey wouldn't have no hammer."

"So, what we gon' do?"

"We not gon' leave 'em in jail, that's for sure. We gon' have to sit here and grind up the money."

Wink sat back and closed his eyes. He couldn't believe they had fucked up that money. Just two more days and they would have been breaking bread, and he'd be that much closer to where he wanted to be, on top. No matter what happened, though, he wasn't about to throw the towel in. Wink wanted it too bad.

He thought about his mom standing in the doorway with Gary looking over her shoulder. The thought of her putting him out made his blood boil, and it gave him the extra drive he needed.

Think, Wink. How am I gon' get this money? Wink thought on that question all day, while Gator continuously brought custos through the spot.

Gator tried his old game of siccing two fresh pink toe turn-outs on Willie and Wink, but Wink shot that shit down immediately. His mission was money, fuck the rest.

"I see you learning," said Gator. "That's right. Don't you be nobody's fool in this world. You hear me?" asked Gator in a fatherly tone.

Wink nodded as he let the two skanks out the spot, along with Gator. Those words were stuck in Wink's head as he sat on the sofa, eyes to the ceiling. *Don't be nobody's fool.*

There was a light knock on the door.

"Go 'head and chill. I got it, my nigga," said Willie as he stood up to get the door.

It was Sheila from downstairs. She was Gator's old lady. "Hey, y'all. Why the long faces? Y'all usually up here laughing and whatnot," she said, stopping in front of the coffee table.

"It's just one of them days." Willie sighed.

"I know what you mean, baby. Which is why I came to get me two of them things." She unfolded a crispy twenty and gave it to Willie.

"Let me guess. You ain't want Gator try'na help you smoke yours up," said Willie.

"How you know?" Sheila laughed. "Shit, I been holding onto that twenty all day. Couldn't wait till his ass left."

"Here you go," Willie said, dropping two dime rocks into Sheila's palm.

Her smile turned upside down instantly. "J-Bo know his ass is wrong as two left shoes and a fat bitch in Spandex."

"What's wrong?" asked Willie.

"These shits are micro-dots. One hit and they gone. Shit, Fat Mike got rocks twice the size of these around the corner."

"What, you want your money back?" asked Willie.

"Nah, I'ma take 'em this time, but tell J-Bo he need to quit it." Sheila tucked the rocks into her bra and started for the door.

Wink was soaking up everything Sheila had said, and a plan had hit him. He knew exactly how he was going to get that money up, and fast.

Chapter Ten

The good news was that the police let Trey go. They tried everything in the book to keep him, but the lawyer J-Bo sent down there was one of the best in the game. He demanded they release Trey because they had nothing on him. The victim, Robert, pointed Krazy out in a lineup as the man who shot him, as did Mandy. Trey was out, but the bad news was Krazy was stuck in jail on a $150,000 bond for attempted murder. The lawyer tried to pull some strings with the magistrate for a reduced bond, but the prosecution argued that he was a flight risk because he lived in another state.

J-Bo was dead set on not forking up any money to get Krazy out of jail. He told them it was a learning lesson in the game, and that Krazy wouldn't do life. Wink wired Trey some money, though, for a bus ticket and fifty dollars to put on Krazy's books. Gator picked Trey up at the bus station in downtown Detroit. He took him to the spot on Linwood so he could talk to Wink and Willie.

"My nigga, what it is?" Willie asked as he rushed to give Trey a hug.

Trey wasn't feeling that hug shit. He pushed Willie back and focused his attention on Wink, who was lying across the sofa.

"I see you made it out. I hope you didn't drop the soap," joked Wink.

"Oh, you think that shit's funny, huh? Y'all still up in here sellin' for that ho-ass nigga, and he won't even post Krazy's bond," said Trey.

Willie saw an argument about to go down, so he made his way over to the love seat. Wink popped up from his spot on the sofa with his face twisted.

"First off, you bogus as mothafucka, you and Krazy. Y'all jacked that money and for what? Some trick-ass bitch," said Wink.

"I ain't do shit. But I still can't see how you sidin' with J-Bo over me and Krazy. We 'pose to be your niggas."

"It ain't about sides. We can't expect J-Bo to put up that kind of money. It'd be different if y'all got jammed up while handling business, then yeah, I'd be like yo, go get my man, but y'all fucked the lick up."

"So, you just gon' leave Krazy in jail?"

"You already know it ain't in me to do no shit like that. I'm in here grindin' twenty-four seven try'na get that nigga's lawyer fee together. We owe his lawyer another seven grand for him to take the case."

"And J-Bo won't front us the money?"

"Fuck J-Bo! We gotta do this shit! Us three right here. We gotta put our heads together, let our nuts hang, and go hard for Krazy." Wink looked from Trey to Willie. "We can't depend on nobody but us. Now, I need to know if y'all with me."

"I'm with you, my nigga," said Willie.

Wink turned to Trey. "What about you?"

"Come on, Trey. Krazy needs us," said Willie.

"I'm in, but soon as Krazy's out, I'm out," said Trey.

"We all out," said Wink. "Not out the game, but we gon' start doin' our own thang."

"That's what the fuck we shoulda been doin' from day one. We don't need J-Bo's sucka ass. All he doin' for real is getting over," said Trey.

"You don't think I know that? But who else was gon' show us the game? I done learned a few tricks, and once I learn a few more, we going solo. In the meantime, though, we gon' continue to work this one trick, here," Wink said, tossing Trey a rock.

"What you give me this for?" Trey asked, looking at the dime rock in his hand.

"You see how big it is?" asked Wink.

"Catch," he said, tossing Trey another rock.

"You see how small that one is?"

"Yeah," said Trey.

"Well, the second one is one of J-Bo's. That's what he got us sellin' around here. The other one is from this nigga around the corner name Fat Mike. They both dimes."

"So?"

"I know you ain't that slow, my nigga. We can buy Mike's shit and cut two dimes out of it. Then sell the shit outta the spot like it's J-Bo's," said Wink.

"I like that," said Trey.

"I was waitin' on you to get out before we put the lick down, 'cause I holla'd at J-Bo about lettin' us open up another spot. I figure if we can pimp two spots at once, we'll have Krazy's lawyer money in no time with cash to spare."

"How many of these you got?" asked Trey.

"Ten right now, but when we get paid, we gon' snatch a thousand dollars' worth. That'll double our money, and we'll just keep flipping until we can find us a connect."

"You know I'm with it. Fuck that nigga," said Trey.

"Word," added Willie.

"We just gotta be careful not to overdo it," said Wink.

"You sound like you been thinking on this," said Trey.

"Yeah, right. Nigga ain't told me nothin', and I been right here with him the whole time," said Willie.

"Nah, I just wanted to make sure all bases were covered so there won't be any more fuck-ups. 'Cause we gotta get this money up before Krazy's next court date," said Wink. He walked around the table and took a seat on the sofa. He leaned his head back and rubbed his face with both hands. Just two weeks in the game, and the stress was already hitting him. They hadn't even had the chance to at least hit the mall and splurge like every other nigga did when they first got in the game. They were facing some grown man shit early in the game, and it was all because of two mistakes, which should have been avoided.

Wink took his hands from his face and sat up. He interrupted Trey and Willie by saying, "Yo, no more mistakes."

Trey and Willie just looked at Wink like, *Where that come from?* But neither said anything. It was at that moment, right there in the front room of the spot, that they became men. Silence filled the room as they all were lost in thoughts of what they had to do to get Krazy out, and what they had to do in order to survive in the game. They realized that it wasn't all about money, cars, and clothes. There's a flip side to the game, and it's called jail.

Chapter Eleven

Everything was going according to plans. Wink played off of J-Bo's greed and talked him into opening another spot on the east side. J-Bo being the larceny-hearted nigga he was, quickly set up shop at this old cleaner's on 7 Mile and Eureka Street. He bought the building a while back, thinking he could crank the cleaner's back up. The Chinese couple who sold it to him were kind enough to leave all the pressing equipment. They just wanted out because they kept being robbed. The cleaner's sat for two years, and J-Bo had finally found some use for it. Only difference was, they wouldn't be pressing nothing except bills after they sold crack out of the drive-thru window.

J-Bo took Trey and Willie over to open the newfound spot. He was determined to get his money back out of that place one way or another. J-Bo showed them a few stash spots in case the task force decided to raid. He told them, if asked, to just say they were watching the building for vandalism. J-Bo thought he had all the sense when it came to running a crack operation, he put an OPEN SOON sign in the window and actually paid a few crackheads to do some minor repairs and cleaning to make it seem like the business would really be opening soon.

Things were going smooth. They had a bedroom set up in the back with a color TV and VCR, so Trey and Willie were chilling, just serving custos through the drive-thru window. Some custos would do a walk-through. They'd slide their money into the glass chute, then wait for their crack. It was a smooth operation, dead smack in the hood, so plenty of action was popping off.

Every morning, Willie and Trey would watch the pretty girls walk past on their way to Pershing High for summer school. They had to fight with all their might the temptations of taking the girls inside the cleaner's and blowing their young backs outs. The thought of Krazy sitting in jail would keep them focused—that and the constant calls they received from Wink to check up on them.

"Let that shit ring. It ain't nobody but Wink's ass. He over there bored as shit. Wanna keep callin' and fuckin' with us," said Trey.

"Yeah, but it might be an emergency," said Willie as he stared at the ringing phone sitting on the front counter.

Trey waved his hand at the phone and said, "I'll be back. I'ma shoot across the street to the store."

"A'ight," said Willie as he snatched up the phone.

"Osborn Cleaner's, how may I help you?"

"Nigga, drop the act. Where Trey at?" asked Wink.

"Damn, do you know any other numbers to dial? You call me more than my bitch," snapped Willie.

"That's 'cause you ain't got no bitch. Now stop playing and put Trey on."

"He just went to the store."

"A'ight, well, check it. When he gets back, tell 'im I said to catch a cab over here. It's on."

"It's on?" Willie repeated excitedly.

"That's what I said. Just tell 'im to hurry up."

Wink hung up the phone and finished sorting through the half of rocks he was going to give Trey to sell out the cleaner's. Wink had spent so much money with Fat Mike that he gave him a deal. Instead of a thousand dollars' worth of dime rocks, he gave him twelve hundred and told him the more he spent, the more of a deal he'd give him. That was music to Wink's thirsty ears. He put six hundred dollars' worth of rocks into a baggie and made up three more the same size. He'd give Trey two and keep two.

It had been almost a week, and the cleaner's was starting to show a consistent money flow on a daily basis. Wink thought that now was the time to start sliding their rocks into the mix of things before J-Bo could actually pinpoint and know how much to expect from the cleaner's on a regular basis. Wink would slide his rocks in on the midnight shift after J-Bo had done his last pickup for the day. Wink had it all mapped out. He figured it wouldn't be nothing to slide in two hundred dollars of his own rocks. J-Bo wouldn't miss it because the night was hard to peg.

Trey showed up in a yellow Checker Cab. He had the driver hit the horn twice, then climbed out. He met Wink on the landing of the spot.

"Here, put this up," said Wink.

"How much is it?"

"It's six hun'd in each one. I got a little deal on it, so keep a hun'd off each one and give me back the rest so we can re-up and get Krazy's lawyer this bread. He talkin' like he ain't gon' be there at his next court date if he ain't got his bread in hand."

"How hard you want me to go with this shit?"

"Just do like two hun'd, and only at night. We don't wanna blow the move."

"What about the work? Is it any good?"

"I done passed out a few testers, and it's actually better, so we shouldn't have no complaints. And I got 'em the same exact size."

Trey smiled, then extended his hand for Wink's. "That's what I'm talkin' about. Let me get outta here. I got the cabbie waitin'. A'ight, one," said Trey. He speed-walked across the street and jumped in the cab.

"Oh, shit. Pull off," he told the Arab driver. Trey ducked low in his seat at the sight of J-Bo's Porsche floating down Linwood in the direction of the spot. The cab passed the Porsche, and Trey sat up.

"You runnin' from someone, my friend?" the driver asked, looking through the rearview at Trey.

"I paid you to drive, so drive." Trey pulled the sandwich bags from his hoodie pocket and looked down at the crack. For once, he felt like he was holding something that belonged to him, and not to some nigga who was trying to work him like a sucka.

Trey didn't want to get in the game to begin with. That was Wink and his crew pressing him to start hustling. But he felt like if he was going to be out there taking penitentiary chances, then he was going to be one of the best that ever did it.

He tucked the rocks back into his hoodie and sank into his seat. Trey thought about his mom and told the driver to drive down his street. He didn't have the man stop. He just needed to see the house so he'd know she was all right. He was just like Wink—a momma's boy and spoiled to death. He already knew both their moms had an APB out on them because neither had bothered to call home. Trey wanted so bad to go see his mom, but he could hear her pitching a bitch about how he shouldn't be out there in the streets. She would beg him to stay home, she'd go to crying and some more shit . . . just a whole bunch of drama Trey wasn't ready to deal with. Krazy needed him right now, and there wasn't no way he was going to turn his back on him. Not for nothing in the world.

Trey felt guilty for Krazy being in jail. He didn't know that he'd snuck his grandfather's .25 along, but Trey felt like if he hadn't went in the bathroom to finish up his head job with Mandy, he would have been out there with Krazy, and none of this would even be happening. That was the whole purpose of them splitting up the way they did. Trey was supposed to keep an eye on Krazy and run the downstairs, while Wink held it down upstairs.

Trey felt even worse when he thought back to the look on Krazy's face when the guards came and told him he was being released. Krazy had a look on his face like, *What about me?* Trey had promised him and swore on his life that he wouldn't leave him there. Trey swallowed the lump in his throat and mouthed the words "I promise" as if he were back at the jail, standing in front of Krazy.

Chapter Twelve

Almost two months had passed since Wink copped his first double-up from Fat Mike. Since then, he had been to see Fat Mike twice a week and was now copping two times the amount as before. Wink wasn't being greedy. He was going hard 'cause Krazy's lawyer was demanding more money to file motions. Money to go out and visit Krazy, money for gas, and money to scratch his ass—the shit was getting out of control, but there was no way Wink was going to stop paying and leave Krazy on ice.

Trey and Willie were over on the east side, going just as hard, and J-Bo was starting to get suspicious. He couldn't figure out why, all of a sudden, the money from both spots was coming in so slow. He'd count behind them when he'd re-up, but the money and crack was always on point. But J-Bo, being in the game as long as he had, knew some shit had to be in the game, especially when he saw no change in traffic at the spots. He got a rental car and watched the spot on Linwood for a couple of days to see if the same custos were coming through, and they were. Even some new ones were showing up.

J-Bo would bend a few corners and watch the passing cars. *Maybe somebody's out there callin' themselves short-stoppin',* he thought, as he drove around the hood only to see no one out there except little kids shooting basketball on a crate nailed to the phone pole. The shit was irking the hell out of J-Bo. Losing money meant losing weight, sleep, and respect on the streets, and he wasn't accustomed to it.

J-Bo circled the block and spotted Rayfield. He was walking down Linwood, carrying two bags of bottles and cans over his shoulder. J-Bo grew up with Rayfield. They played PAL football together and went to the same schools. They used to be friends back in the day, but after high school, J-Bo started hustling, while Rayfield started experimenting with drugs. He finally found his drug of choice when crack hit the city. Who'd have ever thought J-Bo would be the one supplying it to him? But life was funny like that.

J-Bo pulled alongside the curb and rolled down his window. "Rayfield!" he yelled.

Rayfield was in a trance. He had one thing on his mind, and that was cashing in his bottles and getting himself a nice fat dime rock to get off. Then it was off to downtown to see what and who he could swindle.

J-Bo honked his horn, breaking Rayfield from his early morning mission. He turned and squinted with unfamiliarity in his eyes. The crack had really taken its toll on ole Rayfield.

"It's me, Gerald," said J-Bo.

Rayfield pulled back a smile, exposing his yellow, smoke-stained teeth. "I didn't know who you was," Rayfield said, crossing the short lawn.

"Put those in the trunk. You going up to Hank's, right?" J-Bo asked.

He put the bottles in the trunk. "Yeah, gotta cash these bottles in." Rayfield climbed in the passenger seat, out of breath and reeking something awful.

J-Bo rolled down all the windows, then pulled away from the curb with his head leaned as close to the window as possible.

"I see you're out here still doing your thang. That's good, man," Rayfield said, smiling.

"I would ask you when you gon' clean yo'self up, but that's none of my business. I wanted to holla at you 'cause I need you to do somethin'."

"Anything. What's up?"

J-Bo rode past the spot, then asked, "You been coppin' at my spot lately?"

"Yeah, why?"

"Notice anything funny going on?"

"Just the size of them damn rocks. They're small as hell, but that's always been your M.O." Rayfield laughed.

"What about the crack? Is it always the same high?"

"It's never the same. But then it could just be me. You know I been chasing that first high since '85."

J-Bo dug in his pocket and pulled out a hundred-dollar bill. "Look, I want you to go up and get ten rocks out of my spot. I'ma let you keep them, but I just want to see them first."

Rayfield's eyes lit up like he'd just won the Powerball on the Super Lotto. J-Bo handed the bill to him and circled the block, then parked on the corner.

"That's all you want me to do?" asked Rayfield.

"Yeah. I'ma be right here, waitin' on you. And Ray, don't make me have to chase you. I'ma give you all the rocks," said J-Bo.

Rayfield pulled the door handle. "I got you, baby."

J-Bo watched as Rayfield's head got small. He knew Rayfield like the back of his hand. Everybody knew about Rayfield and how scandalous he was. He was known for pulling capers on people's shit and then would have the nerve to show his face in the hood a couple days later. After a while, people got tired of chasing him, and instead, they put the word out there. His grimy ways had earned him a name in the city. People from all over Detroit would be saying, "Don't make me pull a Rayfield move on yo' ass."

J-Bo relaxed at the sight of Rayfield heading back for the car. *Good,* he thought. He really didn't feel like a foot chase through the hood. Rayfield climbed in the car and poured the ten dime rocks into J-Bo's palm.

"You sure you just got these from my spot?" J-Bo asked, looking up from his hand.

"Yeah, that's what the li'l nigga gave me."

J-Bo handed Rayfield the rocks after looking them over once more. He pulled away from the curb and drove over to Hank's liquor store. J-Bo popped the trunk for Rayfield to get his bottles.

"A'ight, good lookin' out, Bo." Rayfield climbed out the car.

J-Bo was furious and had every intention of going around to the spot and putting hands on Wink for insulting his intelligence. But J-Bo was never one to act out of emotion, because he believed an emotional man was a weak man. Half of the rocks Rayfield showed J-Bo were his. The other five he had not a clue where they came from. He could tell that they weren't his because they weren't in the sky blue 20-20 packs he used. They were in sandwich bags.

"Where the fuck is his li'l ass gettin' on from?" J-Bo asked himself aloud.

He bent the corner of Andover and saw Fat Mike standing outside in front of his spot. Fat Mike flagged him to pull over to the curb.

"What's up, big boy?" J-Bo asked.

Fat Mike sank into the passenger seat of the Dynasty. His 380 pounds caused the car to sink. "When you gon' be ready for me? I'm 'bout out around here," said Fat Mike.

Fat Mike was one of the few niggas J-Bo sold weight to. The rest of them niggas he made work for him, or otherwise they wouldn't get any money.

"You flyin' through that shit, ain't you? It usually takes you two weeks to dump a half brick," said J-Bo.

"Yeah, but I got this li'l nigga coppin' from me. He be spending two G's every couple of days. And the thing about it is, he's buying all rocks. Stupid mothafucka." Fat Mike laughed at the thought of him getting over so well. He had started referring to Wink as his "sweet thang."

"What the nigga look like?" asked J-Bo.

"I'm not tellin' you so you can try an' steal him from me. That's my sweet thang."

"Nah, I've got a good feelin' you're talkin' about my li'l worker, Wink. He's pushin' some side shit outta my spot, and I just wanted to know where it was coming from."

"That's crazy. Every time I run across something sweet, shit don't never last long. Yeah, that's his li'l ass." Fat Mike couldn't lie to J-Bo because that would be like biting the hand that was feeding him. "Damn!" he yelled, then slapped the dashboard.

"You know what they say. You gotta get it while the gettin' is good."

"So, what? You gon' give the li'l nigga the pumpkin head for disrespecting?"

"I started to, but nah. I want to show his li'l ass what he's doing is elementary and that school is in. It's time

I teach him one last good lesson before he graduates."
J-Bo was doing what he did best, cooking up a master
plan.

Fat Mike looked over and saw that spaced-out, sinister
look in J-Bo's eyes. "I been knowing you for too long,
Bo. What's that look in your eyes?"

"I need yo' help on baking his cake," J-Bo said. He
snapped out of his trance with a well thought out plan.

"I'm listening."

"You say he be coppin' like two G's every time he
re-ups, right?"

"Yeah."

"A'ight, well, what I want you to do is tell 'im you **got**
a sweet deal for him, but that you can't sit on it. Tell 'im
you'll give 'im twenty ounces for ten grand."

"Then what? You want me to rob him?"

"Oh, we gon' definitely do that., but with no gun," J-Bo
said. He knew just about how much money Wink had
cuffed on him, which was about ten thousand, give or
take. It was ten thousand he was soon to part with.

J-Bo let Fat Mike out and went to put the finishing
touches on his cake bake. There was no way he was
going to let Wink get over, let alone think he was getting
over.

Chapter Thirteen

J-Bo was a master when it came to masking his emotions. He could smile in your face while he was plotting on blowing your brains out. It was no different with Wink. J-Bo played it cool as a fan, acting as if he knew nothing. His complaints about the spot slowing down ceased. He attributed the loss of money to the narcos being out, running down custos as they left from the spot. He told Wink that he'd run into a few custos at Hank's, and they said they stopped coming because they were scared they'd be arrested. He assured Wink that the spot would pick back up and not to worry about it.

This was all, of course, to make Wink feel lax in what he was doing. He was relieved to know J-Bo hadn't suspected any shady dealings on his part. They both smiled in each other's faces during pickups and dropoffs. Wink would be cheesin' right along with J-Bo all the way until he left; then it was back to business.

Wink had another phone line put in the spot so that Krazy could call home collect. J-Bo's petty, penny-pinching ass had already shot down the idea of Krazy calling the spot's phone because he didn't want to be stuck with no high-ass bill. Wink held it down, though. Krazy would call every hour on the hour, worrying the hell out of Wink about his court date and what they might do to him if he lost at trial. They had the same conversation at least fifty times. They'd start out talking about back in the day, remember this, and do you remember that? Then Krazy would go silent. He was beginning to feel like that was what was left on his life, nothing but old memories. He knew if he lost at trial, them honkies were going to roof his black ass.

Wink was sitting on the edge of his sofa seat, leaning forward while counting out the re-up money for Fat Mike. He held the phone to his ear with his shoulder. "Go ahead. I'm listening," he told Krazy.

"My nigga, these crackers is try'na give me forever and a day," said Krazy.

"How many times do I have to tell you stop stressin'? You gon' be straight." Wink tried to assure his friend. He was steady counting out the re-up money and putting it in stacks of a thousand.

"That's easy for you to say. Y'all out there free as a mothafucka, living it up while I'm in here on ice."

"Who's living it up? 'Cause we sure in the hell ain't. Every time you call this phone, my nigga, I'm right here going hard, try'na get this money up for your lawyer. And Willie and Trey on the east side doing the same thing. We done blew the whole summer fuckin' with this shit, but it's cool, 'cause you our nigga, and we got love for you."

"I know, my nigga. It's just good to hear sometimes. These crackers got me 'bout to worry a patch in my head," Krazy said, leaning against the phone with his head down. He was sick that he got jammed up, and of all places, in a small town like Davenport.

The food was garbage. All the guards were locals who had heard about the incident, and some them even personally knew Mandy and Robert. Krazy was real leery of them tobacco-chewing honkies. He didn't know what they might try and pull.

"Just don't leave me in here, Wink."

"We got you. You just gotta ride it out, and hopefully yo' mouthpiece can get your bond reduced. But until then, fall back and bust ya head."

"You got jokes, huh?" smiled Krazy.

"Nah, I'm just fuckin' with you. Damn, yo' phone beeping. It's about to hang up?"

"'Bout another minute."

"A'ight, I wanna ask you one question before you go. What were you thinking about bringing the Donnie Brosco?"

"After that demo happened with you up at Hank's, I told myself not again. Never would we be caught slippin' again, and I meant that."

The phone went dead before Krazy could finish saying what he was saying, but Wink got the message. He figured it was something like that. Krazy was always putting his neck on the chopping block for his crew.

Wink smiled as he recalled the time Krazy took one for the team. Back when they were in middle school, all the other crews were showing up to school in stolen cars. The girls would all pile in and go on a joy ride. Wink never wanted his crew to seem lame or behind, so he paid this junkie Zap to steal him a car.

Wink pulled alongside Trey, Krazy, and Willie one morning in the stolen Toyota as they walked to school. The day played itself back as if it were just yesterday. They all climbed into the *stoly* and took turns joy-riding through the hood.

It was Krazy's turn, and he wanted to ride up to Pershing High so they could floss on some of the older chicks. Krazy pulled up in the Amoco gas station across from Pershing and parked like all the other niggas who were either skipping school or up there to pick up some chicks. He was leaning out the window, trying to get the attention of a pack of thick young girls when the narcos pulled into the rear of the station. All the other cars started pulling off, but Krazy was still shooting his shot at the girls. He hadn't seen the narcs until it was too late.

Krazy locked eyes with Officer Thrashter, who was riding shotgun in the cranberry Crown Victorian. "Oh, shit," said Krazy. He tried to play it cool, but the car stopped, and all four doors opened.

"Get out of the car now!" yelled Thrashter as he and his three partners slowly approached the Toyota.

Willie said from the back seat, "Pull off."

He didn't have to tell Krazy twice. It was right up his alley anyway. Krazy slapped the car down into drive and peeled away from the pump. The four officers dived out of the way and quickly climbed into their patrol car. Within minutes, they were on the Toyota's ass. The little six-cylinder Krazy was pushing wasn't measuring up to the souped-up 5.0 under the Crown Victoria's hood. It was like a mouse trying to outrun a cat. It just wasn't happening.

Krazy took them on a chase, though. He flew down residential streets at speeds of eighty miles per hour, trying to shake the narcs, but they were riding on their bumper. Willie and Trey were holding on for dear life in the back seat, while Wink rode shotgun, with his eyes bugging out of his head. All their hearts were beating a million miles an hour.

Krazy wasn't scared, though, even knowing there was no way out. Krazy figured there wasn't any sense in all of them going down. He made a screeching right down Fenlon Street and looked in the rearview at Trey and Willie.

"This what I want y'all to do," he said. "When I stop, all y'all jump out and run."

"What about you?" asked Wink.

"Don't worry about me. Just get ready." Krazy cut the wheel and slammed on the brakes, making the car do a half donut so that his door was facing the narcs. "Go!" yelled Krazy.

Wink, Trey, and Willie all got out and ran, while Krazy stayed to block them in. The narcs jumped out and snatched Krazy out of the window and beat the brakes off him. Wink looked back over his shoulder at Krazy as the cops continued to put hands and feet on him. Wink wanted to go back and try to help Krazy, but he realized what Krazy had done. He took one for the team.

Krazy spent two months down at the juvey center and came on home. Wink wished it was that simple with this case, but he knew it wasn't.

"One for the team," Wink said as he gathered up the money off the coffee table. He looked at the alarm clock beside him. It was almost one o'clock. Almost time to meet Fat Mike. He told Wink that he had a partner who'd give him a sweet deal, twenty ounces of hard for ten grand. Wink had been stacking the odds for a week, and he finally had the money up. With twenty ounces, he could afford to pay for Krazy's lawyer and have something put away for his bond.

Wink put all the money in a brown paper bag, then stuffed the bag into his drawers. He pulled his hoodie over his pants and patted the bag for safekeeping. He locked the spot up and took the raggedy back staircase down to the backyard. He jumped the back fence into the alley and walked down to Fat Mike's spot on the next street over.

Wink scanned the block as he knocked on the door. Fat Mike snatched the battered door open and moved aside, letting Wink in.

"Wink, my man. What's up, hustla?" asked Fat Mike as he put the two crossboards back on the door.

Wink eyed the man seated on the sofa. "I'm good, but yo, who this?" Wink hadn't taken his eyes off the high yellow man.

"This my man, Tony Long Loot, one of the richest niggas to come off the west side." Fat Mike put his hand on Wink's shoulder.

"Yeah. Well, y'all got that ready or what?" Wink wasn't for all the small talk. He was trying to get what he came for so he could be on his way.

Tony Long Loot stood up and mashed the Newport he'd been smoking into the glass ashtray on the ancient coffee table. "I got what you need. Did you bring the money?" Tony asked, giving Wink his back.

"I got it near," Wink said, following Tony into the kitchen.

Tony opened one of the cabinets above the stove. He pulled down a box of Frosted Flakes cereal, then carried it over to the kitchen table. Tony poured twenty individually wrapped ounces onto the table and waved his hand. "It's all here."

Wink picked up one of the cookie-size pieces and inspected it.

"Money," said Tony.

Wink looked over at Fat Mike, who gave him the nod like it was cool. Wink lifted his hoodie and dug the paper bag out his drawers. He set the bag on the table and said, "That's ten grand."

"A'ight then, young dawg. Good business. Good business," Tony repeated as he counted the money.

"I'ma holla at you later." Wink stuffed the ounces back inside the cereal box.

"I'll be here. Just come through." Fat Mike let Wink out the back door and watched as he leaped the back gate.

Tony kept the agreed-upon five hundred dollars and handed Fat Mike the rest.

"I'm not gon' have to kill his young ass, am I?" asked Tony, real name Fred.

"You saw how frail he is. Wink don't want no problems. He gon' have to just charge it to the game," Fat Mike assured Fred while he separated his cut from J-Bo's.

Chapter Fourteen

J-Bo lay in the cut on Wink. He waited until the night shift, then sent Rayfield up to buy ten rocks. Just as J-Bo suspected, Wink had mixed half of his own rocks in with some of J-Bo's.

J-Bo gave Rayfield Wink's five rocks and watched as he packed his pipe, then beamed up to . . .

"What the fuck is that shit?" yelled Rayfield. He choked and spat from the smoke.

"This what you sellin' these days?" he asked, still gagging.

"Nah, that's what li'l bastard calls himself try'na sell. Just don't know he's gon' get himself seriously hurt out here." J-Bo looked up at the spot from across the street.

"The shit done fucked my pipe up. I don't know what it is, but it sure in the hell ain't crack."

"I got five real ones for you, but I need you to go in there and check the dog shit outta his li'l ass."

"What you mean? Like, beat his ass? 'Cause you know I don't discriminate."

"Nah, just choke his ass up a little. I'ma come in once you spook him."

"Say no more." Rayfield got out the car and crossed the street.

J-Bo watched as he climbed the steps and disappeared inside the spot. J-Bo really liked Wink, so he wasn't going to let anything happen to him, but he still had to be taught a lesson, and who better than Rayfield's crazy ass to teach him?

Rayfield put his screw face on as he climbed the steps. He balled up his fist and pounded on the door like a madman.

Wink's eyes bucked at the sound of the pounding. He jumped to his feet and grabbed everything off the table and rushed over to the stash spot in the fireplace. Who else but the police would be beating down the door like that?

"I know your ass is in there. Open this door!" yelled Rayfield.

Hearing Rayfield's voice sorta put Wink at ease from knowing it wasn't the police. But he was still a bit hesitant to open the door. Why was this nut yelling and banging?

"Open up this fuckin' door!" yelled Rayfield.

"What's up?" Wink shouted from inside.

Rayfield stepped back, then rammed his shoulder into the door, sending it flying open. Wink jumped back. The door nearly hit him in the head.

"What's wrong?" he asked, back stepping into the living room. Fear filled every cell of his body as Rayfield backed him into the corner next to the fireplace.

"You sold me some fuckin' gank. That's what's up. But you knew that, didn't you?" asked Rayfield. The look in his eyes was that of a deranged man.

"You know I wouldn't play you like that, Ray man. We cool. I can make it up."

"Nah, fuck that." Rayfield charged Wink with his hands outstretched. He grabbed hold of Wink's scrawny little neck and commenced to choking the shit out of him. To his surprise, though, Wink was fighting back, or at least trying to. He kicked and swung wildly, but to no avail.

"That's right, go to sleep," whispered Rayfield as he watched Wink's eyes flutter. He was losing consciousness.

J-Bo rushed into the living room and snatched ole Rayfield off of Wink. Rayfield had forgotten he was only supposed to be scaring Wink. He had blanked out in that bitch. J-Bo stood between the two with his arms stretched out.

"Here you go. I'ma catch you later." J-Bo handed Rayfield his well-deserved five rocks.

"Thanks, baby. And you need to teach slim how to throw his hand," Rayfield said on his way out.

"Nah, school's out," said J-Bo as he turned and focused his attention on Wink, who was bent over at the knee, trying to catch his breath.

"Why'd you let him go? We shoulda fucked him up," said Wink, struggling to stand up.

"Never mind that. Stand yo' ass up and look at me."

Wink pushed himself up from his knees and leaned against the fireplace.

"I want you to tell me the truth. You up here sellin' your own shit?" asked J-Bo.

Wink stopped breathing. His eyes grew to the size of two fifty-cent pieces.

"Don't lie to me," warned J-Bo.

Wink dropped his head like a nigga on his way to jail. He shook his head and tried offering his reason. "I was just try'na get this money up for Krazy's lawyer, Bo. I swear it wasn't to try and get over on you."

"Nigga, save that weak-ass shit, 'cause you been pitchin' yo' own shit. But just like anything else that you do in the dark, it'll always come to light. What? You thought I wasn't gon' find out you been buying shit off Fat Mike?"

Wink's face tightened up in shock.

"Yeah, I know all about you buying his rocks, then cutting them in half and mixing 'em with mines. I just wanted to see how long you were going to continue thinking you had a brain. Your first mistake was even tryin' some stupid shit like that, then the baggies you were using are different from mine's. And plus, all this money you keep sending Mr. Hurston for Krazy. You had a plan. You just ain't think it through. Just like your chess game." J-Bo walked over to the chessboard. "Com'ere."

"Remember when I asked you what piece you were on the board, and you said a pawn? You were never a pawn," said J-Bo as he took all the pieces off the board. "You see that?" he said, placing his finger on one of the squares. "That's what you were when you first came into the game, a square. A square represents the road or path all the players in the game use to get to where they wanna be, and that's the top. When I first met you, you were a square because I could use you to further my cause, but somewhere along the lines, you became a pawn. You're learning too fast, and I can't use you anymore."

"So, what you saying, Bo?"

"Wink, I'm not at all mad with you. You did what we all do in this game, and that's try and get over. You just got caught. Pretty soon, I know you're going to be great at this shit, and then I won't be able to catch you. So, it's best I cut ties now. See, Wink, in this game, just like in chess, the object is to keep everyone around you under you for as long as you can. You can't win the game with two kings on the board."

"So, you knew the whole time, huh?" asked Wink.

"Yep."

"What about the twenty ounces? Can't I at least get my money back?"

J-Bo put his hand on Wink's shoulder and pulled back a wide smile. "That was the cost of your final lesson. Consider yourself lucky. Most pay with their life." J-Bo picked up one of the pawns from the table and walked Wink to the door. He stopped to face Wink, then said, "I want you to always remember that it's a cold game, but it's fair. Here," he said, handing Wink the black pawn. "It's up to you if you become a king."

Wink looked J-Bo in the eye and felt mixed emotions. He wasn't sure if he was ready to leave the nest just yet, but he wasn't about to show any signs of weakness. He held his head high and gave J-Bo a nod, then turned to leave.

J-Bo watched from the top step as Wink left the same way he found him—broke. That was Wink's last lesson, and it cost him everything he had and some.

Wink took the walk of shame down Linwood with his hands stuffed deep inside the empty pockets of his jeans. *Damn, ten G's*, he thought. That was a hard pill to swallow. The only thing J-Bo left Wink with was the game he picked up along the way.

"What the fuck am I gon' do now?" The thought of Krazy being stuck in jail ran through Wink's mind. Shit just couldn't get any worse.

Wink flagged a yellow Checker Cab once he reached Dexter. The Arab driver promptly asked for a deposit. Wink tried telling the man he'd pay him once they got to the east side.

"No money, me no drive you. Out!"

Wink felt like shit on a stick. He reluctantly climbed out the cab and watched the cab skirt off in pursuit of someone who had money in hand. Wink looked at the pay phone next to the bus stop and thought to call his mom, but he shook that thought away. He wasn't going to give her and Gary the satisfaction of seeing him down on his knees so they could scold him with a bunch of dumb-ass I-told-you-so's. He tried calling Trey and Willie at the cleaner's, but their line didn't accept collect calls. As he slammed the phone back on the hook, J-Bo bent the corner in his red Porsche. He looked at Wink, hit his horn, and kept it moving.

Wink sucked it up and put one foot in front of the other. It was a long walk to the east side, but Wink figured he could use the time to get his plans together. 'Cause one thing for certain, he wasn't about to give in or give out.

Chapter Fifteen

When Wink finally made it back to the east side, he was drained, his feet blistered, his shirt clung to his back from sweat, and he had a pounding headache. He had thought of every possible way he could to make some money, but Wink couldn't come up with anything. He couldn't get past the ten thousand dollar loss, but he knew he had to do something, and fast.

J-Bo had already beat Wink to the cleaner's. He did the honors of stripping Trey and Willie of all their side cash as well as his, then sent them on foot just like he did Wink. Wink found them at Trey's house down in the basement, eating some of Ms. Shelton's good home cooking. Trey's mom was so happy her baby was alive and home that she cooked him a full meal with fried chicken, mashed potatoes, gravy, corn bread, greens, and a tall pitcher of her famous kiwi-strawberry Kool-Aid. She would cuss him out later.

Ms. Shelton came down the basement to check on Trey and Willie and see if they needed anything else. She stopped in her tracks, put her hands on her hips, then grunted in Wink's direction. She never did like Wink. Ever since he and Trey started hanging out, Ms. Shelton would always toot her nose up at the sight of Wink. She called him the son of Satan. Ms. Shelton always blamed Wink every time Trey got in trouble.

"What is he doing in my house?" she said.

"Ma, can you please not start."

"Do your mom know you're over here? She's been lookin' for you." She frowned at Wink.

"I'ma call her in a minute," Wink said from the love seat. The feeling was mutual; he couldn't stand her either.

Ms. Shelton rolled her eyes and turned on her heels.

"Don't mind her, my nigga," said Trey.

"I never do."

"What happened with J-Bo? How the nigga find out?" asked Willie.

"The bitch nigga Fat Mike sold me out. And he set me up with some pretty nigga name Tony Long Loot. He sold me twenty ounces of gank."

"Word. How much he get you for?" asked Trey.

"You don't wanna know." Wink put his hands to his face and wiped the invisible pain away.

"How much, Wink?" Trey said.

Wink closed his eyes and said, "Everything."

"The whole ten G's?" Willie dropped his fork. He pushed back from the table and stood up.

"Wink, tell me you didn't let that fat fuck clip you for the whole stash," Trey stood beside Willie. They both looked down at Wink while he rubbed his temples.

"When I say everything, I mean every cent. I didn't even have bus fare. I walked all the way home."

"This some bullshit!" Willie yelled. "How the fuck we keep starting from the bottom? We might as well throw in the towel."

"That's what we're not going to do. Krazy's still in jail, remember." Wink stood up and began pacing.

"So, what are we going to do?" asked Trey.

"I say we put J-Bo tiny ass in the trunk and make 'im take us to the money. I know his bitch ass holdin'," said Willie.

"I'm with that," Trey said.

"Slow down, gun slinger. Ain't no sense in diggin' ourselves no deeper hole than the one we're already in." Wink paced.

"You act like J-Bo can't be touched. His ass ain't the Mob. He ain't untouchable," snapped Trey.

Wink stopped dead in his face, chest to chest, and stared Trey in the eyes. "You ready to kill J-Bo? 'Cause that's what we gon' have to do if we go barking. Hell nah, he ain't the Mob, but his hand is way stronger than ours. He knows where yo' moms lay her head at. Willie, you too, and me. This shit ain't no game out here, so unless y'all talkin' 'bout slumpin' his ass, miss me with that shit."

Wink looked from Trey to Willie. Just like he thought, they was just talking. He went back to pacing the floor and trying to come up with something. He had shot down their feeble idea, and yet he hadn't offered another solution.

Wink stopped dead in his tracks at the sound of his mom's voice. She was talking to Ms. Shelton.

"Damn, why yo' momma can't never mind her business?" said Wink. He knew Ms. Shelton went and called Hope. She would do anything to get his demonic self out of her house.

"Wayne, are you down here?" Hope asked as she made her way down the basement. She stopped at the bottom step and put her hands to her face. Tears quickly welled in her eyes.

"Y'all g'on upstairs and let Wayne talk to his mother." Ms. Shelton shooed Trey and Willie up. She patted Hope on the back while looking at Wink with a you-oughta-be-shamed look. "It's going to be all right, Hope."

Wink was burning up inside. Damn, he hated Trey's nosey-ass momma. He wanted to blame something or someone other than himself. He needed to focus on anything other than the beautiful woman standing before him with tears streaming down her face.

"Come here, Wayne." Hope sniffled. She opened her arms and started for her son.

Wink met his mom halfway, and they embraced. He couldn't help but feel bad for having his mom worried sick. She didn't even look her normal self. She looked like she hadn't slept in days.

"Oh my God, Wayne. I thought you were dead." Hope squeezed Wink tight and continued to rub the back of his head while her tears soaked his shoulder.

"I'm okay, Mom. I'm okay."

"Step back and let me look at you," Hope said, wiping tears from her face. "You've lost a lot of weight. What, you weren't eatin'?"

"Yeah, I been eatin'. It just wasn't your good cookin'."

Hope managed a smile. She continued to look her son over. "Wayne, I wish you would leave them streets to their keeper and come on home. Home is where you belong, baby."

"You put me out, remember?"

"I know, and that was the worst decision I ever made in my entire life, and I'm sorry. I should've never kicked you to the streets."

Wink dropped his eyes to the floor. "What about Gary?"

"He's my man, but you'll always be my son, Wayne. I won't let him come between us ever again. I promise. Just come home with me so I can get you out of these clothes and put some food in you."

"Ma, I'm not a child anymore. I need to know you won't be on my back about going to college or working if I come home."

"So, what are you going to do? Huh, Wayne? You've been gone for three months and you're wearing the same clothes you left in. What's the reason you want to be out there so damn bad for?"

"That's what I'm talkin' about right there. Ma, I love you, but I gotta live my life, and this is what I'm going to be doing."

"You're hardheaded just like your father, and you see where it got him. Two life sentences."

"I'm not him, and he ain't never been my father," Wink said heatedly. He hated even thinking about the nigga his mom kept referring to as his father. Wayne, Sr. ain't never did shit for Wink except go half on a baby with his moms.

"I'm sorry." Hope knew how much Wink disliked his father. "Just come home, Wayne, and I'll try to give you your space. I just really need you home."

Wink thought about it for a second and saw the hurt in his mother's eyes. She didn't deserve this, Wink told himself. He reached for Hope's hand and kissed the back of it.

"Let's go home," said Hope as she started for the steps.

Trey was waiting on Wink at the top of the steps and followed them out to the car. Wink waited until his mom got in the car and shut the door.

"I hope you not checkin' out on me," Wink said.

"Wink, you tell me what our next move is gon' be, and I'll be right there beside you."

"For Krazy." He gave Trey a pound. "Tomorrow," he said, then climbed in the car.

When Wink got home, it just didn't feel the same. He felt like a total failure, a little boy running home, scared of the cold world. He felt like coming back home was accepting defeat. His mom scurried to the bathroom and started his bath, set some new clothes out for him, then it was off to the kitchen, where she prepared his favorite meal, smothered pork chops.

When Wink finished showering, his food awaited him in the oven. His appetite was instantly spoiled at the sight of Gary's sucka-lame ass sitting bare-chested at the kitchen table, reading the paper.

Wink had a joke he wanted to ask Gary. "What, you lookin' for a job?" But he kept it to himself, figuring he didn't want to start off negative. He wanted to be civil for his mom.

Hope sat across from Gary, her face lit up like a Christmas tree when she looked up from the crossword puzzle and saw Wink. "Come on and have a seat, baby." She was smiling from ear to ear.

Wink looked at Gary, then said, "I'ma eat in my room, Ma."

"Okay. There's plenty down here if you want more," Hope said.

Wink carried his two-pound plate, along with a two-liter bottle of Coke, up to his master bedroom. He flopped down on his king-size waterbed and turned the TV onto the news.

"Stupid mothafucka," he said of the man being arrested after crashing on a high-speed chase.

Wink was enjoying his mom's cooking when Gary appeared in the doorway. Wink looked up at him but didn't say anything.

"Can I come in?" asked Gary. He was holding a large burgundy photo album in his hand and a shoebox underneath it.

"Yeah," Wink said, really wanting to say, "Fuck nah, beat it." But he was curious as to what ole dusty had to show him.

Gary took a seat on the edge of the bed and set the photo album and shoebox down.

"Wayne, I know—"

"My name's Wink."

"I'm cool with that," said Gary. "A'ight, Wink. As I was about to say, I know we haven't never seen eye to eye, and I want you to know that's my fault. I never took the time to sit down with you and let you really get to know who I am."

Wink was thinking, *I know exactly who you are. You're bum-ass Gary.*

"There's something me and your mom shoulda told you long time ago."

Please don't let this nigga come out his mouth and say he's my daddy. Please . . .

"Wink, your mom and I used to be engaged long time ago." Gary opened the shoebox and removed a stack of Polaroid pictures. He took the rubber band off, then handed Wink the first two pictures.

"That's me and your mom at the prom. That was 1971." Gary, for a moment, was back at the prom, out on the dance floor with the prettiest girl in all of Pershing High. He was prom king, and she was his queen.

Wink looked the pictures over, then handed them back. "I see you had the bell bottom tux with the blowout."

"Yeah, that was the style back then." Gary smiled. "Boy, do I miss those days." Gary's smile slowly faded as he focused back on his reason for pulling out the photos to begin with.

"After high school, I proposed to your mom, and we were supposed to get married a few months later."

"What about, you know, Wayne?" Wink hated calling ole boy Dad—or anything else, for that matter. His name was Wayne.

"I was with your mom first. She was my first love and everything. Somehow, your father, who was my main man at the time, he hooked up with your mom behind my back. Your moms popped up pregnant with you, and the whole time, I'm thinking it's mine. Well, Wayne and me got jammed up by the feds. He got booked at trial, and I did a five-year bid. When I got out, your mom came clean with me about you being Wayne's son."

"That's why y'all never got married?"

"Yeah, and a lot of other things. So much had changed between us. That's why we're on and off like we are."

"What about Wayne?"

"I haven't heard from him since I got out. I was salty with him for betraying me, and more importantly, not tellin' me."

"Does he know that I'm his son?"

"That, I don't know. You would have to ask your mom about that."

Wink wondered if that was the reason his father never got at him. And why, after all these years, was Gary telling him this? He liked it better hating him.

"I know you think that I'm a washed-up old fool and don't know nothin', but I've been down the road you're on and seen everything there is to see. I've been to the top, and I've been to the bottom. You seem to have your mind made up on being in the game, so I'm going to give it to you like I learned it.

"See, ain't nobody show me anything when I started hustling. I had to learn everything by bumping my head. The most valuable lesson I learned is if you're going to do it, do it to the max, 'cause when them people come see about you, that's what they're going for, the max. I just slipped through the cracks. That's why I don't hustle anymore because I know what's waiting—death or a life sentence.

"Wink, if you're going to play this game, just make sure you always go hard. Don't play no games. Get yours, and hopefully, you'll be one of the few who actually make it out." Gary paused for a moment, then looked down at the shoebox. "I left you something at the bottom of the box. It belonged to your dad. I'm sure he'd want you to have it. I'ma leave you with the pictures. Just bring 'em down when you're done lookin' at 'em."

Gary stood up and started for the door, but then turned to face Wink. "If you ever need something, don't be ashamed to ask. This old dog still know all the tricks."

Wink nodded and said, "A'ight." He waited until Gary bent the corner, then opened the photo album. He stared at the flick of Gary with his dad back in the day. They were at the Fox Theatre at some type of shindig. They were suited and gator booted, with black diamond minks draped over their shoulders. Wink took the picture out of its place and set it on the bed. He flipped through the rest of them in awe. He had no idea Gary used to be a money-gettin' nigga. He had pictures with brand new Fleetwoods and stinkin' Lincolns. In each flick, he wore a different suit with matching gators.

Wink had no idea Gary was a major player. His mom never spoke a word about it. But now everything was starting to make sense. That's why Gary never worked. Maybe he still had some of that old-face money stashed somewhere, thought Wink.

He closed the album, then reached for the box. At the bottom sat a gold bracelet that was iced out. It was a custom-made nugget with the letters WAYNE in white crushed diamonds. Wink picked up the picture beside him. It was the same bracelet his father wore in the picture. After all those years, it still hadn't lost its luster. Wink tried it on and stood in the mirror, taking on the B-boy stance.

For the first time in his life, Wink wondered what his father was doing. There were a bunch of questions that answers alone couldn't satisfy. Wink sat down to write him. He stared at the blank piece of paper in front of him, trying to think of what to write. Then he thought, *Maybe I should go see him.*

Chapter Sixteen

Wink was awakened by the smell of bacon and eggs burning. He rolled onto his back and smiled at the scent. He lay staring at the ceiling for a moment. It felt good to sleep in his old bed again. He had clunked out early last night and slept like a baby. Wink let his eyes adjust to the sunlit room, then squinted at his alarm clock beside him. It was going on nine o'clock. Time to get up, he thought, rolling out of bed and stepping into his slippers.

Wink grabbed the old photo album and shoebox off his dresser, then went downstairs. He found his mom and Gary perched at the kitchen table, enjoying breakfast.

"Mornin', baby," said Hope She raised her coffee mug halfway, then stopped. Her eyes locked on the ever-so-familiar photo album in Wink's hands.

"What are you doin' with those?"

"It's okay. I gave 'em to him to look at." Gary nodded at Wink, then continued eating his breakfast.

"Good morning, Ma." Wink walked over and gave his mom a kiss on the forehead.

"I'll take those. Here, have a sat, Wink." Gary got up and cleared his plate.

"Since when you start calling him Wink? His name is Wayne in this house."

Wink took a seat across from Hope and dug into his bacon and eggs. He looked up from his plate to see his mom staring at him. The look in her eyes asked, *How much did he tell you?*

"Why you lookin' at me like that?"

"You are mine's. I can look at you. So, what all Gary tell you?"

"Not enough. I was hoping you'd fill me in." Wink bit into a crispy slice of bacon.

Hope sipped her coffee, then pushed her chair back and stood up. "Maybe later. Right now, I've gotta get ready for work."

Wink watched his mom's back as she rinsed her dishes. He could tell by the sound of her voice that she had no intention of having that conversation. Wink decided not to press the issue because, after all, she was his mom. She had been the one there his whole life. So what if she made a few mistakes? She didn't owe up no explanations. His love for Ma Dukes would never waver, but those thoughts of his father still lingered in the back of his mind.

"I'll see you when I get off?" Hope said.

"I'll see you before you close your eyes tonight."

"Fair enough. I want you to be careful, and I left you some money on the mantle."

"Thanks, Ma."

Hope gave Wink a hug around the neck and kissed his cheek before telling him, "I love you."

"Love you too." Wink watched as his mom bent the corner out of the kitchen. *Probably on her way to cuss Gary's soft ass out,* he thought with a smirk.

The phone rang, and Wink leaped to his feet. "I got it!" he yelled, then snatched the phone off the wall.

"Hello."

"Ay yo, meet me at my crib," said Trey.

"What's up, my nigga? You sound like it's an emergency."

"Nah, but it's 'bout this money. Just get around here. Me and Willie gon' be in the basement."

"Yo' momma there?"

"Nah, she at work."

Good, thought Wink. "A'ight, I'm on my way."

Wink scraped his plate, then rushed into the bathroom to take a quick shower. When he came out, he found his clothes already set out on his bed with a brand-new pair of Patrick Ewings. He smiled at the thought of his mom always looking out for her baby. He slid into his crispy new Boss jeans, then stepped into the Ewings.

Wink walked over to his dresser and opened the top drawer. He unfolded the sweater and grabbed the gold nugget bracelet. He looked at it for a moment, then tucked it inside his pants pocket.

Wink grabbed the fifty dollars off the mantle. Gary was stretched out across the sofa, watching *The Price is Right*.

"Remember what I said. You need anything, don't hesitate to ask," said Gary.

"A'ight," said Wink. He left out the house, thinking that maybe he was wrong about ole Gary. He never really gave him a chance because he didn't want to see him with his mom, but looking at the pictures of Gary from back in the day gave him a different outlook. Wink smiled to himself as he thought of Gary's skinny ass out there hustling.

Wink knocked on the basement window where Trey and Willie were seated, playing that stupid-ass game Contra on Nintendo. He could hear the theme music blasting from the surround sound system. Trey paused the game and got up to let Wink in.

regret for making the trip suddenly vanished. Wink could deal with all the country talkin', dirt roads, and being over a thousand miles away from the crib. The money would make up for all that!

Trey had just finished taking a shower. The long bus ride, then stepping foot inside Willie's people's shack, had him feeling grimy.

"My nigga, I knew you was a country 'bama," Trey said to Willie. "You down here livin' like you in *Roots*."

"I can't laugh with you on that, Trey. It's money down here, and I'm feelin' this shit already," said Wink.

"He don't know nothin'," said Willie.

"Look, I'ma be next door gettin' this shit bagged and ready. Y'all post over here. You know the same one-two how we did it in Ohio," said Wink, standing at the door.

"How long we gon' be down here?" asked Trey.

"Shit, we gotta get it while the gettin' is good," Wink said then left the room and went next door to his room. He spread all the work out on the kitchen counter and started making twenty-dollar rocks and fifty pieces.

Wink was in no rush to leave Mississippi. When he went back to Detroit, he wanted to have enough money to buy his first kilo, a whole brick. No more petty ounces or double-ups, but his own bird. Mississippi seemed like just the place to get him there.

"Whenever we're ready."

"A'ight, well, be ready in the morning, 'cause we on the first bus going that way. I'm out," said Wink. He gave Willie and Trey some dap, then left.

Wink walked up to 7 Mile Road and flagged a Checker Cab.

"Where to, my friend?" The driver looked at Wink through the rearview mirror.

"Zeidman's on Gratiot." Wink passed the man a twenty-dollar deposit, and they pulled into traffic.

The cabbie parked in front of Zeidman's and checked his meter. Wink still had a few dollars left on the deposit. "Leave the meter running. I'll be right back."

Wink climbed out the cab and stepped inside the crowded pawn shop. Zeidman's was the oldest pawn shop in all of Detroit. They had everything in there from Rolex watches to drum sets. If you needed it, you could always find it at ole Zeidman's. It was owned by some Arabs, and they were known to play fair whenever you bought something off them or pawned your shit. All other pawn shops were looking to get over.

Wink make it to the front of the line. He stepped to the window and dug in his pocket, pulling up his father's gold bracelet. He stared at the diamond-encrusted WAYNE for a moment. Even though his dad hadn't been the one to give it to him, for some reason, it still had some sentimental value.

"Can I help you?" the Arab behind the bulletproof glass asked, breaking Wink's train of thought.

"Yeah, I want to know how much you'd give me for this." Wink placed the bracelet inside the slot. "I want to pawn it, not sell it." Wink watched the man as he did his ghetto assessment.

"You mean *we*. Shit, I'm ready to jump clean and see some of these country-toe bitches y'all got down here," said Trey.

"I'ma fall back and see if I can't find us some more work," said Wink.

"A'ight. Well, we be back. Come on, Trey. We can have Ball shoot us to the mall."

"That nigga gotta get a new car. We can't be pulling up in that silver bullet try'na holla at no chicks," Trey said as he closed the room door.

Wink reached over from the bed and grabbed the phone off the nightstand. He dialed his home number and waited while the line rang.

"Hello," answered Gary.

That was just the person Wink was looking for. He was hoping his mom wasn't there, because he didn't feel like hearing it.

"It's me, Wink. Is my mom around?"

"Ah, what's up, Steve man?" Gary said, pulling the sheets back and rolling out of bed. He walked into the kitchen, leaving Hope asleep in bed.

"What's up, Wink?" whispered Gary.

"I need you."

"Where are you?"

"I'm down in Mississippi with a couple of my partners, you know."

"Yeah, yeah. Well, what's up? Is you a'ight?"

"I need you to go see your friend for me and have me six this time."

"You finished already?"

"Done. I'ma catch a bus back in about another day. Can you have that for me when I get back?"

"You sound like you're going right back?"

"I'm sure I can get it at a playa's price, but I'ma say eight hundred."

"I want two." Wink dug in his drawers and began counting out sixteen hundred dollars.

"If your momma knew what we was sittin' here talkin' about, she'd kill us both."

"You ain't never gotta worry about me saying nothing.'" Wink handed Gary the money.

"Good, 'cause I don't need to hear her mouth. I normally wouldn't do this, but I told you I'd look out if you needed anything. You sure ain't waste no time." Gary laughed.

"Something came up." Wink followed Gary to the front door.

"Whoa. I'ma go by myself this first time. These some real shifty mothafuckas I'm dealing with, but I'll see about getting you plugged in."

"You just want me to wait on you to get back?"

"Yeah. I shouldn't be too long."

Wink watched as Gary climbed in his cocaine-white Fleetwood and disappeared into the horizon with his sixteen hundred dollars. Wink stepped back inside the house and started pacing the floor and making plans. If Gary came back with some decent coke, and for only sixteen hundred, it was on, Wink told himself. He just hoped Willie's cousin wasn't selling them a dream about how sweet Mississippi was. With just one flip, Wink could finish paying for Krazy's lawyer, have enough to grab four ounces, and still be able to get his father's bracelet out of pawn.

Wink damn near paced a hole in the floor while he waited for Gary to get back. He heard a door slam and ran to the window. It was Gary climbing out of his Caddy.

needed it. He laughed at the thought of the police trying to bust people for selling drugs when they were moving it without even knowing it.

Wink reached in his pocket and looked at the pawn receipt. "Dad, as soon as I get back to the D, I'ma get this bracelet back." The thoughts of his father were starting to get the best of him. When he wasn't counting money or thinking about selling drugs, the only thing Wink could think about was his father.

When he got up to his room, he dug in the front pouch of his carry-on bag and removed the photo of Gary and his father. He looked on the back of the picture for the first time. There was some old blue ink scribbled across the photo. It read: *Wayne "Gunz" Stewart*. Wink reached for the phone and dialed information.

"Information," answered the operator.

"Federal Bureau of Prisons, please."

"One moment." The operator clicked off and put Wink straight through. The phone just rang and rang.

Wink was about to hang up, but at the last second, someone answered the line. "B.O.P."

"Yes, can you tell me where you have Wayne Stewart located at in prison?"

"Wayne Stewart?" asked the clerk.

"Yes."

Wink heard the operator typing on a computer keyboard. There was a moment of silence before she came back. "I'm sorry, sir, but I'm not showing that we have an inmate by that name. Are you sure that's the name he's serving his sentence under?"

Wink looked at that back of the picture again.

"I don't know," he said, frustrated. "Sorry I wasted your time."

continued to run cold water over it. He set the crack on a paper towel so it could dry.

"There you are."

"That's it?" Wink asked.

"That's it. There's a few more tricks to the trade, but I'll show you those when you ready."

"Good lookin' out, Gary man. I really appreciate it."

"A'ight, just remember no mention of this to your mom or anyone else. I'm supposed to be retired."

"I got you," said Wink. He focused his attention back on the glob of crack sitting on the counter.

That shit was easy, he thought. I can do that. Wink fingered his investment.

"Yeah, it's on," he said aloud. He cleaned up the mess, then headed up to his room to get ready for their trip to Mississippi.

Wink was one step closer to where he wanted to be, which was to the top. He told himself that he had to make it. *Third time's a charm.*

Chapter Nineteen

The next morning, Wink woke up at the crack of dawn. He was waiting across the street at the Waffle Hut, watching the Ave. for any sign of a brown UPS truck. Gary hadn't said exactly what time to expect the package. He just said in the morning, so Wink was up and ready. He sat at a booth next to the window, sipping coffee and nibbling his strawberry waffles and eggs. Wink, paid Beats twenty dollars to sign for the package once it got there. Out of all people in the world, he picked Beats' sheisty ass. It wasn't like Wink had much of a choice. The truck could pull up at any moment, and ole slick Beats was the only one up at the time.

Wink watched Beats as he loitered around the lobby area, sippin' on a pint of Wild Irish Rose. He paced the sidewalk. The twenty dollars was burning a hole in his pocket. He couldn't wait to give it right back to Wink so he could get a taste of that good butta. Beats stopped his pacing at the sound of a diesel engine approaching. He could hear the gears shifting, then the brown UPS truck appeared in the distance. Beats nodded at the Waffle Hut, and Wink jumped up from his waffles.

The UPS truck stopped at the curb, and a young white man jumped down with a small box in one hand and a clipboard in the other. Beats met the man at the lobby door and signed for the package. He said something to the driver, and they both started laughing.

each handed the short, wide-body woman their stubs so they could get some good seats.

"How long they say the ride is?" asked Willie.

"About eighteen hours, plus I think like ten layovers and pit stops," said Wink.

"Yeah, so you might as well get comfortable, Cram. That's yo' new name: Cram." Trey laughed. He wasn't letting up on Willie's ass.

The bus filled up about halfway, and they made their departure. Wink sat up and looked out the window, while Willie and Trey dozed in and out of sleep. Wink thought about his mom and her being worried. Gary said that he would explain to her that he'd be all right. He figured maybe it would sound better coming from him. Wink thought about his main man, Krazy, and how he wished he was sitting beside him on the bus. Things just weren't the same without him. But mainly, Wink thought of his father. Those thoughts of him doing life in the fed haunted him. Wink told himself that when he got back, he was going to find out exactly what happened with his dad.

Their first layover was in Ohio, just outside of Toledo. Wink saw the setup of sheriffs and woke Willie and Trey up.

"Y'all be on point. I think they pullin' everybody off the bus and searching they stuff," said Wink. They each had a little carry-on bag with a few outfits, but Wink wasn't worried about their bags. He was worried about the crack packed in Willie's ass.

He took a deep breath and remembered everything he learned off J-Bo. *The K-9 can't smell it if it's in a nigga's ass.* Wink could hear J-Bo's raspy voice. He remembered also what Gator had told them about having the same story.

"In a minute," said Wink.

He looked at the powder chunks sitting on the counter, and his stomach filled with butterflies. He was overanxious to try to cook it, to the point he was scared he'd mess it up. Wink took a deep breath and tried to remember everything he saw Gary do. He walked back into the kitchen and went to work. He grabbed the lone box of Arm & Hammer baking soda from the mini fridge. He put a pot of water on the electric stove and searched around for a jar. He found an old pickle jar full of rubber bands on the top shelf.

"This oughta do," Wink said. He poured the rubber bands on the counter. He measured out about an ounce worth of coke, then about seven grams of baking soda. He poured them both into the jar, then ran a little water over the mixture. He swirled the jar around just as he saw Gary do, then put the jar inside the boiling pot. Wink waited until he saw the coke take on the form of gel and pulled the jar out the pot.

"Shit," he said, burning his fingertips on the rim of the jar. He endured the stinging pain while swirling the jar. He took the jar over to the sink and ran some cold water inside.

Clink. Clink. Clink.

"Hell yeah!" shouted Wink. The coke turned to crack right before his eyes. Wink pulled his small cookie fortune from the jar and stuck it under the water for a moment. He could feel it hardening even more from the shocking cold water. He carried the ounce over to the counter and let it air-dry on a napkin.

While the crack dried, Wink raced back to the phone to call Gary. "It worked. I got it!"

said Wink as he watched the caravan of crackers pile into their cars.

Willie's cousin Ball was waiting on them at the bus station. He hit his horn at the sight of Willie as he walked out the terminal.

"Over here, Buddha!" yelled Ball as he leaned his fat face out the side window of his silver used-to-be police car. It was an old Diplomat he bought at an auction.

"Buddha?" Wink teased.

"They don't call me that no more." Willie was all uptight about his childhood name.

Trey chimed in as they tailed Willie over to his cousin's car. "Buddha," Trey said in a scary low voice like he was worshipping an actual Buddha statue. He ran past Willie and rubbed his stomach.

"See what you started?" Willie asked Ball as he opened the passenger door.

"What?" asked Ball.

"From now on, don't call me Buddha."

Trey and Wink climbed in the back seat. They had to sit sideways with their knees touching because Ball's fat ass needed all the room he could get. His seat was all the way leaned back, and yet his gut was still beefing with the steering wheel. It was impossible for him to turn and introduce himself. His lack of room and no neck stopped that, so he adjusted the rearview mirror.

"Ball, this is my nigga Trey, and this here is Wink," Willie said.

"They call me Ball."

"A'ight," Trey and Wink said together.

"Pussy, nigga. Or you done forgot what it looks like?" snapped Trey.

"Yeah, my nigga. You been on some robot shit since we been out here. Niggas still gotta get they dick wet," said Willie as he climbed back in the bed with his beast. Trey was laying on the floor with his.

"Y'all would want a nigga to be on some robot shit too if you were sittin' in jail. Anyway, I'm not hearing that shit. The party's over." Wink turned all the lights on and started shaking the girls to wake up.

"What the fuck is you doin'?" asked Trey.

"It's early as shit. We'll be up in a minute," said Willie. "You trippin'."

Wink wasn't hearing that shit. "Come on, baby girl. Get all ya stuff. Rise and shine. Get ya weave and Reeboks. They gon' holla at y'all later."

The girls were looking at Wink with the screw face. "Fuck nigga, who is you?"

"Never mind all that. Here, put these on," Wink said, handing one of the girls her polka dot panties.

She snatched them from Wink and mumbled under her breath while getting dressed. Her and the other young tackhead were dressed and out the door in minutes. They let the door slam hard.

"My nigga, you fucked up the pussy," said Willie.

"Fuck them raggedy-ass bitches. We back on, and custos is waiting, so here. Get up." Wink tossed the sack of rocks on Willie's chest.

"Where you get on at?" asked Trey.

"That's not important," snapped Wink.

"Oh, so what, we keepin' secrets now?"

"Nah, I'ma put you on it, but not right now. Y'all niggas get up and let's get this money. Oh yeah, all we

"I might be drunk, but it's still my damn house," Uncle Lonnie said.

The boys entered the shack. In the living room sat more kids. They were all packed onto two aging sofas, with their eyes glued to the small TV mounted on two milk crates. Wink noticed four women sitting around the kitchen table, looking rough as all outdoors. If there was any question as to who all those rugrats sitting in the front room belonged to, that question was answered.

"Close the door," said Ball. He flopped down on two mattresses sprawled out on the floor. The room was completely out of order. Empty chip bags and quarter water jugs lined the floor. Dirty clothes decorated the dresser and floor as well, and there was this stomach-turning stench coming from somewhere. It smelled like baby shit, and the heat was cooking it.

Wink flipped his top lip under his nose and looked around with his eyes in search of a shitty Pamper.

"Ay yo, how many people stay here?" Trey couldn't help but ask.

"I lost count about two years ago. But this here is my room. Don't nobody share this with me," said Ball. He bit into a half-eaten Snickers bar.

Trey scrunched up his face. There was no telling how long that candy had been sitting out.

"This ain't gon' work, my nigga. I'ma be honest. Y'all got any hotels around here?" asked Wink. He had seen poor, but this was on some other type level of being poor. They was living like they were over in a Third-World country.

"Yeah, it's a couple up on the Ave. That's where all the money is at anyway." Ball licked his fat fingers of the smeared chocolate.

Wink walked down to the parking lot and climbed in the passenger seat. "What's good?" he asked, giving Ball a play.

"Shit, you," said Ball.

"What's up?"

"I got a few niggas asking if they can grab some weight off you. They heard you got straight butta, and they wanna know what's up."

Wink thought for a second. "How they know I got anything in the first place?"

"They don't know you're the one, but you know how people talk."

Wink looked at Ball like, *Yeah, I do.*

"What are they looking to grab?" Wink didn't plan on selling them any part of the six ounces, but he was curious, seeing how everybody else seemed to be asking questions. "These niggas got money. They'll buy whatever you bring their way. I'm talkin' 'bout whatever."

"What they paying for an ounce down here?"

"Like two G's, sometimes twenty-five hun'd. It just all depends on if there's some coke in town, which it hardly ever is. That's why niggas is pressed to hook up with you."

"I'm not try'na meet nobody right now, but I'm gon' definitely do something with you." Wink thought about how easy it was for him to receive the work through the mail. He figured once he went back to Detroit, it wouldn't be nothing to send Ball some work, and it would be just like he was still out of town, hustling.

"Yeah, we definitely gon' do something."

ment on the Ave. ceased until they saw it was nobody but Ball's fat ass.

"Boy, you gon' get enough of ridin' through here in that fuckin' thing!" yelled Beats, a local crackhead. He earned the name Beats because he was known for always beating people out of their money. He was an old, slick-talkin', oil-black nigga who lived to get high.

Ball waved Beats off as he held the door open to the front lobby of the hotel. Wink walked up to the window and got two rooms side by side. He handed Trey one of the room keys and kept one.

"Why you get two rooms?" asked Willie.

"The same reason J-Bo had two rooms. Never put all ya eggs in one basket," said Wink.

They stepped outside the lobby and crossed the parking lot. Ole Beats was on their heels. "Fat boy, you hear me talkin' to you," said Beats.

Ball stopped and slapped his hands on his pants. "What, Beats, what? I ain't got a a dollar today."

"Nah, is you on? I got fifty dollars I'm try'na spend." Beats unfolded a soiled fifty for Ball to see.

"Give us a minute," said Ball, taking the weathered fifty from Beat. He checked it for authencity, because it just wasn't no telling with Beats.

It took Ball a minute to climb the two flights up to the second floor of the hotel. Wink had wanted the rooms upstairs so they'd have time to get rid of the work in case the police showed up.

"Next time, get some rooms downstairs." Ball closed the door to the room and leaned against it for a moment. "Here," he said, extending the fifty-dollar bill.

"Who this from?" Wink asked, taking the bill.

"Beats. He downstairs, waitin' in the parkin' lot."

There was a knock on the door. Ball turned and looked through the peephole, then snatched the door open to a crack. "I told you to wait downstairs."

Beats was trying to look over Ball's shoulder. "Shit, I gotta keep an eye on mine's," he said. He had beat so many people over the years that it was automatic he thought someone was going to try to get out on him.

"I'll be out in a minute." Ball closed the door and locked it. "I'm tellin' y'all right now, that nigga there is slick as goose grease, so watch 'im, and don't credit him shit."

"Who that, ole Beats?" Willie laughed.

"You already know," said Ball.

"You got that out already?" Wink asked Willie.

Willie dug in his bag and pulled out the cucumber-size package of crack. He tried to hand it to Wink, but Wink stepped back.

"I'ma need you to unwrap that."

"Yeah, Cram. Ain't nobody 'bout to be touching that shit after you done had it all up yo' ass," teased Trey.

"Nigga, fuck you," said Willie. He walked the package over to the counter in the small kitchen and tore the plastic open.

"Ball, come show me what a fifty looks like," said Wink.

Wink watched over Ball's shoulder as he broke off a piece of crack, then he scooted a small dot to the center of the counter. He stepped back and waved his hand at the pebble.

"That's fifty dollars?" Wink asked in total disbelief.

"All day 'round here."

Wink gave Ball the pebble to go serve Beats, then packaged the remainder up in a Ziploc. All the feeling of regret for making the trip suddenly vanished. Wink could deal with all the country talkin', dirt roads, and being over a thousand miles away from the crib. The money would make up for all that!

Trey had just finished taking a shower. The long bus ride, then stepping foot inside Willie's people's shack, had him feeling grimy.

"My nigga, I knew you was a country 'bama," Trey said to Willie. "You down here livin' like you in *Roots*."

"I can't laugh with you on that, Trey. It's money down here, and I'm feelin' this shit already," said Wink.

"He don't know nothin'," said Willie.

"Look, I'ma be next door gettin' this shit bagged and ready. Y'all post over here. You know the same one-two how we did it in Ohio," said Wink, standing at the door.

"How long we gon' be down here?" asked Trey.

"Shit, we gotta get it while the gettin' is good," Wink said then left the room and went next door to his room. He spread all the work out on the kitchen counter and started making twenty-dollar rocks and fifty pieces.

Wink was in no rush to leave Mississippi. When he went back to Detroit, he wanted to have enough money to buy his first kilo, a whole brick. No more petty ounces or double-ups, but his own bird. Mississippi seemed like just the place to get him there.

Chapter Eighteen

Soon as the word got out that there was some niggas from out of town with some good butta, as they called it, them country 'bamas were beating the door down, coming to get they issue. They were spending no less than fifty dollars each, so Wink started taking two twenties and selling them for fifty. He was lovin' it, because the money was coming in so fast and nobody had complained once about the size of the rocks. They just wanted more and more.

Wink ran out in two days. He was sitting on thirteen thousand dollars and some change off just two ounces. They all took turns counting the money and making plans on what they would buy.

Wink let Trey and Willie indulge in their pipe dreams for a minute. Then he reminded them that one-fourth of the crew was sitting in jail. "Let's not forget about Krazy. He needs this money for more than anything we could ever think to buy," said Wink. "But that don't mean we can't splurge a little something. Here." Wink counted out three thousand dollars and tucked the other ten grand.

He handed Trey and Willie a thousand dollars each and kept a grand for himself. "We outta work, so I guess niggas can chill or do whatever."

"I'm 'bout to hit the mall up," said Willie, counting his stack.

"You mean *we*. Shit, I'm ready to jump clean and see some of these country-toe bitches y'all got down here," said Trey.

"I'ma fall back and see if I can't find us some more work," said Wink.

"A'ight. Well, we be back. Come on, Trey. We can have Ball shoot us to the mall."

"That nigga gotta get a new car. We can't be pulling up in that silver bullet try'na holla at no chicks," Trey said as he closed the room door.

Wink reached over from the bed and grabbed the phone off the nightstand. He dialed his home number and waited while the line rang.

"Hello," answered Gary.

That was just the person Wink was looking for. He was hoping his mom wasn't there, because he didn't feel like hearing it.

"It's me, Wink. Is my mom around?"

"Ah, what's up, Steve man?" Gary said, pulling the sheets back and rolling out of bed. He walked into the kitchen, leaving Hope asleep in bed.

"What's up, Wink?" whispered Gary.

"I need you."

"Where are you?"

"I'm down in Mississippi with a couple of my partners, you know."

"Yeah, yeah. Well, what's up? Is you a'ight?"

"I need you to go see your friend for me and have me six this time."

"You finished already?"

"Done. I'ma catch a bus back in about another day. Can you have that for me when I get back?"

"You sound like you're going right back?"

"I am. It's sweet down here."

"Well, listen. There ain't no sense in you doing all that back and forth on them highways. Give me an address, and I'll get it to you."

"What do you mean?"

"Just trust me. Give me an address."

"Hold on," said Wink. He got up and walked over to the window and peeked down at the address painted above the lobby door. He read the address off to Gary and gave him the street.

"In the morning, be on the lookout for a UPS truck. It's coming under the name Clarence Thomas. Have somebody else sign for it, though."

"You sure that's—"

Gary cut him off. "Trust me, Wink. It'll be there."

"A'ight. What about my mom?"

"She's okay. You just be careful out there. And I'ma tell you something. Don't you go gettin' laxed down there. Get what you come for and get your ass back home. You hear me?"

"Yeah."

"A'ight then, in the morning."

"Bye."

Wink locked up the room and stepped down to the lobby of the hotel. He peeled five hundred off his share of the money and sent Krazy a MoneyGram. He had to make sure his main man knew they hadn't forgotten about him and that they were handling business.

Wink thought about his call with Gary and wondered just how much game that old nigga was sitting on. He had never heard of anyone using the mail to send dope. If that shit worked, Wink told himself, then the sky was the limit. He could send work at will, whenever he needed it. He laughed at the thought of the police trying to bust people for selling drugs when they were moving it without even knowing it.

Wink reached in his pocket and looked at the pawn receipt. "Dad, as soon as I get back to the D, I'ma get this bracelet back." The thoughts of his father were starting to get the best of him. When he wasn't counting money or thinking about selling drugs, the only thing Wink could think about was his father.

When he got up to his room, he dug in the front pouch of his carry-on bag and removed the photo of Gary and his father. He looked on the back of the picture for the first time. There was some old blue ink scribbled across the photo. It read: *Wayne "Gunz" Stewart*. Wink reached for the phone and dialed information.

"Information," answered the operator.

"Federal Bureau of Prisons, please."

"One moment." The operator clicked off and put Wink straight through. The phone just rang and rang.

Wink was about to hang up, but at the last second, someone answered the line. "B.O.P."

"Yes, can you tell me where you have Wayne Stewart located at in prison?"

"Wayne Stewart?" asked the clerk.

"Yes."

Wink heard the operator typing on a computer keyboard. There was a moment of silence before she came back. "I'm sorry, sir, but I'm not showing that we have an inmate by that name. Are you sure that's the name he's serving his sentence under?"

Wink looked at that back of the picture again.

"I don't know," he said, frustrated. "Sorry I wasted your time."

"It's okay. If you get another name, don't hesitate to call us. We encourage family contact. Are you a family member of the prisoner?"

Wink hung up the phone. He didn't mean to be rude, but he couldn't yet answer that question. Family was more than being related. Wink stood up and put the photo back in the bag, then lay across the bed. He closed his eyes. Thoughts of his father dominated his mind. Eventually, he started to think about all the money they were about to make. He fell asleep with a smile on his face.

Chapter Nineteen

The next morning, Wink woke up at the crack of dawn. He was waiting across the street at the Waffle Hut, watching the Ave. for any sign of a brown UPS truck. Gary hadn't said exactly what time to expect the package. He just said in the morning, so Wink was up and ready. He sat at a booth next to the window, sipping coffee and nibbling his strawberry waffles and eggs. Wink, paid Beats twenty dollars to sign for the package once it got there. Out of all people in the world, he picked Beats' sheisty ass. It wasn't like Wink had much of a choice. The truck could pull up at any moment, and ole slick Beats was the only one up at the time.

Wink watched Beats as he loitered around the lobby area, sippin' on a pint of Wild Irish Rose. He paced the sidewalk. The twenty dollars was burning a hole in his pocket. He couldn't wait to give it right back to Wink so he could get a taste of that good butta. Beats stopped his pacing at the sound of a diesel engine approaching. He could hear the gears shifting, then the brown UPS truck appeared in the distance. Beats nodded at the Waffle Hut, and Wink jumped up from his waffles.

The UPS truck stopped at the curb, and a young white man jumped down with a small box in one hand and a clipboard in the other. Beats met the man at the lobby door and signed for the package. He said something to the driver, and they both started laughing.

"Let the man go, Beats," Wink said aloud. He was watching the transaction from the foyer of the Waffle Hut. He looked down the Ave. and didn't see any signs of a sting. The white man jumped his goofy ass back in the truck and pulled down the road. Wink pushed the glass door open and stepped outside. He waited for two cars to pass, then crossed the street in full pursuit of Beats, who was already headed up the stairs.

"Slow down, Beats. I'm coming." Wink took the steps four at a time. He took the box from Beats and put his key in the door.

"I'll be down in a minute," said Wink.

"When you gon' be straight?" asked Beats.

"Soon as I get on, you gon' be the first one to know." Wink stepped inside the room and locked the door. He carried the box into the kitchen and used his key to cut the tape open. At the top of the box sat a bunch of different exotic soaps. Wink looked at each of them, then removed the plastic wrap from the center of the box. He unwrapped the plastic, and it was the coke in its rawest form.

Wink was happy that it had made it, but why hadn't Gary cooked it? He walked in the front room and picked up the phone. He called his mom's number.

"Hello." Gary's deep voice sounded on the other end.

"I got it," said Wink.

"Good. So, you're cool then?"

"Yeah, but why you didn't you do like last time?"

"I showed you. Now it's time to see if you were paying attention. You remember what I showed you, right?"

"Yeah, I think so."

"Just don't do nothin' extra and you'll be all right. Call me back if you can't get it to come back."

"In a minute," said Wink.

He looked at the powder chunks sitting on the counter, and his stomach filled with butterflies. He was overanxious to try to cook it, to the point he was scared he'd mess it up. Wink took a deep breath and tried to remember everything he saw Gary do. He walked back into the kitchen and went to work. He grabbed the lone box of Arm & Hammer baking soda from the mini fridge. He put a pot of water on the electric stove and searched around for a jar. He found an old pickle jar full of rubber bands on the top shelf.

"This oughta do," Wink said. He poured the rubber bands on the counter. He measured out about an ounce worth of coke, then about seven grams of baking soda. He poured them both into the jar, then ran a little water over the mixture. He swirled the jar around just as he saw Gary do, then put the jar inside the boiling pot. Wink waited until he saw the coke take on the form of gel and pulled the jar out the pot.

"Shit," he said, burning his fingertips on the rim of the jar. He endured the stinging pain while swirling the jar. He took the jar over to the sink and ran some cold water inside.

Clink. Clink. Clink.

"Hell yeah!" shouted Wink. The coke turned to crack right before his eyes. Wink pulled his small cookie fortune from the jar and stuck it under the water for a moment. He could feel it hardening even more from the shocking cold water. He carried the ounce over to the counter and let it air-dry on a napkin.

While the crack dried, Wink raced back to the phone to call Gary. "It worked. I got it!"

"I knew you could do it." Gary laughed. "When you get back, I got another trick I wanna show you."

"A'ight. Thanks, Gary man."

"You're welcome. Just hurry back home."

"I will. Bye."

For the first time in his life, Wink was starting to feel some type of connection with Gary. He wasn't that bad of a dude after all. It was just too bad that they only got to talking on the strength of some coke.

Wink carried his thoughts back into the kitchen. He took a razor blade and cut the ounce dead in half, then did the same with the two chunks. He decided that all he was cutting this time was hundred-dollar pieces, since it would be their last run and then back to Detroit. Wink wanted every penny off them six ounces, and he was set on getting it. He cut one twenty-piece for Beats and packed all the rest into sandwich baggies.

Wink stashed the other five ounces and locked the room up. He pounded on Trey and Willie's door. They both were in there, passed out sleep, drunk and some more shit. Wink pounded some more.

Willie reluctantly rolled onto his back and managed to ask, "Who is it!" Those few words made his head ring from his hangover.

"Get the fuck up and open the door," snapped Wink.

"Who . . . is . . . that?" asked Trey.

"Sound like Wink's ass." Willie rolled off the bed and snatched the door open and squinted from the morning sun beaming in his face.

Wink brushed past him. "Get up. It's time to get this loot." Wink paused in his sentence at the sight of two naked, nappy-neck chicks. He waved his hand at the sleeping beasts and asked, "What's this?"

"Pussy, nigga. Or you done forgot what it looks like?" snapped Trey.

"Yeah, my nigga. You been on some robot shit since we been out here. Niggas still gotta get they dick wet," said Willie as he climbed back in the bed with his beast. Trey was laying on the floor with his.

"Y'all would want a nigga to be on some robot shit too if you were sittin' in jail. Anyway, I'm not hearing that shit. The party's over." Wink turned all the lights on and started shaking the girls to wake up.

"What the fuck is you doin'?" asked Trey.

"It's early as shit. We'll be up in a minute," said Willie. "You trippin'."

Wink wasn't hearing that shit. "Come on, baby girl. Get all ya stuff. Rise and shine. Get ya weave and Reeboks. They gon' holla at y'all later."

The girls were looking at Wink with the screw face. "Fuck nigga, who is you?"

"Never mind all that. Here, put these on," Wink said, handing one of the girls her polka dot panties.

She snatched them from Wink and mumbled under her breath while getting dressed. Her and the other young tackhead were dressed and out the door in minutes. They let the door slam hard.

"My nigga, you fucked up the pussy," said Willie.

"Fuck them raggedy-ass bitches. We back on, and custos is waiting, so here. Get up." Wink tossed the sack of rocks on Willie's chest.

"Where you get on at?" asked Trey.

"That's not important," snapped Wink.

"Oh, so what, we keepin' secrets now?"

"Nah, I'ma put you on it, but not right now. Y'all niggas get up and let's get this money. Oh yeah, all we sellin' from now on is hun'd pieces. We gotta kill 'em before we leave, so even if it takes us a little longer to dump, so be it."

"Go to the store and get me a beer to knock this hangover off," mumbled Willie.

"Yeah, and bring some waffles back," said Trey.

"A'ight, but be up when I get back. I'm 'bout to let mothafuckas know it's back on." Wink stepped outside and flagged ole Beats up.

He had been diligently waiting on his taste, as he called it. Beats jogged up the steps with the sweaty twenty in his hand. "Let me get one of them butta pieces from you," said Beats as he tried to hand Wink the money.

"Nah, hold onto that. Here," Wink said, handing Beats a lookout rock.

"That's real classy and playa-like of you, young blood. Thank you."

"You take care of me, I'ma take care of you."

"Without a doubt. You need me for anything else before I get going?" Beats was stepping in place as he clutched the rock in his palm for dear life.

"Yeah, I need you to bring me two orders of waffles and eggs and a forty-ounce of Old E." Wink dug in his pocket and gave Beats another twenty.

"I'll be right back." Beats jogged down the stairs on his mission.

As Wink stuck his key in the door, he saw Ball pull into the parking lot in the silver bullet. He honked once and stuck his fat arm out the window. Wink waved him up, but Ball waved him down. His heavy ass wasn't trying to see those two flights of steps again unless two Big Macs was waiting at the top.

Wink walked down to the parking lot and climbed in the passenger seat. "What's good?" he asked, giving Ball a play.

"Shit, you," said Ball.

"What's up?"

"I got a few niggas asking if they can grab some weight off you. They heard you got straight butta, and they wanna know what's up."

Wink thought for a second. "How they know I got anything in the first place?"

"They don't know you're the one, but you know how people talk."

Wink looked at Ball like, *Yeah, I do.*

"What are they looking to grab?" Wink didn't plan on selling them any part of the six ounces, but he was curious, seeing how everybody else seemed to be asking questions. "These niggas got money. They'll buy whatever you bring their way. I'm talkin' 'bout whatever."

"What they paying for an ounce down here?"

"Like two G's, sometimes twenty-five hun'd. It just all depends on if there's some coke in town, which it hardly ever is. That's why niggas is pressed to hook up with you."

"I'm not try'na meet nobody right now, but I'm gon' definitely do something with you." Wink thought about how easy it was for him to receive the work through the mail. He figured once he went back to Detroit, it wouldn't be nothing to send Ball some work, and it would be just like he was still out of town, hustling.

"Yeah, we definitely gon' do something."

Chapter Twenty

Trey and Willie focused up and helped Wink grind out for five days straight. The only sleep they got was in between blinks. Crackheads were coming like they knew it was going to be their last time smoking some butta for a minute. Wink had made fifty-seven thousand and still had a half ounce left. He had never seen that much money before in his life, let alone called it his. He took another page out of J-Bo's book and started sending MoneyGrams home every five grand he made. Gary was to hold the money until they got back.

The crackheads weren't the only ones circling the Knights Inn. Undercover cops started showing up in tinted-out Crown Victorias. They'd cruise through the parking lot and be over at the Waffle Hut, asking people questions about the young boys from out of town selling crack. That's how Beats brought it to Wink. He said that was their way of sending a warning shot.

Well, they didn't have to tell Wink twice. He got the message loud and clear. It was time to take the show on the road or risk going to jail. It was all good, though, Wink had gotten what he came for. They murdered the town, and now it was time to keep it moving.

Wink walked into Trey and Willie's room. "Y'all almost ready? Ball downstairs waitin' to take us to the airport," he said.

"Airport?" Trey stopped packing his bags.

"Yeah, nigga. We rich now. I know you ain't scared to get on no plane?"

"Nigga, the only thing I'm scared of is dying broke. I was just asking," Trey said, zipping his two bags, then throwing them over his shoulder.

"Shit, I ain't gon' lie. I'm scared as a mothafucka to get on a plane," Willie said.

"That shit ain't nothin'. Come on. That's Ball hittin' his horn now." Wink stuck his head out the door and nodded like, *Here we come.*

"For real, I was thinking about staying for a little while and help Ball set things up," Willie said.

"I mean, if that's what you wanna do, I ain't got no problem with that."

"Shit, I don't give a fuck if we ridin' a donkey back. I'm ready to get back to the city," said Trey.

"So, what you gon' do? You staying?" asked Wink.

"Yeah, I'ma stay for a couple more weeks. Go see my grams and them, and wait on you to get it going."

"A'ight. Well, here. Take this." Wink counted out a thousand dollars and handed it to Willie.

"Oh, yeah. And here. That's about a half ounce."

"A'ight, bet." Willie tucked the crack into his sock and folded the money.

"Let this hotel die down, though. We don't need you sittin' in jail too, my nigga," Wink said.

Willie gave Wink and Trey a hug. "I'ma miss y'all niggas. I'll be home in a minute."

"We'll be waitin' on you when you get back," Trey said.

They hit rocks one last time, then Wink opened the door and walked out the room.

"Call a nigga, Cram." Trey laughed as he closed the door.

Ball drove Wink and Trey to the McCall International Airport. He pulled the silver bullet around to the valet and parked. Wink reached over and gave Ball a play.

"We 'bouts to get this money, big baby, so I hope you're ready."

"I'm ready whenever you get settled."

"Yeah, and we gon' get you outta this *In the Heat of the Night* jump-off. Get you in some new shit," Trey said.

"I left Willie with something. That should hold y'all until I can put something together," said Wink as he reached for the door handle. "I'ma call you," he said, closing the door.

Trey fell in step with Wink as they entered the terminal. "My nigga, we might as well get used to walking through airports, 'cause we gon' be doin' a lot of traveling when this money starts rolling in," said Wink as they approached the counter.

"Stewart. I should have three tickets to Detroit," Wink told the clerk.

"Yes, here you are." The white woman handed Wink three tickets to Detroit. Gary had booked their flights the day before. He didn't want Wink riding that Greyhound anymore.

"I got one question," said Trey.

"And what's that, my nigga?"

"What are we going to do once we get back to Detroit? I mean, just because we got some money, where we gon' hustle at?"

"That's all I've been thinking about. You know, me and J-Bo still got some unfinished business."

Wink led the way through the terminal and onto their plane. A petite, short-haired black woman showed them to their seats in coach. "If you guys need anything, let me or one of the other flight attendants know, and we'll get it for you," said the woman from the aisle.

"Are all the attendants as pretty as you?" asked Trey.

The woman smiled. "Thank you, but you'll have to be the judge of that. You guys buckle up and enjoy your flight."

Trey watched from the aisle seat as the woman gracefully swished away. The tight-fitting black skirt emphasized every curve down to her shapely legs.

"Did you see those?" Trey turned to Wink. "I gotta start gettin' me some old pussy. That's probably some of the best pussy, 'cause it ain't being hit like that. What you think?" Trey had locked eyes on the woman as she stood at the front of the plane, talking to some passengers. "You hear what I said?"

"Huh?" Wink was lost in his world of thoughts. He stared out the window into the horizon.

"That's crazy. You ain't heard nothin' I done said. You over there in la-la land, missing all this pussy squishing around here." Trey flagged down a thick white brunette as she passed down the aisle.

"Uh, yes, can you please help me with this seat belt? I'm having trouble tightening it."

The woman leaned over Trey's lap and pulled on the strap. Trey smiled at her breasts, then at her after she finished. "Thank you."

"Anything else?"

"Yeah, we can start with your number, Sue," Trey said, reading from her nametag. "I'm Trey."

"Maybe before you get off. Enjoy your flight."

Trey nudged Wink. "I got one." He could already see himself lost between the thickness of her thighs.

Trey was having himself a good ole time, while Wink plotted on how they were going to get that money when they got back to Detroit. Trey's question lingered in Wink's mind. Where would they set up shop? Niggas in the city were playing for keeps.

I guess that's what we're gonna have to start doing too, Wink told himself, then closed his eyes.

When Wink woke up, the plane was touching down at the Detroit City Airport on Gratiot Ave. He sat up in his seat and looked out the window as the plane raced down the runway, coming to a screeching stop. He pulled back a smile, knowing that they were back on familiar ground. The plane did a lap around the tarmac, then hooked up to the terminal.

Trey was in Sue's ass like the IRS about her math. He cornered her in the back by the coffeemakers. "Here, write your number down," he said, taking a pen from her shirt pocket.

Sue blushed from his persistence and the way he was handling her. Trey wasn't taking no for an answer. Sue scribbled her number down on a napkin, then handed it to Trey.

"Where's this?" Trey asked, not recognizing the area code.

"Dallas."

"Texas?"

"One and only. Call me," said Sue as she walked past Trey.

"There you go. Come on, nigga. We got shit to handle," Wink said after finding Trey in the back of the plane.

"Don't hate me 'cause yo' dick on strike." Trey followed Wink off the plane. He had never been to Texas, but for a piece of that ass, he'd travel to hell and back.

Wink power-walked through the terminal, while Trey scanned for potential booty calls.

"Damn, nigga, wait the fuck up," he said, realizing Wink was no longer inside the terminal. He caught up with him outside the double door, getting in the back of a black Lincoln Town Car. Trey slid in beside him. "Damn. What, we too good to take a cab now?"

"I keep tellin' you we rich now. Just sit back and enjoy the ride. Driver, can you please take us to Zeidman's off Gratiot?" said Wink.

"Hello, can I speak to Sharon?" Trey had picked up the car phone between them. He wasn't wasting no time in letting people know they were back and that it was on for the night.

Wink let him have his fun. He gazed out the window while clutching the pawn receipt and the twenty-five hundred it was going to take to get the bracelet back. "Pull over right here," he instructed the older black man. "I'll be right back."

"Hold on. You want me to come in with you?"

"Nah, finish setting things up for the night." Wink climbed out the Lincoln and entered Zeidman's. There wasn't much of a crowd. Only two people stood in line ahead of Wink.

When he reached the window, the same Arab who pawned the bracelet stared him in his face. Wink could tell by the look in the man's eyes that he wasn't pleased to see him, especially if he was there for his bracelet. The actual value of it still, after nearly twenty years, was eighteen thousand dollars.

"I'm here to get my bracelet out of pawn." Wink pushed the receipt through the slot.

"You have the money along with the interest?" the man asked with a hint of an attitude.

Winked pushed the twenty-five hundred through the slot and watched the man briskly count the bills. He looked up from the money and disappeared into the back. His funny-lookin' ass was taking too long back there.

Shit. It didn't take this long to pawn my shit, thought Wink, as he started to get impatient. He dinged the silver bell a few times. *Funky mothafucka probably back there switching the diamonds.*

A few minutes later, the man appeared with a manila envelope in his hand. He broke the seal in front of Wink, then slid the bracelet through the slot. Wink inspected the diamonds, then nodded at the man as he slid the bracelet onto his wrist. The diamonds sparkled under the lights, and Wink pulled back a closed smile. He left out Zeidman's feeling a great deal of relief, having the bracelet back in his possession. He wondered what-all his dad went through to afford the thing. For Wink, it represented his platform, his means to coming up in the game. And for that, he would never part with the bracelet until death.

"You just bought that?" asked Trey. His mouth was draped to the floor as he turned Wink's wrist.

"Nah, it belonged to my . . . to my dad. I pawned it so we could get on. Now that we're in the game, it's time to put this boy up."

"This shit is fly. It's a little old, but it still looks like money. When we get straight, I wanna have one made," said Trey.

"We all can get something done up. Just give it some time. We gon' have the world."

Wink had the driver drop Trey off at home first. He promised they'd hook up later and go downtown to mess with the girls on Belle Isle. It was the last week of summer, and Trey wanted to make it memorable.

"I'ma call you in a couple hours. Be ready," Trey said as he climbed out the car.

"I'll be at the crib," said Wink. He watched Trey to the door, then instructed the driver to pull off.

Wink sank into the plush black leather seat and gave the old man directions. Wink watched the happenings of his hood from behind the tinted windows of the Lincoln. He envisioned himself taking over all the crack houses and eventually, the city. He knew what he had to do in order for that to become a reality.

Chapter Twenty-one

Gary had everything in order when Wink got home. He handed him all his money, not a dollar short except for the six ounces he sent him. Wink spread all the money across his bed and just looked at it. Almost every dollar down to the cent was going toward something. The first priority was finishing up Krazy's legal fees. Second, Wink was going to buy his first kilo. Gary told him that he could get it for an even twenty thousand. The rest he promised to split with Trey and Willie.

Wink heard his mom climbing the steps to his room. He rushed over to the bed and tried to hurry up and put the blanket over the money.

"Wayne, are you up here?"

"Yeah, Ma." Wink rushed over to the door to try to block his mom, but she pushed past him. She searched the room with her eyes. Wink nervously stood behind her, hoping she wouldn't move the blanket. She turned to face Wink.

"When you come in this house, you make sure you at least say hello to your mother."

"I'm sorry, Ma," Wink said. He kissed Hope on the forehead.

Her eyes turned to his bed. She pushed away from Wink and snatched the blanket off the bed.

"Oh my God. Wayne! Where did you get all this money from?"

"Ma, calm down."

"Don't you tell me to calm down. Wayne, who's going to come lookin' for this money?"

Wink walked over to his mom and put his arm around her. "Ma, it's mine. Nobody's going to come lookin' for it, me, or nobody else. It's mine. I swear."

Hope crossed her arms and shook her head, then looked down at the bed. She reached down and moved a stack of bills. The clip from Wink's dad's bracelet was sticking out.

"Where'd you get this from?" She recognized the bracelet immediately.

"I gave it to him," Gary said from the door. He walked in the room and took the bracelet from Hope and handed it back to Wink. "It belonged to his father, so it's in the rightful hands. Come on, Hope," said Gary, wrapping her into his arms and starting for the door. Gary looked over his shoulder at Wink like, *I'll take care of her.*

Wink paced the floor. He was kind of glad his mom had seen the money, because now it was all out in the open. There wasn't any question as to what he was out there in those streets doing. But still, Wink felt some type of way about having to answer to his mom. He was a grown man and didn't need to answer to no one. Wink looked at the money and added one more plan to his list of things to do. He had to get his own space, and soon.

Gary came back upstairs after seeing Hope off to work. He walked over and took a seat on the bed and crossed his long, skinny legs.

"What she say?" asked Wink.

"She'll be all right. But that doesn't mean she won't worry. That's your mom, so she going to do that."

"I think that it'll be best if I got my own li'l apartment or something. That way, she won't have to see me doing what I'm doing."

"I was going to say something to you about that, but it's good to see you're already thinking ahead. I mean, yeah. I think that's a good move, 'cause you don't want to have that stuff around your mom. Even when you get your own spot, you still don't want to have no whole bunch of money laying around, and you definitely don't want to have no drugs where you lay your head at."

Wink nodded at this. He hadn't thought that far.

"But that's why I'm here to show everything you need to know."

"So, can you help me get an apartment?"

"Sure, I can do that. You ready to go meet my partner?" Gary stood up and started for the door.

"Yeah, just let me put this away. I'll be down in a minute," said Wink. He gathered up all the money with the exception of the twenty thousand he was taking with him. Gary was going to introduce Wink directly to the man himself so they could do business in the future without having to use Gary as the middleman. Wink couldn't believe he was already going to meet his connect. He thought Gary would be dealing with him for a while until Wink proved himself. Gary was a realer nigga than Wink ever gave him credit for.

Wink stashed everything, then scanned the room one last time before hitting the light and leaving out. Gary was waiting in his pearl-white Caddy at the curb. Wink climbed in the passenger seat and kicked back. Gary pulled the neck shift down to drive.

"You know, outta all these years, this is the first time I've rode in your car," said Wink.

"You can get it any time. I got a few other toys you might like as well," said Gary as he laid the pedal down and opened the boat up.

Gary drove deep on the west side, taking 7 Mile Road the entire drive. He pulled into the parking lot of an Ace Hardware store across the Southfield Expressway.

"Come on," he said as he got out the car.

Wink didn't want to be making a pit stop at a hardware store. He was too eager to be making his connect. If Gary needed to do some handyman shit, he could have done it some other time. Now was the time for gettin' that cheese.

"You doing some home repair?" Wink asked.

Gary said nothing and walked to the entrance. Wink fell in step with Gary. They entered the store.

"Who's this you got with you?" a wide-body black man behind the counter asked Gary.

"This is my . . . my son, Wink. This is Mr. Fatts." Gary stepped aside so that Wink could shake Mr. Fatts' hand.

"Wink, huh? Why they call you Wink?" When he talked, it sounded like he was on a respirator. He sounded like he was always out of breath, and his tongue protruded from his fat face.

"Just a name my friends call me."

"So, you're the one Gary's been tellin' me about. What a young man like yourself doin' in the streets? You look like you should be in somebody's college."

"Looks are deceiving." Wink shrugged.

"Ain't that the truth." Mr. Fatts laughed. "Y'all come on around back."

Wink followed Gary around the counter and into the back room. Fatts stood at the refrigerator, pulling brown bricks from the shelves. He grabbed the one he was looking for, then carried it over to a workbench where Gary and Wink stood. Wink's eyes widened. This was Gary's man. They weren't there to buy hardware; they were there to buy coke.

"You know what you're buying here?" asked Fatts as he set the brick on the bench.

"A kilo," said Wink.

Fatts laughed. He looked up at Gary and said, "I assume you're going to lace him so that he knows the difference between flake and something some nigga done smashed with ten toes."

"I'ma give 'im the game. When I get done with him, he's gon' be the coldest young nigga in all of Detroit." Gary smiled at Wink.

"You see that?" Fatts busted the kilo down the middle with a knife and pulled up a chunk of powder. "You see all the oils and flakes. If it ain't like that, then you don't want it."

Wink nodded as if he understood, but he had no clue what Fatts was talking about. It looked like regular cocaine to Wink. He watched as Fatts stuck the chunk back in its place, then wrapped tape around the brick. Gary nodded at Wink for him to pay Fatts.

"Oh." Wink understood the look and dug in his drawers. He handed Fatts the rubber bands and watched his stubby little fingers fan through the bills.

"There you go." Fatts nodded to the kilo. "You can come see me anytime, but just make sure it's by yourself."

"I got you," Wink said. He cradled his first kilo in the game as if it were his first born child.

Gary handed him a brown Ace Hardware bag to put the key in. "A'ight, Fatts, I'ma get going. I'll call you later."

"Y'all be easy," Fatts said.

Wink tailed Gary out the store and climbed in the Caddy. Gary leaned over and opened the glove box. He did something with the windshield wiper controls and pumped the brake, then the inside of the glove box fell down. Gary took the key and stuffed it inside the secret compartment, then closed up the box and locked it.

"Where you get that done at?" asked Wink.

"I got a few partners who own collision shops. When you get some wheels, I'll have one put in your car."

Wink sat back and thought about how much game ole Gary had. If Gary had never said anything to him, Wink would have continued thinking he was just a bum living off his mom. Wink was grateful that Gary had stepped up.

When they got back home, Gary showed Wink one last trick in the kitchen. He showed him how to stretch coke into more coke and how to whip crack. As good as the coke they just copped off Fatts was, Wink could turn that one kilo into one and a half kilos easy. Gary showed him step by step and gave him the cuts he'd need in the future. When they finished, Wink was staring fifty-six ounces of crack in the face. He was awestruck watching Gary do his thing.

"One more thing. I need you to show me how you packaged that box up you sent me. I want to send one of my partners something."

"Wink, all this game I'm giving you, I don't want you teaching no one. This is for you and you only. Hear me?"

"I hear you." Wink hadn't planned on showing anyone anyway. If he was going to be top dog, he needed to be the one everyone relied on. His crew would have to pay for the game he was learning.

Chapter Twenty-two

Two weeks had passed, and everything Wink planned was coming together. He had sent two shipments down to Willie and Ball. The demand for that butta was growing fast.

Gary helped him get an apartment and a pearl-white El Dorado. He decked it out with Vogue tires and an Alpine sound system. Gary advised him to buy a new outfit. He told Wink that in order to be respected on the street as a major player, you had to dress the part. Wink obliged. Gary had him wearing linens and starter gators, as he called them, the ones that were only costing six hundred dollars. Gary took him down to Broadway's and City Slicker to shop. He said Wink couldn't be pushing no Caddy wearing rags.

Trey bought a triple-black El Dorado on Vogues. They said as soon as Willie got back, he'd get one, and whenever Krazy came home, they'd pitch in and get him one too. Trey had a bracelet custom made similar to Wink's. They'd ride back to back, trying to make a name for themselves.

It was all fun, but Wink still had one more part of his plan that he had yet to accomplish. He wanted the city, and he was going to start with his hood.

They were parked outside Trey's momma's crib, leaning against their shiny new Caddies. Trey was making all these grand plans on what they should buy next and where they should travel to. Wink wasn't listening. He was lost in his world of thoughts. He still hadn't forgot how J-Bo got over on him for that ten grand. No matter what J-Bo said about teaching Wink a lesson, Wink knew he had been taken advantage of. It would never sit right with him.

Gary had told him that in the streets, you can never let a man take anything from you because once they start, they'll never stop. These words played over and over in Wink's head. Here it was they had all this money in their pockets, yet no one knew who they were because they were still nobodies. They hadn't earned respect in the streets of Detroit. All their game was being played down south. Wink wanted his name known throughout Detroit.

"Ay yo, I'ma holla at you later, my nigga." Wink pushed off his Caddy and gave Trey some dap.

"What you think about that?" asked Trey.

"Yeah, that sounds good. Just let me know." Wink hadn't heard a single word Trey said.

"A'ight. I'ma hit you on the hip later," said Trey.

"In a minute." Wink climbed behind the wheel of his El Dogg and pulled away from the curb. He reached over in the glove box and pulled his 9 mm Berretta from the stash spot. He massaged the handle while he planned his next move. It had to be done, he told himself. It was the only way niggas would give him his respect and he'd be able to sell crack in the city.

J-Bo may have been one of the sharpest hustlas in Detroit and one of the richest, but one mistake he made was thinking he would rule forever. Niggas didn't know how to get theirs and pass the torch. They wanted all the money and didn't have no plans on ever letting the next man get any. Another mistake greedy niggas like J-Bo made was they never really changed their schedules.

Wink looked at the dashboard clock. It was going on three o'clock in the afternoon. Every day at exactly 3:30 p.m., J-Bo would make his pickup and drop off a fresh sack at the spot on Linwood. Anyone slinging dope for J-Bo knew this. The dope fiends most assuredly knew this. On any given day, you'd start seeing an uptick in fiends roaming the streets around Linwood starting at around 2:30.

Wink got on the Davidson Expressway and leaned his seat back. He couldn't wait to see the look on J-Bo's face when he pulled up in his El Dogg, leaning to the side. It hadn't been a full month, and Wink had surpassed half the niggas calling themselves hustlas. In a sense, Wink felt like he owed a great deal of his success to J-Bo for taking him under his wing.

"Nah, fuck that," Wink said aloud. He shook those thoughts, thinking back to what J-Bo had told him about being a square on the board and him using niggas like him to get to the top.

Wink shifted in his seat as he turned down Linwood. He was trying to see which side he looked better on, leaning against the door or the console. He turned up the radio and stretched his arm out on the steering wheel, letting his dad's bracelet gleam under the sun.

Wink parked across the street from the spot in front of Kennedy's penny candy store. He watched as Gator fast-talked some white man parked in a brown tow truck. Wink laughed to himself. The spot hadn't missed a beat in his absence. He looked up at the top window and wondered what young, dumb nigga J-Bo had sitting up there.

Wink looked at the clock, 2:28 p.m. Just like clock-work, J-Bo bent the corner in his navy-blue Porsche. Wink watched his former idol climb out the Porsche and start barking orders. He honked the horn twice, and J-Bo turned around, squinting to see who was behind the wheel of that pretty mothafucka.

Wink climbed out the car and tried to conceal his Kool-Aid smile. He folded his arms into a B-boy stance with his bracelet showing.

J-Bo pulled back a phony smile, then crossed the street. Instead of giving props where props was due, he said, "Who you out here workin' for that was fool enough to let yo' young ass borrow they car?"

"I work for me. I'm my boss," Wink said proudly.

"Wink, you know better than to lie to me. You know I can find out who you workin' for," J-Bo said. He walked around the car, looking for any clues.

"Well, when you do go asking around, they gon' tell you she's mine. And my man Trey's got a black one."

"You left me what, a month ago? Well, who you done robbed?"

Wink was starting to get pissed. J-Bo refused to give him his props, but he let it pass, because he hadn't come to shoot the bobo, and at the end of the day, he didn't need J-Bo's nod of approval.

"Hop in and let me take you to get something to eat. We'll hit Red Lobster's," said Wink.

"This car isn't hot, is it? 'Cause I ain't got time to be downtown about no stolen car."

"Hell no, it's not hot. Just come on. It's my treat."

J-Bo looked at Wink suspiciously. "Let me grab this money and I'll be right back."

Wink climbed behind the wheel and adjusted the Berretta under his shirt. A few minutes later, J-Bo came walking out the spot with Gator in tow. He pointed across the street at the Caddy, and Gator pulled back a wide grin, exposing his hideous grill. He rushed over to check the wheels out.

"My young playa, you ain't waste no time getting y'all fronts up, I see," said Gator as he leaned in the driver-side window. "That's a mean bracelet. How much it run you?"

"That's slum," said J-Bo as he climbed in the passenger seat.

Gator peeped jealously, so he didn't press the issue. He shot a wink at Wink, then said, "Take care of yourself out here, and you stop by and see me whenever you want."

"A'ight, Gator."

Gator tapped the roof, and Wink pulled away from the curb. He cruised down Linwood while thinking to himself how tight-faced J-Bo was about his come-up. It was exactly what Wink thought would happen. He knew the J-Bo was a jealous nigga that couldn't stand to see anyone else get theirs. His plan was to flaunt his success in front of J-Bo in order to get his ass heated. Then he would sit back, watch, and wait for J-Bo to slip up because he was too emotional and his rage and jealousy would cause him to lose focus. Wink was loving every second of it.

"I'm really not all that hungry. Why don't you stop at Henry's so we can grab something to drink, then we can go downtown to Belle Isle," suggested J-Bo.

"That's cool." Wink busted a U-turn, then headed up to Henry's on Dexter.

"I'ma grab a fifth of Hennessy. You want me to get you anything else while I'm in here?" asked J-Bo.

"Nah, just get a bag of ice," said Wink. He wasn't big on drinking. He felt like it slowed him down and prevented him from being on top of his game. He would let all these other niggas get drunk and high while he planned and executed. His advantage would be to make clear decisions all the time, no weed and alcohol to cloud his mind.

Wink was getting a little nervous. He felt like J-Bo was setting him up. The pit stop to the liquor store felt off. But he kept telling himself that he was the one in control. This was what had to happen if he wanted the respect of the streets and his right to hustle in the city. If that meant a few drinks with J-Bo, then so be it.

J-Bo walked out the store carrying a bottle of Henny, two plastic cups, and a bag of ice. He climbed in the car and set everything on the floor between his legs. He cracked the seal and poured them a drink. Wink cruised down Jefferson while taking an occasional sip from his cup.

"So, where you getting your work from?" asked J-Bo.

"Here and there. You know how it is."

"How much you moving?"

"Enough to buy this car. You hear me?" Wink laughed.

J-Bo did not find it as funny as Wink. "Where you set up shop?"

"You know, here and there."

"Nigga, you a tight-lipped mothafucka."

"Come on, we all good. We can all enjoy a piece of this game. Like chess. All of us have a position."

J-Bo squinted his eyes at Wink, looking as if he was trying to read his mind. Wink took a sip of Henny and raised his cup in salute to J-Bo.

J-Bo smiled. "Look at you. Young gun is moving up from a square to a pawn. You know I'll never let you be king, though."

Wink raised his cup again and gave another salute and a head nod.

"Now to business. You know I can give it to you for a good price. How much you paying?" asked J-Bo.

"The last time I bought something off you, I lost ten grand, remember?"

"Wink, we already know whose fault that was. I'm just trying to look out for you."

Yeah, right, thought Wink. *The only person you care about is J-Bo.* Wink looked for a good spot to park at on Belle Isle. He pulled near the river and killed the engine. There wasn't but a few cars scattered around the island and a few joggers. For the most part, the Isle was deserted. The weather was changing, and nobody liked hanging on Belle Isle around that time of year because the water whipped the wind something serious. Wink checked all his mirrors and made a mental note where everyone was situated.

"You know, Wink, I knew you'd figure it out once you were forced to. I don't think that I ever told you this, but you remind me so much of myself when I first started hustlin'." J-Bo laughed, then took a sip from his cup. He continued, "You actually made out good having me as your turn-out. When I came up, them old niggas who put me down were heartless. They didn't care if ya ass lived or died. Long as you had their score straight, they could care two shits less."

Wink was wondering what angle J-Bo was trying to scheme. He ain't never heard J-Bo be so complimentary toward anyone. There must have been some ulterior motive, but Wink didn't know what that would be. In the end, Wink figured it must be the liquor talking.

"What I'm try'na say, Wink, is that had you not gone through the little tribulations of bumping your head, you might not be right here having this conversation with me. You'd still be at the bottom somewhere." J-Bo raised his half-empty cup and said, "So, good job." He downed his drink, then reached for the door handle. "I'll be back. I'ma step over here and use the bathroom."

Wink downed his drink and pounded his chest, trying to get the burning to go away. He watched J-Bo cross the street and enter the little public restroom. Winked pulled his Berretta from his waist and cocked one round into the chamber. He tucked the gun underneath his shirt, then got out the car and quickly crossed the street. He could hear piss splashing into the toilet as he leaned against the brick wall of the building.

He gave himself a pep talk. "Come on, Wink. Don't freeze up on me now." He heard the toilet flush. He may never get this clear of an opportunity again. *It's now or never*, he thought.

Wink slid into the bathroom with his gun drawn. When J-Bo looked up from the sink, his shock and confusion looked like he'd seen Satan himself. Wink tossed a black pawn piece at J-Bo. As soon as J-Bo caught it, Wink pulled the trigger. *Boom! Boom! Boom!* Three gut shots sent him to the floor. He walked over to J-Bo and put two more slugs in his dome. *Boom! Boom!*

"Now I'm the king of the chessboard." Wink spit on J-Bo and walked out.

Chapter Twenty-three

Wink left J-Bo on the bathroom floor with his brains hanging. He thought about it all night. He lay in his bed at his new apartment in downtown Detroit off Jefferson. He stared up at the ceiling with his mind locked on when he squeezed the trigger and the amount of blood pouring out of J-Bo's skull. Wink had no intention of telling anyone about what he did, not even his main man Trey. He was going to the grave with that secret. If one person knew, eventually everyone would know. Wink wasn't about taking any chances, so he'd keep this to himself.

It was almost eight o'clock in the morning, and the sun was peeking its way through the blinds in Wink's room. He snatched the sheets off his frail frame and rolled out of bed. It was time to hit the streets and claim what he took yesterday: his throne, his respect, and right to hustle. Wink knew that there was going to be a battle for who would take J-Bo's throne, so J-Bo wouldn't be the last nigga he put in the dirt. If he wanted to stay above ground himself, he'd have to bury niggas. The quicker he squeezed the trigger, the faster he could get the job done. It was all part of the game.

After Wink killed J-Bo, he threw his Berretta over the Belle Isle Bridge, so he was going to need a new piece. He called Gary on his car phone as he drove down Jefferson.

"What happened to the one I just gave you? It was brand new," said Gary.

"Something came up," said Wink.

There was a short pause on the other end. Gary knew exactly what *something* meant. "You make sure you stop by the house and talk to me before you get lost in them streets for the day."

"A'ight." Wink hung up the phone and pressed down on the gas. He was on his way to scoop Trey from his mom's crib.

When Wink pulled up on Trey's house, his mom stood on the front porch with her hands on her hips. She flashed at the sight of Wink sitting in front of her house.

"Trey! This nigga is out here!" she yelled at the top of her lungs.

Wink honked his horn out of spite and waved. "Hi, Ms. Shelton!" he yelled. He got a kick out of mocking her because he knew she couldn't stand his black ass.

Trey came walking out the door, fastening his Marc Buchanan leather jacket. He kissed his mom on the cheek, then started down the stairs. His face tightened as Ms. Shelton scolded his back for having that heathen at her house.

"What up, doe." Wink laughed.

"You," said Trey as he climbed in the car. "Pull off," he said, looking up at his mother, bitching her heart out.

Wink gladly laid rubber to the street, drowning Ms. Shelton out as they sped away.

"What you need to do is get your own spot. They got some empty units in my building," Wink said.

"I might fuck with it. But what's up? Where you was at all yesterday? I kept paging you. I had these two young freaks."

J-Bo lying in a pool of blood flashed through Wink's mind. "I had to take care of some business. You got yo' heat on you?"

"Yeah, why? What's up?"

"Nah, we 'bouts to take over all of J-Bo's old spots."

"What you mean, his old spots?"

"Somebody killed J-Bo last night."

"Word? You bullshittin'."

"Nah, I'm not. They found him on Belle Isle this morning. Somebody blew his candle out."

"Daaaaamn. I can't believe somebody touched his ass. Who do you think it was?"

Wink shrugged his shoulders. "It could have been anybody. You know how it is out here. Niggas probably wanted him outta the way."

"And them same niggas gonna want J-Bo's spots."

"That's why we strap our nuts and go to war. Sooner or later, somebody's gonna try us once they see how much money we gettin'. My nigga, we can't be scared to kill, 'cause you know damn well they won't hesitate to kill us too." Wink looked over at Trey. He could tell that he was a little shaken up. If J-Bo could get his shit pushed back, that meant nobody was exempt.

Wink pulled up on the spot on Linwood. He parked behind J-Bo's Porsche. It hadn't moved an inch since yesterday. Wink popped the glove box and pulled out the stash box. He cuffed the plastic bag into his drawers, then grabbed the door handle.

"Come on," he told Trey.

Trey fell in step behind Wink as they climbed the porch up to the front door. They didn't bother knocking. Wink pulled the screen open and walked right in and up the stairs to the spot. Two young niggas were sitting in the front room, smoking weed and playing Nintendo. They looked to be no more than fifteen years old. Wink elbowed Trey with a smile. He couldn't believe that J-Bo started getting them this young. It was brilliant, thought Wink. The younger the better, because you could use their dumb asses even longer.

Wink walked around the coffee table and paused the game. He and Trey stood blocking the TV.

"Nigga, who the fuck is you, and how'd you get in?" snapped the young nigga seated directly in front of Wink. He reminded Wink so much of himself, and the little yellow nigga sitting beside him looked just like Trey. "What, you deaf? How'd you get in here?"

"You left the door open. And if you're going to be working for me, that can't happen again," said Wink.

"Nigga, we don't work for you. This J-Bo spot," said the other li'l nigga.

"Nah, it used to be J-Bo's spot. But he's no longer with us, so you'll be working for us." Wink pointed at Trey. "This is Trey. I'm Wink."

"What happened to J-Bo?"

"He, unfortunately, came to the end of his game. What's y'all names?" asked Wink.

The one sitting in front of Wink spoke first. It was obvious he was the leader of the two. "They call me JT, and this is my man, Dilla."

"What was J-Bo payin' y'all a week?"

"Seven hun'd," said JT.

Wink pulled back a smile. J-Bo was a stingy bastard. "Well, I'ma pay y'all a thousand dollars a week, and the more the spot picks up, the more money y'all gon' get." Wink waited for the teeth to show, as JT and Dilla high-fived each other. They had forgotten all about J-Bo.

"Where's the rocks he had y'all sellin'?"

JT dug around the sofa and tossed Wink the remainder of what they hadn't sold. Wink looked at the pebbles and tucked them in his pocket. He tossed JT his own sack of fat rocks. "That's what we're sellin' from now on. Don't open them, tamper with 'em, or nothin'. Give the fiends exactly what they comin' for and the more they gon' come. I catch y'all fucking with those rocks and it'll be hell to pay. Y'all hear me?" snapped Wink as he was running down his house rules just like J-Bo did with them.

"We got you," said Dilla.

Wink looked at Trey. "You got anything you wanna tell these li'l niggas?"

"If they ain't coppin', no stoppin'. No trickin' with the fiends or these hoes strolling 'round here," said Trey.

"Definitely no tricking. Let's see. What else?" Wink's thoughts were interrupted by the sound of footsteps in the kitchen.

Gator bent the corner, not looking his normal upbeat, ready-to-fast-talk a nigga self. The look in his eyes said that he knew what happened.

Wink turned to Trey and said, "Why don't you take Dilla and JT up to Coney Island and grab something to eat. I need to holla at Gator."

Trey nodded at JT and Dilla. They got up from the sofa and followed Trey out the front room. "I'ma need your keys," Trey yelled from the stairs.

"I'll be right back. Have a seat," said Wink. He dug in his pocket for his car keys. He whispered to Trey at the steps, "Give me your strap."

Trey pulled his 9 mm from his waist and whispered, "What you 'bout to do?"

"Hopefully nothin'. Just stay gone for a couple hours just in case."

Trey nodded with fear in his eyes. He turned and walked down the stairs. Wink tucked the black Berretta in his waist, then locked the door up. He found Gator pacing the floor in the living room, mumbling something under his breath about J-Bo. He looked up at Wink and stopped.

"Why'd you do it, baby boy? Why?" Gator had tears in his eyes. He had raised J-Bo in the game.

"You know why, Gator. The same reason every other nigga gets killed. He was in the way," said Wink.

"But J-Bo had love for you. You may not had believed this." Gator threw his hands up in the air, then let them fall to his side as he began his pacing.

"Maybe this will help take your mind off of it. Here." Wink tossed Gator the rocks he took off JT.

"He's gone. Ain't nothin' we can do about it now except live on," said Wink.

Gator wanted to grieve and hate Wink for what he did, but the rocks he clutched in his hand were calling his name.

"G'on and clear ya mind, Gator. I'll be out here when you get finished." Wink put his arm around Gator's shoulder and walked him toward the back of the house. He opened one of the bedroom doors, then patted Gator on his back. "It's just you and me now, Gator. G'on and get straight. I'll be out here."

Gator walked in the room, tearing at the plastic of one of the rocks. Wink closed the door. Gator was about to be on cloud nine, right where Wink wanted him so he wouldn't have that far to go up.

Wink walked in the living room and turned up the stereo to blast. He pulled the Berretta from his pants and walked back to the bedroom. When he opened the door, Gator didn't even see it coming. He was on his knees, tweaking, looking around like he dropped a crumb of crack. Wink walked up behind him and shot him once, execution style. *Boom!*

Chapter Twenty-four

Two months had passed, and Wink, along with Trey and Willie, took over all of J-Bo's crack spots and even opened a few new ones. Wink had mastered the art of setting up shop, following J-Bo's blueprint and adding some of his own techniques. Wink would find abandoned houses throughout the city and pull a "kick door," just taking over the property by vandalizing the interior of the house. Wink, Trey, Willie, and their workers would kick the door in to the house and bust all the light sockets out, bash holes in the walls and ceilings. They'd spray paint the outside of the house and garage. They'd do all this for two reasons: one, so no one would want to move in the house, and two, the landlord wouldn't want to invest the needed money to repair the home. And if he/she did, they'd double back and fuck the house up again and again until the landlord got the picture that their property had been lost to the DOT (Department of Thugs). Wink started spray-painting *DOT* on the sides of his houses. His plan was working well. There just weren't enough police to combat the shady tactics Wink and his crew had been putting down around the city.

Niggas fell in line because word was getting around that Wink would bust his gun and put a nigga in the dirt about his. A few old heads wanted to try their hand just to test the waters and who knows what else. Old niggas were just stubborn like that. They'd make you kill their old asses. But Wink didn't have to wage war, because he had what every nigga in the city needed—good coke at the best price.

Mr. Fatts saw that Wink's hand called for more work, and he didn't hesitate to hit him off. Wink was coppin' thirty bricks every week off Fatts, and sometimes he'd have to make a trip to the store in the middle of the week just to keep up with the demand. Wink got smart and formed allies with other hustlas without them really knowing it. He figured if he sold them weight at a decent price, in a time of war, they'd be more likely to aid and assist because they stood to take a loss if he lost.

Willie was handling things down in Mississippi. He and his cousin Ball were working on expanding the operation in other cities and hick towns down south. Wink was no dummy, though. He kept everybody at an arm's distance. He never let Willie and Ball know the game on how to mail the coke. Wink made sure he packaged every box, and he'd pay a crackhead to mail it off. He didn't even put his main man, Trey, up on game because he couldn't afford niggas trying to grow a brain, figuring they no longer needed him.

When Wink was out working the streets, he preferred to park his El Dogg on the corner of his street in front of the old transmission shop. He'd be out there, sippin' Henny with Trey and Willie, flodging on hood rats dying to take a ride in their Caddies.

Wink chose that spot because that's where he officially met J-Bo, the day when J-Bo told him that if he made it that far in the game, he would understand. Wink would look up at the sky and tell him how he understood and that he was willing to die for what he had.

"Y'all know Krazy's trial is next week," Wink said, then took a long swallow from his cup of Henny.

Trey shook his head while staring off into space. He still couldn't believe Krazy was MIA. "You think he's going to beat it?"

"It's a fifty-fifty chance. If them two rat-face moth-afuckas show up, it's cancel Christmas. But if they don't show, he'll walk. Well, that's at least how his lawyer put it to me the other day when I spoke with him."

Wille poured himself another cup from the fifth, then set the bottle back on the hood of his burgundy El Dogg. He took a sip from his cup and tried to think of something meaningful to say. Every time somebody brought up Krazy, silence soon followed.

"What if we get them two crackers missing?" Willie said.

Wink shook his head. "Tried that. Can't find 'em, though. I even told Krazy's mouthpiece to go holla at their cracker dog ass and tell 'em I got fifty stacks for them to not show up."

"And what he say?"

"Can't find 'em. I don't know where they're at, but I got a feelin' they're somewhere with police at their side," said Wink.

"So, we just gon' have to wait and see how shit pans out, huh?" Trey poured the last of the Henny into his cup, then chucked the bottle onto the roof of the building with the rest of their empty liquor bottles.

The liquor was starting to talk for Willie. "I say we just wait for they cracker asses to show up for court and blaze all they ass. Police, news, whoever!"

"If it were a life or death situation, then yeah. But Krazy's got a shot. Let's just hope all goes well and that next week this time, we'll be throwing him a welcome home party," said Wink.

"Yeah, and I'll be in charge of gettin' all the bitches." Trey smiled.

"I don't know, my nigga. Them hoes you had with you last night look like some down-bads. Where'd you find them at, Grand River?" Wink said.

"Yeah, you do be having some bucketheads with you," Willie said. They all laughed at their jokes.

Gary pulled up in his Fleetwood and rolled the passenger window down.

"Cool . . . daddy." Trey laughed, making fun of Gary's long white Caddy. "Superfly. Doom-doom. Superfly."

"You's a nut, my nigga." Willie was holding his side, laughing so hard at Gary's ass.

"Y'all chill out," said Wink, grinning.

"Superfly . . . a goldie," shouted Trey.

Wink walked around the car and leaned in the window. "What's up?"

"Hop in and take a ride with me. I need to show you something," said Gary. He had this li'l smirk on his face, which meant good news. Wink had known the man all his life, and the only time he smiled, smirked, or laughed was when some good news had come his way.

Wink looked over the roof at Trey and Willie, who were still clowning Gary. "Ay, y'all. I'ma take a few laps with my old head. If y'all leave, lock my car up for me."

"What, you gon' leave us to go hang with Ron O'Neal? Jive turkey." Trey and Willie laughed.

"I don't know why you hang with them simple-ass niggas," said Gary. He pulled away and into traffic.

"They're cool, just a little buzzed." Wink laid his seat back and flipped down his visor. His buzz was nice too.

Gary pulled back a wide, teeth-bearing smile as he dug in his coat pocket. He pulled up a little black box and handed it to Wink. It was a ring box from Tiffany's.

Wink's stomach did a back flip, then rested near his ass. He nearly lost his eyesight when he opened the box. The five-carat ring bling-glowed in the sun.

"I'm gon' ask your mom to marry me tonight at dinner. I think we're finally ready to do it. Time has healed our differences, and to be honest, I never did stop lovin' her."

Wink hadn't heard a word past *mom to marry me*. He was having mixed emotions about the shit. He shut the box and handed it back to Gary while looking out his window. "What you think?" Gary was smiling from ear to ear.

Wink took a deep breath and thought about his mom. She was getting up there in age, and he wouldn't always be around to take care of her. Hell, he was already now deep in the game. And besides, she deserved to be happy.

Wink turned to Gary and smiled. "I think y'all should do it."

"Thanks, Wink. You don't know how good that feels to have your blessin' on this. I'ma go all out for the wedding, maybe have it down in the Bahamas." Gary leaned over and stuck his hand out, real cool-like. "I'd like for you to be my best man, Wink. It'll really be an honor." Gary said this as if it were a question. He held his hand steady until Wink grabbed it and shook it.

"My man, or should I say son?"

The only thing Wink could think about was his dad. Here it was Wink had given Gary his blessing to marry his mom, and his father was somewhere doing life in federal prison. Wink decided he was going to find Wayne, Sr., and more importantly, he was going to go see him for the first time in his life. It was time.

Chapter Twenty-five

The courtroom was scarce, with the exception of a few news reporters, uniformed Davenport police officers, the stubby redneck prosecutor, and the racist white supremacist judge perched high on his throne. Through the entire proceedings, Judge "Hang-em" Gault gripped his gavel in his wrinkled white hand like he was ready to skip all the bullshit and just go ahead with sentencing.

Wink, Trey, and Willie sat behind Krazy at the defense table. They were his only supporters. Not even his lawyer seemed to be on his team. All he kept saying was that maybe Krazy should consider taking a plea.

"A plea. Bitch mothafucka, my people paid you to fight, not to sell me out." Krazy had to lightweight collar his pink-faced attorney up at the start of the trial.

"Okay, I'll do my best."

Krazy slowly released the man's tie and dusted his suit jacket. "Your best betta be me walkin' outta here today."

Things weren't looking up for Krazy. His supposed-to-be lawyer faked a fight, while the prosecutor painted his case like he was Picasso himself. The victim, Robert, took the stand and pointed Krazy out as the man who shot him, as did his wife, Mandy. Krazy wanted his lawyer to raise the question of her being a crack addict and that she was the cause of the ordeal. Krazy's defense was that Robert attacked him, and so he did as any other red-blooded man would've done, he defended himself. Just so happened it was with a gun.

Krazy's sell-out attorney raised no such argument. He kept whispering to Krazy at the defense table that he had it under control, but closing arguments opened and closed with no certainty that Krazy would walk. His lawyer had thrown him under the bus.

Krazy turned in his chair and tried to flash his crew a *I'm all right* smile, but they knew him too well. The look in his eyes said, *I won't see y'all for a long time. Don't forget about me.*

When the jury re-entered the court room, Krazy's lawyer strategically positioned himself on the side of the podium away from Krazy. The white woman serving as the lead juror stood with an envelope in her hand, which contained Krazy's fate.

"Has the jury reached a verdict in the matter?" asked the judge.

"We have, Your Honor." The woman tore the seal on the envelope and unfolded the piece of paper.

"And how do you find the defendant?"

"They jury finds the defendant guilty of attempted murder and guilty of possession of a firearm."

Krazy went crazy. He leaped from his set at the reading of the verdict. He chased his bitch-ass lawyer around the podium until he caught him. Krazy grabbed that cracker by the back of his suit jacket and tripped him. Krazy jumped on the man's back and commenced to beating the sleeves off his ass. He had nothing to lose. What were they going to do, give him some more time? Krazy already had his mind made up that if he lost at trial, his lawyer had to wear it. And boy, was he wearing that ass-whooping Krazy was putting down.

The judge banged on his gavel relentlessly, but Krazy wasn't stopping. He punched, kicked, and bit the four officers as they attempted to pry him off the lawyer's ass. They had to mace Krazy to get him up off the man.

More police rushed into the courtroom and stood between Trey, Wink, and Willie as they tried helping Krazy. The police drew their weapons and backed them out of the courtroom. Wink was left with the haunting image of Krazy being hog-tied and dragged out.

The whole ride back to Detroit, nobody spoke a word. Wink pushed his El Dogg down the interstate. Trey and Willie passed each other joints, trying to take the pain away and block their mind from thinking about Krazy. *Guilty* was the only thing that kept playing through Trey's mind. All of them felt guilty for Krazy sitting back there on his way to do at least twenty-five years. And knowing Krazy, he was bound to run his number up with all that time. Twenty-five years was like a lifetime, and his crew was starting to realize that they might not ever see him walk the streets again.

It's funny what a few months can change when you're out there running in the game. They went from B-boys to D-boys in what seemed like overnight. The stress of the streets was already starting to show on their young faces, Wink's especially. He was starting to be more withdrawn every day. All he wanted when they first started hustling was the glitz and glam you see when you're on the side-lines watching playas and hustlas alike do their numbers. Wink knew that niggas got killed and some went to jail, but it didn't stop him from wanting a taste because he'd never personally had to kill anyone, and besides his father, no one else close to him had gone to jail.

Wink looked at the sign on I-94, which read: DETROIT
NEXT EXIT. He sighed and thought, *Why didn't I just go
to that picnic?* Krazy would be right home with them if
he had. Wink just needed something other than himself
to blame. He had no intention of leaving the game, and
besides, Krazy needed them now more than ever. Wink
told himself that he was going to personally find the best
appeals attorney and hire him to take Krazy's case, no
matter how much it cost. Krazy was going to know that
he was gone but not forgotten, and that his crew was out
there going hard for him.

Wink parked across the street from Ms. Shelton's
house and two cribs down. He wasn't in the mood to hear
her bitching, 'cause he just might nut the fuck up and
snap on her old ass. Wink killed the engine, then reached
under his seat for a fresh bottle of Henny. He held the
bottom of the bottle up for Trey and Willie. They both
slapped the ass of the fifth, then Wink cracked the seal
and pulled the cork out. They ain't have no cups. Today
they were hittin' it straight from the neck. Wink took a
long gulp and passed it to Trey.

"What y'all 'bout to get into?" asked Wink.

"Get ready for this trip in the morning," said Trey.

"You taking Willie with you?"

"You know it," Willie said with a little rhythm. He sat
up from the back seat and grabbed the Henny, trading
Trey for a joint he just lit.

"I wish you'd come with us. I hear them Texas chicks
are all thick as a mothafucka. And Sue says she got a few
friends," said Trey.

"Maybe next time. I got something that I gotta handle.
I been putting it off for too long."

"A'ight, well, I'm 'bout to go in here and try to get some sleep." Trey reached over and gave Wink a play.

"I'ma see y'all when y'all get back," said Wink.

"A'ight, my nigga," said Willie.

"Y'all just gon' take my liquor, huh? Nah, it's cool, go ahead." Wink turned the key and waited for them to cross the street. He pulled the neck shift down to drive and peeled away from the curb.

He drove past his mom's house, but her car wasn't in the driveway. Wink figured her and Gary were probably out somewhere, still celebrating their engagement. Wink hadn't seen his mom smile so much in his whole life. Thinking about his mom being happy, it brought a closed smile to his face.

At least somebody's happy, Wink thought. He wouldn't be happy until Krazy was home where he was supposed to be, and until he buried the hatchet with his father.

Wink drove to his apartment so he could kick back and try to relax. It had been a long, stressful day. He kicked his shoes off at the door and allowed his toes to sink into the plush, cream-colored wall-to-wall carpet. It felt like a sponge massaging the arches of his feet as he walked over to the phone sitting on the small table in his living room. The red light on his answering machine was blinking, so he pushed the message button.

You have two messages. Beep!

"Wayne, it's Mom, I was just calling to see if you wanted to have dinner with me tonight. I really miss you being home. You give me a call. Love you. Bye."

Beep!

"Hello, Mr. Stewart. This is Charmene Wilson. I have some good news. I was able to locate the prisoner you inquired about."

Wink's stomach dropped to the floor. That was the call he'd been waiting on for two weeks. He rushed into the kitchen, grabbed a pen and a yellow sticky pad, and wrote down the information: *Yusuf Al-min, United States Penitentiary Leavenworth, Kansas.*

Wink pushed the END button and walked slowly around to the sofa and sat down. He looked at the sticky pad. His dad had changed his name. No wonder he couldn't find him.

"Yusuf Al-min." Wink struggled to pronounce the name. He couldn't believe it. The man who he heard so many war stories about had flipped Muslim.

Chapter Twenty-six

A thousand butterflies danced around in Wink's stomach as he rode in the back of a cab down some rural road in Leavenworth, Kansas. His stomach had been playing tricks on him since he boarded the plane and took his seat. Wink hadn't told anyone he was going to see his father in prison. Not his mom, Gary, his crew, no one. The only person who knew that he was coming was his father, and that's because Wink had to fill out some visitation forms and mail them back to the prison.

Wink didn't know what to expect when he got there. All he had was the lone picture he clipped from Gary's old photo album, and the many legendary stories niggas would tell from time to time about Wayne, AKA Gunz. Wink kept telling himself not to expect anything. How could he when eighteen years were lost between them? Wayne, Sr. had never held his son, talked to him on the phone, saw him on a visit, nothing. Eighteen years gone by and not a card, picture, money order, birthday gift, shit!

Wink was getting angry the closer they drove to the prison. He wasn't going to see his father to lash out and vent on him. He wasn't going with a list of questions demanding satisfying answers, because answers alone could never satisfy the pain and hurt built up inside. Wink wasn't sure of the reason he was going. Something in him needed to see his father face to face.

Wink took a deep breath and let out the frustration as the cab turned inside the complex. The stone sign out front read: USP LEAVENWORTH. The prison was situated in the middle of nowhere, and nowhere was exactly where it had been sitting for the past sixty-five years. Leavenworth was the third oldest USP in America, next to Lewisburg and Terre Haute.

Wink paid the cab driver, then stepped out into the sharp wind. It was dead winter, and the freeze was out and biting. Wink flipped his collar and shoved his hands deep inside the side pockets of his mink bomber. He regretted not wearing a heavier coat, but he wanted to be fly when his father saw him for the first time. Wink stomped the snow slush from the sole of his triple-black small-block Maury gators. He dusted the snowflakes from the shoulders of his mink, checked his reflection in the window, then pulled back the handle.

The prison lobby looked more like a hunting lodge with all the trophies and pictures dangling from the wooden walls.

Where the hell they got my daddy at? Wink thought as he approached the full-blooded hillbilly working the front desk.

"Visitation?" the freckle-faced worker asked with a strong accent.

"Yes. I'm here to visit Yusuf Al-min."

"Your driver's license."

Wink handed the man his license and watched as he punched some keys into some aged computer.

Nasty mothafucka, Wink said to himself as he looked the man over. His hair hung over his ears, hair protruded from his chest and the back of his neck, where a dirt ring lined his collar. He looked like the first man God put on this earth, like a cracker straight out of the Caucasus mountains.

He finally handed Wink his license back, then pointed down a long hallway full of gates. "Down four gates and to your left."

Wink felt like he was going to jail. Walking through all those gates, them slamming shut behind him, and the constant buzzing sent a chill down Wink's spine. He wondered what kind of niggas the feds had hid in a place like that. Breaking out was out of the question with all the security checks jumping off around there. And so far, the only color Wink saw was white. Them crackers all probably went to school together and were related somehow, thought Wink.

He made it to the fourth gate and waited to be buzzed inside the visiting hall. Minutes later, the Yankee working inside control decided to buzz him in. Wink walked inside the massive visiting hall. Little kids were running around, some screaming. People stood in a line for pictures, others for the vending machine. And of course, you had those out there making moves.

Wink saw a young black guy, couldn't have been no older than himself. He was over in the corner, trying to boof something up his ass while his girl kept an eye out. Wink caught an eyeful as he faced the section toward the back. A woman's head was going up and down on some Mexican's dick. Despite being in the middle of nowhere, niggas was still making it happen. This made Wink relax and think about his father. If those two crumb niggas were busting moves, he knew his pops was running the jail.

A female C.O. seated behind a desk waved him over. "Name, please."

"Wayne Stewart, Jr."

"Your visitor will be out shortly. Please take a seat in the second row." The woman pointed to an empty row of hard plastic chairs bunched together on a steel bench.

The butterflies returned at the sight of a huge, light-skinned man wearing a kufi coming his way. It was his father, Wayne, Sr. Wink slowly stood up and faced the man he'd longed to meet all his life. His father hadn't aged a day from the photo. His skin was clear, as were his eyes. His chest bulged from under the tan khaki shirt, and he smelled like some type of oil.

Wayne, Sr. pulled back a million-dollar smile and opened his arms. Wink gave him a brief hug. For that short moment, Wink felt something he had never before felt in his life except when hugging his mom. Love.

"Thanks for coming," Wayne, Sr. said as he stood back and checked Wink out.

"I had to," said Wink. He had to clear his throat because he was starting to get a little emotional.

"Let's have a seat." His father waved to the chairs, and they sat.

"Can I get you anything out of the vending machine?" asked Wink. He was so nervous he didn't know what to do with himself. His hands were shaking, and the hairs on his body stood up.

"No, I'm okay. I'll eat something when I get back to the block. That stuff's bad for you anyway."

There was an awkward moment of silence until Wayne, Sr. noticed the gold nugget bracelet dangling from Wink's wrist. "Ah, man. That bracelet brings back so many memories. Who gave it to you, your mom?" He leaned forward to inspect the diamonds. "The stones are still shining."

"Nah, Gary gave it to me. He said that you'd want me to have it."

The bright smile disappeared from Wayne, Sr.'s face at the sound of Gary's name. He clenched his jaws, and Wink saw a flash of hate in his eyes.

"Alhumdullah," said Wayne, Sr., then he took a deep breath, obviously trying to calm himself. "So, you're eighteen now."

"Yeah, I'll be nineteen in a couple more months."

"Wayne, I know why you come all this way, and I'm willing to answer all the questions you may have. I owe you that much."

"I mean, really, I just wanted to see you. For years, all my life I wanted to come visit you, but it was always a touchy subject 'round the house."

"Well, I'm glad you came. I can tell by the mink and gators that your hustlin'. I'm not gon' tell you a bunch of reasons why you shouldn't. Just look around where I've been for the past eighteen years."

"I'm not going to hustle forever."

"At least you know that much. Man, I can't believe how much you've grown. You look just like Hope. By the way, how is she doing?"

"She's doing good. She and Gary are about to get married soon."

"What?" yelled Wayne, Sr. That flash of hate appeared back in his eyes, but this time it stayed.

Wink didn't understand why his dad was so bent out of shape. He hadn't been with his mom in nearly twenty years.

"You mean to tell me she's still foolin' with that nigga?" snapped Wayne, Sr. He didn't wait for Wink to answer. "Don't you know he's the reason I'm serving two life sentences? The reason why I've never been a part of your life. He's the reason!"

Wink frowned out of sheer confusion. He had not a clue what his dad was talking about.

"I can't believe this. How could Hope do this to me?" Wink's dad had tears in his eyes.

"What are you talkin' about?" asked Wink.

"What, you mom didn't tell you? Gary testified against me and gave me all this time. He's the reason I'm sittin' in here with two life sentences."

The news hit Wink like a ton of bricks. It was all starting to make sense why Gary only got five years and his dad got all day.

"Does my mom know?"

"Of course she knows. She was at my trial, pregnant with you, when Gary took the stand on me. All these years, you mean to tell me that she's been dealing with that rat while I'm here with life."

Wink didn't know what to say. There wasn't anything that he could say. He knew there was a reason he hated Gary when he was coming up.

"And you say that they're getting married, huh?"

"They were getting married. That nigga ain't marrying nothin' except a casket," Wink promised his father. He couldn't wait to get back to Detroit so he could push Gary's shit back. His mom would just have to be mad with him, because it was already sketched in stone. Gary had to die.

Chapter Twenty-seven

Wink thought about what his father had told him. He closed his eyes and leaned his head back against the soft headrest so that not a tear would escape. He could feel the plane's engine come to life as it roared and hummed in his ear. Wink promised his father that retribution would be paid for the dishonor bestowed upon him.

Wink couldn't believe that his mother hadn't told him the truth. And why was she marrying the very man who had buried his father alive?

If she wasn't my mom, I'd blow her fucking brains out too, just 'cause she knew, Wink thought to himself as the plane began rumbling down the runway.

Wink opened his eyes reluctantly to look out his window. He sighed out of frustration, then leaned back on his seat and closed his eyes. Eighteen years later, and the truth finally found him. Wink felt bad for his father, sitting back there in those white folks' prison, serving a natural life sentence, and for what? All because Gary couldn't hold his own nuts when the pressure hit. Wink's dad told him all about how they used to get money, how Gary was his stickman. They started off doing petty drug runs for an old head from their era. Back then, heroin ran the city with an iron fist, and only a few niggas actually had real connects with getting the shit. Wink's dad wasn't one of them, but he was a natural born hustla with green flowing through his veins, so when coke started making its impression, he made sure to have two hands in it. Wayne, Sr., was soon known as Gunz because he took every rival to war over the drug trade and won.

Just like every other kingpin, there was a rise and there was a fall. Gunz's fall just so happened to be by the hands of his right-hand man. Gary got caught out of town, selling coke to an undercover agent, and instead of going and doing his number, he gave the time to Gunz. Gary told about all the murders Gunz committed on his way to the top. The feds gave Gary five years for snitching, and they roofed Gunz with two life sentences.

There was no way Gary or Wink's mom could explain themselves or try to rationalize the situation. There was no way to clean it up, except with more blood—Gary's blood. Wink fumed over the thought of Gary having the nerve to lay up around his mom for all these years, and then to top it off, the nigga had the balls to ask Wink to be his best man. Wink figured so much time had passed that his mom and Gary never thought he'd reach out to his father. They thought their secret was safely buried in USP Leavenworth, and that Wink could never find out.

Wink couldn't wait to see that look of death he had seen in J-Bo's eyes right before he killed him. He needed to see it in Gary's eyes, that fear of knowing he was about to die. That was the only way to make it right.

Wink's plane landed at the Detroit City Airport. He took a cab to his apartment so that he could take a shower and wash all that travel grime off. He had been in those woods for three days, visiting his father, trying to catch up on eighteen years of absence.

Wink stood under the steaming hot shower and let the tears go. Wink was hurting because there was nothing he could do to help his father's situation. Over eighteen years, he had exhausted every last one of his appeals, so the court wasn't an option. Basically, he was just waiting to die. Wink just wished that there was something he could do to help ease the pain. He promised his father that he wouldn't forget about him and that as long as there was air in his lungs, he had him on anything he needed.

Wink turned the shower off and reached for his towel. He stood in front of the mirror, looking into his own bloodshot eyes. He could see the stress of the game taking its toll, and more so, he could see his father.

"You can live through me," he said.

Wink threw on some clothes, grabbed his new Glock, and was out the door. He decided to get a head start on the plan he and his father had cooked up. Wink parked across the street up on 7 Mile. He hugged the side of his car while waiting on the busy traffic to clear up. The parking lot was empty as usual. Hardly no one ever shopped at the store except Wink and a few other dealers Fatts was supplying.

Wink entered the store and hurriedly locked the front door, and then casually walked down the middle aisle around the front counter. Wink didn't see any signs of ole Fatts. He called out, "Fatts, you back here?"

Fatts was in the back room, sitting on one of the stools, hunched over the workstation, devouring his second lunch. His back was to the door, but he raised his head from the hoagie sandwich and waved Wink over. With a mouth full of salami, lettuce, onion, and tomato, he still managed to say, "Have a seat."

Wink took a seat on the stool beside Fatts and turned sideways to face him. He stuck both hands inside the side pocket of his hoodie, clutching the handle of his Glock while watching Fatts wipe mayo from the side of his face onto the sleeve of his shirt.

"Where you been at? I thought you were coming yesterday to pick up. You had me worried for a minute, 'cause I called Gary and he said he hadn't seen you either."

"I took a trip," said Wink, short and flat.

"Oh, yeah? Where'd you go?" Fatts took a gulp from his two-liter of Pepsi.

"To see my father." Wink watched the lump form in Fatts' throat. He nearly choked on the Pepsi.

"Your father? You mean . . . Gunz?" he stuttered.

"The one and only."

Wink could tell by the way Fatts was fidgeting with the hoagie wrapper that he was nervous as shit and, without a doubt, wondering how much Gunz had told him. More so, he was wondering how his fat, stinkin' ass was going to make it out of there alive.

"So, how's he doing?" asked Fatts. He tried to stand up, but Wink pushed him back down by the shoulder.

"He's doing two life sentences. How do you think he's doing?"

Fatts' heart started pounding through his chest, and his entire body began to sweat from his head to his toes. Wink came out of his hoodie with his Glock in hand. He slid off the stool while pointing the gun low at Fatts' gut.

"He told me everything."

"Wink, I swear it was all Gary. He brought me into their conspiracy. They were going to give me life," pleaded Fatts.

"So, you traded my dad's life for yours?"

"I didn't want the shit to go down the way it did, but I'm telling you, it was all Gary. He put the feds on all of us."

"I'm not hearing that shit, nigga." Wink became so angry his dick got hard. He raised the gun to Fatts' dome and said. "Nigga, you did just what you're doing right now, lyin' and snitchin'. All you niggas told on my dad, and all y'all gon' die, starting with yo' bitch ass." Wink waited to see that look of death in Fatts' eyes, the one a nigga wears on his face right before death seizes his ass.

Before Fatts could try and plead some furtherance of his rationale as to why he snitched, Wink let the 9 mm rain on his fat ass. The first shot hit him in the right-side temple, knocking him from the stool. As he fell sideways, Wink continued to let the nine-milly spit. Wink stood over Fatts' lifeless body and squeezed the trigger repeatedly, even after he had emptied all seventeen shells. He was in a trance that only another killer could identify with.

He stood there for a long moment, watching the blood slowly rise up and spill over from the bullet holes in Fatts' head. For what he had done to his father, Fatts deserved to die like that ten times.

"Rat bastard," said Wink. He came back to his senses and quickly snapped into the second reason he was there. Shit, there wasn't no sense in leaving empty-handed after spilling all that blood.

Wink walked over to the refrigerator, where Fatts kept all the kilos, and snatched the door open. Staring him dead in the face were two stacks of kilos wrapped in red duct tape from the floor of the fridge to the ceiling. Wink grabbed two large Ace Hardware bags from the front counter, then unloaded the fridge. In all, he came up on sixty bricks of some of the best cocaine Detroit had ever seen. It was the closest thing you were going to get to being pure, and if Wink wanted to, he could have easily stretched each key to two and still would have had some grade-A coke. Wink was counting the dollar signs in his head already. He knew Fatts' old ass was holding way more than that, and for a second, he wished he hadn't killed him so soon, 'cause he could have gotten his fat ass to take him to the vault, and it would've really been a sho' enough lick.

Oh, well, Wink thought as he tossed the bags over his shoulder. *Sixty's good enough.*

Wink took one last look at Fatts as he lay stretched out in a pool of blood, dead as a mothafucka. Wink promised him this, "Don't worry. Gary will join you real soon."

Wink left out the back door and walked down the alley to the side street and back up to 7 Mile Rd. He power-walked across the street to his Caddy and tossed the bags in the back seat. He checked his side mirror, then pulled into the afternoon traffic. It was just like he had bought the keys from Fatts. That's how calm and collected Wink was. He leaned his seat back and gripped the wheel with one hand, while he slid a Newport into his mouth with the other hand. He pushed the cigarette lighter in for a few seconds, then lit his square. He took a long pull off the square and let out a cloud of smoke.

Part one of his plan was completed. He had killed Fatts, who was, come to find out, supplying damn near the entire east side of Detroit with coke. Even if he wasn't directly dealing with a nigga, still nine times out of ten, the shit was coming from Fatts after it been stepped on, stomped on, and sometimes even danced on.

Wink's dad put him all the way up on game. He said that Gary and Fatts told on him for two reasons: one, so they could save their own asses, and two, 'cause niggas feared and respected his gansta. But when he fell, Gary and Fatts started getting major money after Fatts back-doored Gunz and started copping from his Texas connect, some Mexican Mafia mothafuckas who also snitched on Gunz at trial. They kept the operation moving, and them niggas were blessing Fatts with all the work he could stand. The niggas in the city stayed copping from Fatts too, even though they knew he took the stand on Gunz. Them niggas' only concern was how cheap Fatts was slanging them bricks for. They let money abolish loyalty and the unwritten rules of the game, and for that, they would all pay. Wink was on a blood-thirsty mission, targeting all old niggas from his dad's era. If he ran across them and his dad remembered them, it was casket season, because they didn't honor the game.

Wink felt like it was ole niggas like them who were killing the game. There were no consequences for snitching anymore. Niggas talked that *murder, death, kill* shit, but truth was, they wasn't gon' kill nothing and wasn't gon' let nothing die. There was no fear of what would happen to a nigga if he snitched, and that's what Wink vowed to bring back to the game, that fear.

Wink had plans already for the sixty bricks, but in the meantime, he was gon' sit on them. Kicking it with his dad about the game gave Wink a whole new outlook on hustling. His dad made him realize that shit was real, and if he was going to be in the game, then he would be the best. From then on out, Wink was playing for keeps. There would be no more petty dime rocks or Greyhound trips with his ass packed to the hilt with coke. Wink wanted it all, and from listening to his father, he knew the only way he was going to get it was if he played the game on the higher level. So, all the crack houses he took from J-Bo, Wink had no plans on ever returning. As far as he was concerned, all his workers could keep what they owed him. They'd eventually figure it out that he wasn't coming back.

Wink drove deep west to his storage unit he had rented a few weeks back. He stashed his kilos inside his garage unit, then jumped on the Lodge Expressway and came up on Jefferson Ave. He drove down to Chene Park and pulled over next to the river. Wink climbed out the car and flipped his collar up and ducked his head inside his coat to block the whipping wind coming off the river. He walked over to the railing and pulled out the gun he'd just used to kill Fatts. Wink used the tail of his shirt to wipe the gun clean, then he chucked it deep into the water and watched as it splashed and sank.

Don't ever use the same gun twice. Wink could still hear his father's deep, serious voice. Besides Gary and Fatts snitchin', the feds were able to corroborate their tales because Gary knew where Wink's dad stashed all his murder weapons. His dad told him to rob, steal, and especially kill by your lonely. He said, "If you're too scared to do it by yourself, then don't do it, 'cause a murder is like a get out of jail free card. Niggas use 'em when they need 'em."

Wink looked out across the water and promised his dad that he wouldn't make the same mistake. "I got you, Dad."

Chapter Twenty-eight

Since the last episode with Krazy beating his lawyer's ass in the courtroom, the judge decided it would be best to hold a closed sentencing. No one was permitted inside the courtroom except the victims, the prosecutor, and Krazy with a host of police standing around ready to beat his ass if he felt froggy and tried to leap.

The judge lived up to his nickname and hung Krazy with a 25-year sentence, not a day less. "You are a cancer on society, and today I am here to surgically remove you. Twenty-five years in the eyes of this court is far too lenient, but then again, I am not responsible for the maximum penalties. You're not fit to function—"

Krazy interrupted the judge. "First off, fuck you, cracker. You don't know me." He didn't care how many police were standing around him. He wasn't about to let that wrinkled devil get his nut off by talking down on him.

"Quiet him down!" The judge pounded his gavel.

Two police officers took a step forward, one with his hands spread wide. He was trying to calm Krazy, but all the talking was finished. Them crackers were out their rabbit-ass minds to even think that they could give a nigga like Krazy all that time and expect him to stand still. He threw his hands up and popped off.

The only thing Wink could hear from outside the

courtroom was a loud ruckus. He knew Krazy was in there getting in it. Four police decorated the outside of the courtroom, all standing. They put their ready-to-shoot pale hands on their holsters at the sound of the ruckus. Wink, Willie, and Trey wanted so bad to help their man, but it was futile.

The ruckus seemed to abruptly cease, then a few seconds later, Krazy's new attorney, Mr. Cunningham, violently pushed the double doors open. He seemed to be pissed, but to Wink's observation, it was all an act, because he hadn't done a single thing he promised. Wink was quickly learning that those greedy lawyers would fix their lips in a heartbeat to see you dream about what they could do for you—at least until they got paid, and then it was "I tried" or some other sorry shit.

Wink followed Mr. Cunningham over to a corner. His cracker dog ass broke into a spill as he loosened his tie. "I tried. It's that freakin' judge. We never had a chance with the case in front of him."

"What'd they give him?" asked Wink. Willie and Trey were standing over his shoulder.

"Twenty-five years, and I'm assuming they might pursue assault charges after that scuffle in there."

Wink turned to leave, but Mr. Cunningham wasn't finished sucking the blood out of Wink's pockets. He had already juiced him for fifty thousand dollars, and now he was going for fifty more.

"I can file this appeal if you'd like. We've got ten days exact to file a notice of appeal."

Wink looked the round-face devil square in his eyes and said, "I'll stop by your office." Wink could see the dollar signs appear in his eyes. Little did he know, it would be a cold day in hell before Wink let him scorch him out another fifty thousand dollars.

Wink stopped by the jail and put fifty thousand on Krazy's books. That would be enough to get his bid started while they worked on getting him the best appeals lawyer money could buy.

Trey tried to lighten up the mood by recalling his trip to Wink. He and Willie had spent the past two weeks parlaying down in Dallas with a flight attendant Trey met on the plane. He was flying down to Mississippi when he met her.

"I can't believe you don't remember Sue. She was the thick white broad you had to pull me away from, remember?" asked Trey. He had been trying to jog Wink's memory, but Wink had far too much other stuff on his mind to remember some flight attendant.

"Nah, I don't remember her, my nigga. But what's up with her?" asked Wink.

"Oh, she's official. Some of the best pussy I ever had. But that wasn't why we stayed down there so long," said Trey. He paused as Willie leaned forward to pass him a joint.

"I'm listening," said Wink as he looked in the rearview at Willie, who was cheesing.

"That's right, make 'im sweat." Willie smiled. They knew Wink would be wide open at the sound of money.

"We met some amigos down there, and they got it for cheap." Trey took a couple tokes off the joint, then passed it back to Willie.

Wink's wheels were turning. He already had a new connect set up through his dad, but he still wanted to see what Trey had come up on.

"How cheap?"

"Ten thousand a brick. And they say it's that flake."

"You didn't get their hookup?"

"Yeah, *I* got it." Trey put extra emphasis on *I*, and Wink peeped it, but he let it pass. For whatever reason, Trey felt like he had to let it be known that it was his connect.

There was a still silence. The tension was thick.

"How much money we sittin' on?" asked Trey.

Wink's blood started boiling, 'cause he knew Trey and Willie had talked about this while they were away.

"Why? Y'all plan on pullin' out?" Wink watched Willie drop his eyes through the mirror.

"Nah, I just wanna know what's in the pot to see if my count is right," said Trey.

"What, you counting behind me now?" snapped Wink.

"That's what niggas do. Every so often you wanna count ya money. We bustin' all these moves, and yet I feel like I'm on an allowance. Why we even holding all the money in the pot?"

Wink didn't bother answering. He reached forward and turned the radio on, then pressed down on the gas. Wink figured Trey was high, which would explain his boldness. But nevertheless, he had said the words. Here it was, Wink called himself taking care of everything, making sure Krazy's lawyer fees got paid, the re-up money was straight, and even put all three of them in brand-new El Dorados, and this nigga had the audacity to ask what was in the pot. Wink was steaming, but he tried his damndest not to let it show.

Trey was down with his main man, but he just felt like it was time to see some ends and not continue to blind hustle. He wanted to see the money, hold the money, spend some money—all when he wanted to. Krazy had lost his trial, they all put in mad work to pay for his lawyer, and Trey had no intention of leaving Krazy out there to hang. But still in all, he had some of his own plans. Wink never once asked him and Willie what they wanted to do. Willie brought them to Mississippi, and when they got there, Wink set everything up like it was his operation. The shit was cool for a minute, but Trey started peeping little shit like when Wink never wanted him going with him to meet the connect, but his money was going there. Trey just felt like he and Wink were equal. That's at least what he thought it was going to be.

When they made it back to Detroit, Wink drove straight up to the storage unit. He parked at the entrance and got out. "I'll be right back." He didn't want Trey and Willie knowing exactly what garage he was going to. They didn't even know why they were there. Ever since Wink found out how Gary snitched on his father, everything and everybody was a suspect. Nobody was above suspicion.

Wink unlocked the garage, then lifted it from the bottom. He grabbed the large green duffle bag from on top of the two car tires. He checked under the first one and nodded at the sixty bricks he'd taken off Fatts.

Y'all just sit tight. I got plans for y'all, Wink thought as he replaced the tire. He tossed the duffle bag around his shoulder, then locked up the garage.

Trey's eyes lit up with greed. He sat up in his seat and began rubbing his hands together at the sight of the green bag wrapped around Wink's shoulder. Trey already knew what was in the bag. Money. His money!

Wink locked the bag in the trunk, then climbed behind the wheel. He turned up the radio to prevent any idle chatter. In his mind, he figured, *Y'all want y'all money? Well, I'ma give it to you.*

Wink pulled out the parking area and drove straight

to the hood. He opted to not go to Trey's crib because his bitchy mammy always seemed to be home. Wink didn't want to go over to Willie's crib because he had too many people living there. He had been trying to avoid his mother's house because he wasn't ready to kill Gary yet. He needed that day and moment to be grand. So, in the meantime, Wink just tried to keep his distance.

They rented a room at the Suez up on 8 Mile Rd. Wink closed the curtains tight, locked the door, then shoved a chair under the doorknob. Trey and Willie were promptly seated on the bed, staring down at the closed green bag like it was a pot of gold.

"How much is it?" asked Trey. He could no longer conceal his excitement.

Wink walked over to the bed and undid the black steel hooks on the bag, then turned it upside down. Nothing but hundreds, fifties, and twenties poured onto the bed. Wink shook the bag clean, then tossed it on the floor.

"This is it, every last dollar," said Wink. He watched the looks of awe on their faces. Willie and Trey were stuck. There was so much money piled up that it blew both their highs.

"I'll count it," Trey volunteered as he dug into the pile of money.

Willie couldn't count his toes, so he slid off the bed and over to the table, where he promptly rolled another joint.

Wink knew exactly how much money was there. He smirked to himself at the thought of making Trey count the money over. He would be there all night, counting.

"I'ma go across the street to grab something from the Coney Island. Y'all want me to grab anything?" Wink asked.

Willie yelled for a cheeseburger deluxe with a side of chili cheese fries. Trey was too busy at the bank. Wink laughed, then unlatched the chain and opened the door. He crossed 8 Mile Rd. on foot over to Robert's Coney Island. There weren't any customers inside the restaurant, but it was still in somewhat of the hood, so Wink proceeded with caution. He didn't like the feeling of being naked with no gun on his hip.

All those feelings of paranoia vanished when Wink stepped inside the restaurant and looked into the lustrous eyes of the most beautiful woman he'd ever encountered in his life. The woman must have sensed the attraction, because she pulled back an inviting smile.

Wink stepped up to the bulletproof glass that separated them. *Damn, she's beautiful.*

"May I help you?" She had the softest voice.

She was so fine, Wink forgot what Willie ordered. Hell, she was so fine, Wink forgot what he wanted. It was obvious that he wanted her, but he had to play it cool, calm it down.

Wink stared up at the menu, trying to jog his memory. *Oh, yeah.*

"Three cheeseburger deluxe, with three side orders of chili cheese fries."

The woman scribbled the order down on the pad, then rang up the total. Wink paid with a twenty-dollar bill and told her to keep the change.

"Thank you." She smiled.

Wink stood at the counter and enjoyed every stride she took to and from the counter. The black Spandex complemented her hourglass frame, and the tight-fitting teal blue Robert's Coney Island polo shirt accentuated her perfect breasts.

Wink didn't know Arab women were so beautiful. He really hadn't paid them any attention because their men were racist and very protective over them—kinda how the old man was staring at Wink. *She must be his daughter*. Wink played with his pager to throw the old fart off his sins of lust. His order was up, and the woman slid his Styrofoam trays into two plastic bags, then put them in the window. The old man gave Wink the break he needed. He walked into the freezer.

"What's your name?" asked Wink.

"Armeeah."

"I'm Wink. When are your off days? I want to take you out. A pretty girl like you shouldn't spend all her days working."

Armeeah blushed, but she quickly thought about her lurking father. "I don't know," she said, looking over her shoulder.

She didn't say no, Wink told himself as he jotted his pager number down onto one of the napkins.

"Page me," he said, sliding the napkin through the money slot. Armeeah quickly cuffed the napkin into her bra. Her dad walked out of the freezer with some onions and bell peppers in his hand.

"Armeeah," he said, then the rest of his conversation was in Arabic.

Wink grabbed the bag and headed out the door. When he got back over to the room, Trey hadn't knocked a dent in the money stack. Wink and Willie sat at the table and punished their food while occasionally laughing at Trey, but Wink saw something in his eyes that made his skin crawl. He was zoned out and full of greed.

Chapter Twenty-nine

When Trey finally finished counting the money, it came out to $850,000 and some change, the exact amount Wink knew it would be. Trey divided the money into three piles of $280,000 and some change. He began separating his from theirs, but Wink leaped from his chair, stopping him.

"You forgot a pile," said Wink.

Trey looked down at the bed. "Nah, there's three piles," he said.

"Exactly. It should be four. Remember Krazy, our nigga, the one doing twenty-five clocks? He's still crew, and he still needs us." Wink led by example and started making a fourth pile for Krazy out of his own money.

Trey hesitated for a moment, but he didn't want to seem petty or selfish. He and Willie followed suit, taking money from both their piles. When they finished, they each had about $212,000, the way it was supposed to be. Wink wrapped his money along with Krazy's into one of the Coney Island bags, then stuffed it inside his duffle bag.

"I'ma use this money to pay for Krazy's appeal, and the rest I'ma send it to him as he needs it, so he should be straight," said Wink.

"You think he got a chance at getting back?" asked Willie.

"Time will tell. But in the meantime, I'ma hold 'im down." Wink knew he had to be the one to handle all Krazy's affairs because Trey and Willie didn't understand being in the land of the forgotten. They would soon forget about Krazy, maybe in a year or a couple of years. But one thing for certain, they were going to forget. Wink's dad told him all about the meaning of loyalty. He said that it's not mandatory like the air we breathe, but it's expected of real men. He said that loyalty goes beyond not snitching. It's about wanting for your brother what you want for yourself. He said never to expect loyalty, because only a few men understand its depth.

Wink watched Trey stuff money into every pocket he had. He crammed his sleeves, shoes, and socks with bills, then rushed to the table for the other Coney Island bag. He wrapped the money up and shoved it down into his briefs. The nigga looked like he had just gained his independence. And Willie was no better. He did the same thing.

Wink laughed at the thought, *They'll be broke in two weeks*. Then it would be back to the drawing board. Wink expected they'd come running back to him, admitting their foolish mistake of taking their money out the pot. Of course, he would then turn them away and see them fucked up. But maybe they all needed this experience to distinguish clearly who the leader was.

When they left out the room, it was almost midnight. Wink could see Armeeah's silhouette from the parking lot. She was standing at the drive-thru window. Wink remembered her every curve. He smiled, then closed the trunk. He doubted if she would call.

Wink dropped Trey and Willie off in the hood. He could tell they both had big plans to burn the mall up in the morning. *That's right. Spend, spend, and spend till it ain't no more,* Wink thought as he pulled in front of Trey's momma's house. He reached out his hand for a play, which Trey gladly accepted.

"Why don't you come to the Brass Key with us?" asked Trey. He and Willie were going to look at some titties at this new strip club on the west side.

"Nah, I'm tired. Plus, I got some shit to do in the morning," lied Wink. He hadn't a thing to do, at least not for a couple of days. He just didn't feel like looking at his niggas. They really fucked up his day with the greedy shit they were on.

Trey and Willie climbed out the car, and they all knew that shit was sour.

"I'ma fuck with y'all in the a.m.," said Wink.

"A'ight, my nigga," said Willie, and then Trey.

Wink pushed off in his Caddy. Usually, he'd at least wait until they made it in the house, but today, it was *fuck them*. They were being selfish. Maybe they all were, but Wink justified his selfishness by being the one to make shit happen. If it weren't for him, Trey would still be driving around in his momma's Honda with that played-out flat top on his head, looking for a house party him and Willie could crash so they could do their latest break dance routine. Instead, they both were slamming Cadillac doors with damn near a quarter mill to the good. Wink had done everything he said he would. He figured niggas just needed to bump their head a few times.

The next morning, Wink woke up to the familiar smell of bacon and eggs. The aroma drifted upstairs and through his nostrils. He rolled onto his back and smiled, not because his mom was down in the kitchen, putting it together, but because he knew Gary was perched in his seat, looking at the morning paper. Wink had sneaked in his mom's house at one o'clock in the morning. He was careful not to wake his mom or Gary. He tip-toed upstairs and climbed into bed. Morning would be the perfect time to stank Gary's ass. If he hurried, Wink could catch the trash crew with Gary's body.

Wink rolled out of bed. He tucked the .38 he took last night from Gary's glove box into his waist, then reached for the manila envelope on the dresser. Wink had played it out step by step in his mind a million times how he would kill Gary. It had to be memorable, life-lasting, like his father's sentence. Wink decided killing Gary after he ate his last meal would be some classic Mob shit.

Wink found his mom seated across from her husband-to-be. She was sipping coffee while doing her ritual morning crossword puzzle.

"Hey, baby!" Hope said excitedly as she leaped from her chair and rushed over to hug and kiss her son.

"Where have you been? No, never mind that. You come on and have a seat and let me fix you a plate."

"Good morning, Ma." Wink gave his mom a peck on the cheek, then she scurried to fix his plate.

"Gary, what's up? You looking all down." Wink took his mom's seat.

"He ain't been doing too well, baby. Somebody killed his best friend," Hope said from the stove.

"They found Fatts shot to death at his store the other day. His wake is today," said Gary.

Wink could hear the hurt in his voice, and from the redness embedded in his eyes, it appeared he'd been crying.

"They didn't have to kill him," said Gary. He was staring at a picture of Fatts in the Detroit Free Press.

They had a picture of the hardware store and a column, but Wink couldn't care less. He knew the details.

"Who would want to kill Fatts?" asked Wink.

"Nobody. He ain't never done nothing to hurt no one. All he did was sit at that store all day, and when he wasn't doing that, he was somewhere helping somebody."

Wink thought, *Yeah, right. That nigga deserved to die. He was a rat just like yo' ass.*

"Here you go, baby." Hope set Wink's plate in front of him. She stood with her hands on her hips and a smile on her face. She loved cooking, but she enjoyed watching men eat her cooking even more.

"What's this envelope, Wayne?" she asked. She pointed to the manila envelope sitting beside her coffee.

"It's for Gary," said Wink. He pushed the envelope across the table and watched as Gary frowned down at the envelope.

"I need something to drink." Wink scooted back in his chair, then stood up and walked to the fridge. He pretended to be looking for something to drink, but he was really watching Gary as he pulled the papers from the envelope. His mom was standing over Gary's shoulder, being nosey.

Gary's forehead formed into a million lines. He quickly lowered the papers and said, "Where'd you get . . . these?" His words slowed down at the sight of Wink pointing his chrome .38 Special dead on him.

"Your best friend gave 'em to me," said Wink.

"Why would Fatts give you these?"

"Wayne, baby, please put the gun down," pleaded Hope. She tried to take a step toward Wink, but he cocked the hammer and shifted his aim at her.

"Back up and stand by your man," ordered Wink.

"You killed Fatts, didn't you?" asked Gary.

"Yeah, just like you and that fat bastard killed my dad when y'all took the stand on him."

"Wayne, I can explain," said Hope. She had her hands to her face and tears in her eyes.

"Explain what? How can you explain what y'all did?" Wink pointed the gun back at Gary's chest and waited for that look of fear in Gary's eyes that he needed to see before killing him.

"Yeah, I did it." Gary let his nuts hang. "Ask me if I'd do it again, and the answer is yes. Your daddy made his own bed. Now he's got to lay in it."

Boom! Wink shot Gary in the shoulder and watched as he spun out of his chair, down to the floor. Hope was crying and begging Wink not to kill him.

"What you gon' do, kill me? Go ahead. I done lived my life," said Gary. He managed to prop himself up against the kitchen wall.

"Wayne, please put the gun down. Please," pleaded Hope.

Wink stood over Gary, looking into his eyes. He didn't see a hint of fear. *Rat bastard shoulda had the same heart instead of snitching on his partner.* The thought made Wink flash.

Boom! Boom! Boom! He was so angry, he was throwing them shits at Gary. His body slumped over to the floor, making a dead thump upon impact. Blood and brains smeared down the wall onto the kitchen floor.

Hope was down on her knees, cradling Gary's lifeless body. His blood soaked her entire nightgown and her hands. Her mouth was wide open, but the screams wouldn't come out. "Why?" she managed to ask.

Wink squatted beside her, still clutching the .38. He got in his mom's ear and spoke in a possessed voice. "You shoulda asked this dead rat why. Why he gave my father two life sentences? Why his life for his? What you need to do is ask yourself why. Why would you stay with a man who testified against your son's father? Or better yet, why would you agree to marry him?"

Wink stood up and enjoyed the only satisfaction he was going to get, the sight of his mother crying and grieving over Gary's dead body. It was her punishment, seeing as though he could lay her ass out beside Gary. Wink purposely killed Gary in front of his mom. He wanted her to see it, so she'd have to live yet another dark secret.

"What are you going to do, turn me in?" Wink asked, taunting his mother. He took his seat at the table and finished eating his food, showing complete disdain for the dead rat sprawled out in a pool of blood. Things between Wink and his mom would never be the same again. He just wanted to hate her forever until she died. That was the only way to make things right.

Chapter Thirty

Wink stretched across the sofa in the living room of his apartment. He stared at the lone picture frame mounted on the wall. It was a picture of him and his mom on his prom night. Wink felt nothing. No remorse, sorrow, nothing. She deserved a lot worse, he told himself.

Beep! Beep! Beep!

Wink's pager broke his train of thought as it lit up on the table beside him. Wink reached for the cordless phone and held the pager up. He didn't recognize the 248 area code. Detroit was 313. He called the number back and lay back across the sofa while the phone rang.

"Hello," answered the voice of a woman.

"Somebody page a pager?"

"Yes. May I speak to . . . Wink, is it?"

Wink sat up after recognizing the voice. It belonged to the pretty Arab woman from the Coney Island.

"This is Wink. Armeeah, right?"

"Yes. How are you?"

"I'm doing all right. Was just laying around the house."

"I'm sorry, did I wake you?"

"Nah, you're okay. I'm actually glad you called. I was beginning to think you weren't."

"No. It's just my parents. They're very strict on me and my sisters. They keep an eye on us."

"Yeah, I saw the way the old man kept watching you the other day."

Armeeah laughed. "That's my father. I'm the baby, so he's really watchful of me."

"Where are you now?"

"At home, in my room."

"You sound bored."

"I am. There's nothing to do on my days off besides sit in the house and watch TV."

"Let me take you to lunch and maybe a movie."

"I don't know."

"What's wrong? You afraid to be alone with me?"

"It's not that. It's my father. He's going to wonder where I'm at."

"We'll skip the movie and just do lunch. I just want to see those beautiful eyes again. Come on. What do you say?"

"Where are we going, so I can meet you there?"

"There's a Red Lobster on Hoover and 10 Mile Rd. Meet me there in about a half hour."

"I will be there."

"Okay. Bye." Wink stood up from the sofa and walked into the bathroom to start a shower. Hearing Armeeah's soft, innocent voice had made his day. Having to sneak and meet her seemed a little weird and elementary, but thinking back to her flawless frame and long black hair, she was most definitely worth the hassle and then some. She had the ability to bring a smile to a dead man's face. She was so beautiful.

Wink showered while thinking about her—what she liked, disliked, what made her smile. Wink had forgotten all about his mom, who was somewhere, probably over his aunt's house, still crying and grieving. Wink had already made his mind up regarding his mom's side of the family. He wasn't messing with none of them on no level, because as far as he was concerned, they all knew the deal with Gary snitching on his father, and for all those years, they helped keep Hope's secret.

Wink dried off, then sprayed some Joop cologne on. He walked into his room and into the closet, looking for something to wear. He grabbed a brand-new Ralph Lauren Polo outfit and a crispy pair of Gucci gym shoes. All the clothes Wink had been buying, he wasn't even wearing them because he hadn't the reason to jump fresh. Lately, it had been all business. Wink couldn't even remember the last time he took a girl out. All the chicken heads in the hood didn't appeal to him anymore. They all had too much shit with themselves and a lot of mileage.

Wink dusted the invisible dust from the shoulder of the cocaine-white Polo shirt he was rockin'. He turned to the side and looked down at his shoes, then at the entire outfit. He walked away from the mirror over to the dresser and contemplated wearing his bracelet.

Nah, that'll be doing too much, he told himself. Wink wanted to impress Armeeah, but at the same time, he didn't want to come off as being phony or trying too hard. He grabbed his car keys off the kitchen counter and was out the door.

Armeeah beat Wink to Red Lobster's. She was seated near the entrance at a booth for two. She waved him to come over. She stood and greeted Wink with that inviting smile of hers.

"I'm sorry. Am I late?" asked Wink.

"No, I got here a little early. My house is only minutes away."

"You look amazing." Wink looked Armeeah over from head to toe. She wore skin-tight jeans, some type of loose but sexy sweater, and some designer boots. To Wink's surprise, the girl had style like a sista.

"Thank you. You're casual and comfortable. Let's have a seat," said Armeeah. She slid into her side of the booth and swished her long black hair over her shoulder.

Wink was absolutely mesmerized by her beauty. He had his share of bad chicks, but Armeeah was on another lever bad. She resembled the Disney cartoon character Pocahontas.

"Why are you looking at me like that?" Armeeah blushed.

"Because I didn't know you were this beautiful."

"Stop. You're making me blush."

"I'm serious. I see why your dad keeps you in the house."

"Don't mention him, please."

"It's that bad?"

"Yes. And then some."

The waitress interrupted. "Are you all ready to order?"

Wink hadn't looked at his menu. He was too busy lost in Armeeah's beauty. "Uh, yeah. I'll have the catfish platter, and whatever she's having."

Armeeah ordered a shrimp platter and a chef salad.

"Finish telling me about yourself," said Wink.

"Well, I'm a student at Wayne State University. I'm studying business management. My parents want to open more locations of Coney Island, and they want me and my sisters to run them."

"You don't sound too excited about it. That's what you want to do?"

"No, it's not. It's what my parents want me to do."

"And what do you want to do?"

Armeeah sighed and looked up at the ceiling. "You know, I don't know because I've never had a chance to think about it."

"What do you mean?"

"My family came to America in 1960 from Iraq, and they still follow our strict Muslim beliefs. Women don't have a say or thought in what they want. So, I never thought about what it is I want because it doesn't seem possible. I work all day, only to go to night school, and then home. It's like my dad has planned everything for me before I even live it."

Wink listened to Armeeah as she vented, and he wished there was something he could do to help her. "What would happen if you didn't want to, you know, open up more Coney Islands? What would your family do?"

"Probably disown me, or consider me a kafir."

"What's that?"

"A kafir is a non-believer, one who's on the wrong path of life."

"And what am I?"

Armeeah smiled. "I don't know. Are you a bad person?"

Wink didn't acknowledge her question because deep down, he knew the answer was yes. "I'ma ask you this. What would your parents think if they knew you were here with me?"

"They'd kill me. I don't know," Armeeah said.

"Is it because I'm black?"

"Yes and no. They'd be upset because first, you're not Muslim, and also because you're not Arabic. We're not a racist people. We just strongly encourage marriage for religious reasons. So, it wouldn't matter if you were white. They'd still hate you."

Wink joined Armeeah in a laugh. Their food arrived, and they both dug in. Wink liked the fact that Armeeah wasn't shy. Her being herself made it easy for him to relax.

"So, you mean to tell me that every time I take you out, we're going to have to sneak out?" asked Wink.

"I think I'm worth it," said Armeeah. She shot Wink a devilish grin and did that thing with her eyes.

Wink definitely couldn't argue with her on that. She was most worthy of whatever it took to be in her presence. Wink would have walked through Hell wearing gasoline drawers if Armeeah was there waiting on him.

"Enough about me. Tell me about you, Wink. What's your real name?"

"When I tell you, you've gotta promise to never call me by my name. It's Wayne."

"That's not a bad name. But I'll call you Wink if I must. Tell me about your family. Are you close to your parents?"

Wink dropped his eyes to his plate. Mixed emotions ran through him as he thought about his mom and dad. "I'm the only child, and my parents are separated."

"So, who did you grow up living with?"

"My mom. But we're not really talking right now."

"You don't want to talk about it?"

"Nah, not for real. Ask me something else."

"Okay. What do you do for a living?"

"You don't look like the judgmental type, so I'ma be honest with you. I hustle."

"You mean, like, drugs?"

"I guess if that's what you wanna call 'em."

"I understand you've got to survive. I have uncles who sell drugs. It's not right, but I understand."

That was like music to Wink's ears. Could she be any more perfect? The hustla in him wanted to ask her where her uncles were at and what type of drugs they dealt with, but Wink didn't want Armeeah knowing that's all he thought about.

"I don't know, maybe one day we can help each other figure out what it is we want," said Wink. He stared deep into Armeeah's eyes and watched her smile.

"I'd like that," she said.

They finished having lunch, and Wink walked her out to her car. Her parents may have been strict, but they kept her laced and pushin' in a brand-new Audi 5000. Their whole thing was, if they spoiled Armeeah and her sisters, then they wouldn't have to worry about them seeking these things from men. But Armeeah was seeking something else that they wouldn't dare let her have in a million years: a bad boy.

"I gotta watch out. You're ridin' harder than me. You sure you're not the one hustlin'?" Wink said.

"No, silly." She laughed.

"I really enjoyed your company. When can I see you again?"

"I have to work the next five days, and I have school right after. Next weekend, maybe."

"I tell you what. Call me sometime during the week, and we'll have dinner at your school." Wink handed Armeeah his house number he had scribbled onto a napkin.

"I will call you," Armeeah said softly. "And thank you for lunch, Wink."

"You're welcome." Wink opened her door and watched her get in. He wanted so bad to kiss her pretty, full lips, but it was too soon for a girl like her, with her Muslim upbringing and all. Wink didn't want to come on too strong and scare her off. He watched as she pulled away. She honked her horn with a smile and waved goodbye.

Wink thought to himself, *I gotta cuff her.* He walked over to his Caddy and climbed behind the wheel. His thoughts quickly flashed back to his father and their plan. It was time to get back to business.

Chapter Thirty-one

With Fatts dead, there was a lot of street-level hustlas scrambling around the city in search of some coke. There was plenty of coke in Detroit. Other niggas had connects and were making moves, but they did what any other hustla with some brains would do—they all lied and said that they were getting on through Fatts, and the little work that they did have was the last of the last. Them faggot niggas knew exactly what they were doing. They were all in it together. It was always like that. The hustlas shared certain information to keep control of the street economy. The rich vs. the poor, so to speak.

Everybody knew Fatts was rumored to be that nigga, so it made their stories believable. And most importantly, it caused everyone to scream, "Drought!" When there's a drought, the price of pussy goes up drastically. It's like you're hustling out of town, making money hand over fist. In this case, pussy was coke, and the major players were lookin' to rape the city with the coke they were sitting on.

Wink put his ear to the street, and as soon as he heard that there was a drought, he pulled those sixty bricks out. His father's plan was about to come together. He called good money, play by play. Gunz helped found the shady tactics of the game, so he knew them niggas would cry drought. But that's when Wink would make his intro into the big leagues and start rubbing elbows with the niggas who really ran the city, the street hustlas Wink was about to take over in a major way, and not a soul saw him coming.

Gunz told Wink that niggas would be thirsty to find some work, anything that they could get their hands on. Thus, they would be more willing to deal with him, or anybody else, for that matter, who had some work. They just needed the work so they could supply their customers.

Gunz gave Wink the game play-by-play on the visit. "Here's what you do. After you kill Fatts and take what-ever bricks he's sitting on, wait a week or so until the city starts hollering it's a drought. That's when you come out with the bricks you took off Fatts. It's going to be the best coke in town, so they're comin'. Don't try to step on the coke, not even a little. Sell 'em the bricks as is. Once they see how good our coke is and that you have it, they'll become loyal customers. While all those other fools are wondering why they can't off their shit, you'll be stealing their clientele right from under them. Just re-member this, son, and you'll be all right. Forget about the glory and just get the money."

Those words stuck with Wink, and he would remem-ber them until his death. He did exactly what his dad told him to. He didn't take or try to add anything to the plan, and as a result, he was seeing the results. The first thing Wink did was set up a shield around himself. Like his father said, forget about the glory. It was about money. Wink paid this African cab driver two thousand dollars to act like he was this drug lord from Nigeria. The plan was, Wink would introduce and turn on niggas to Offy, the African, for a fee. He'd tell them that he had a connect with the primo who was charging twenty-two thousand a brick, even though it was a drought. Like his father said, niggas would be thirsty, so their judgment would be off. They'd jump at the sound of coke. All the while, Wink would really be the man, the connect, but he'd also be able to protect his identity, which was the important thing. Niggas can't rob, kidnap, or snitch on what they can't see. Wink was to be a ghost.

The inside of Timbo's after-hour was packed to the hilt with hoes, and of course, you had the tricks. For every ho, there were ten tricks impatiently waiting their turn to perform whatever freaky fantasy they had yet to live out. Cars wrapped around Gratiot Ave. down to Harper and back as people hoped a parking spot would open, while some struck side deals right there on the strip.

Wink parked down the street at the Better Made Potato Chip Factory. He knew that if there was anyplace full of hustlas on a Friday night going into Saturday morning, it was Timbo's. He had been in there a couple times with his crew, but they felt out of place because they weren't getting any money at the time, and a piece of pussy cost a month's allowance.

Wink laughed at the memory as he climbed the steps up to the entrance. In a couple weeks, he'd have enough money to buy Timbo's and open up ten more locations if he wanted. It was funny how the game worked. One day, you were at the bottom, not knowing where your next meal was coming from; the next, you were sitting so high you were next to God, having a conversation.

Wink paid the twenty-dollar door fee and let the bouncer frisk him. He stepped down to the basement where all the lap dances and bargaining went down. All the fucking took place upstairs in the rented rooms, which would cost a trick another twenty dollars, plus the cost of pussy, head, and any other weird shit he wanted done. You'd be surprised at what some of those suppose-to-be hard niggas were up there doing. A lot of them were borderline faggots for real, up there getting they ass tickled with chicks' tongues, and some even went so far as to let women strap a dildo on and fuck them in their ass. Long as they were spending, any fantasy could come to life up in Timbo's.

Wink wasn't there for that, though. He was strictly business. He scanned the dimly lit basement for any familiar faces. He spotted his money-gettin' nigga, JC, from the west side, over near the speakers. He was all leaned up against some ho, all in her ear, probably trying to hook it up for later.

Wink didn't know the nigga per se. He just knew of JC because his name was ringing in the city. He supposedly had the west side in a chokehold on the coke. The nigga was only a few years older than Wink, but he was already pushing Benzes with an S on the end. He had mad jewels, but most importantly, he had that dust, which was all Wink wanted.

The skank JC had been rapping to walked away, leaving JC alone. Wink saw his opening and quickly walked over to JC. He was downing the last of his drink when Wink pulled up.

"JC, you mind if I holla at you a minute?"

"Who you?" JC looked Wink up and down like, *Nigga, I don't know you.*

"They call me Ghost. I want to holla at you 'bout some business."

"I ain't never heard of you, so what business do we have?" JC looked sternly into Wink's eyes.

"I know you don't know me, and that's cool. But I think that after I tell you my reason for hollering at you, you'll want to know me."

"I'm listening." JC raised his finger to the ho waiting for him on the steps. He was telling her to wait a minute.

"As you know, it's a drought right now, and niggas is charging an arm and two legs for some work."

"Tell me something I don't know. I got some ass lined up, feel me?"

"What if I told you I had a connect on some primo right now, and the price is the same as if it weren't a drought?"

"I'd say you're lying."

"Well, I'm not. I can plug you in with my man, and y'all can go from there. He's got whatever you need."

"If I ain't know no better, I'd say you're try'na set me up."

"Look, here's my pager number. If you try'na get on, holla at me. If not, you be easy." Wink handed JC a piece of paper with his name, Ghost, written beside his number.

As he walked away, JC stopped him. Wink turned around, and JC being thirsty, said, "I'ma hit you up in the morning."

Wink nodded, then kept it moving. He walked over to the bar and ordered a double shot of Hennessy. He sipped his drink and waited for JC to descend the stairs with baby girl. Then he moved in on this north end nigga named Gucci. They called him Gucci because that was all he rocked from head to toe, every day all day. He was a little black bugger-lookin' mothafucka, so his ass had to stay fresh to give people something to focus on besides his face.

Wink slid up on Gucci real playa-like and disarmed him with a compliment on his Gucci loafers.

"You like these?" Gucci asked, looking down at his white loafers.

"Yeah, I just snatched them today. I see you in step. I got a couple pair like 'em."

Gucci returned the compliment on Wink's Gucci sneakers.

"By the way, they call me Ghost."

"Gucci. What can I do for you, young blood?" Gucci was touching forty and looked every day of it, but he'd live every day like he was twenty-five.

"I think that I'm the one who can do something for you, and at a playa's price."

"Money, my favorite language. Talk to me."

"I got a connect right now who's lettin' 'em go for twenty-two even. Primo."

"In this weather? It's drought season."

"Not for him, it ain't. The nigga got it."

"What's his name?"

"We'll get to that. But if you try'na get on, it'll have to be through me. He's an African from Nigeria, and he wants me to turn him onto some serious niggas."

"I'ma fuck with you on the strength 'cause I like ya style. But youngin', I deal pawns up. I don't want no B.S. about mine's. We clear?"

"That's what I don't do, play games. Here. Hit me when you're ready and have twenty-two racks for every bird you want." Wink handed Gucci his number, then pushed on.

He caught Squirt on his way upstairs. Squirt was off the east side. He ran the Mack Ave. with his brothers. There had to be at least ten of them niggas, but Squirt was the oldest and was the man. He had two yellow-bone skanks tailing him upstairs for their duck-off session.

"Squirt, let me holla at you," said Wink. He was one of the few niggas Wink actually knew personally and not just on some *I heard about you* shit.

Squirt turned around and squinted down the dark steps.

"It's me, Wink."

"Oh, what's good, my nigga? You down here on the same mission I'm on, huh?" Squirt pulled back a wide smile and nodded at the two hoes lingering at his side.

"Nah, I'm on B.I. Let me put something in ya ear real quick. Excuse us, ladies," Wink put his arm around Squirt's neck and walked him upstairs.

"What's up?" asked Squirt.

"Have you been able to find any work in the city?"

"Yeah, but that shit is garbino. Niggas taxing like shit."

"Well, look. You always played it fair with me, so I'ma look out for you. I got a connect, and he's not taxing. The work is A-one, too."

"Shit, where he at? I'm try'na see him right now. What he chargin'?"

"Twenty-two a brick. I'ma plug you in with him so y'all can deal. Just throw yo' man a few dollars for pluggin' you."

"I got you. When can I meet him?"

"Tomorrow! Here. This my number. Hit me in the a.m. and I got you." Wink tapped Squirt on his back, then walked out the front door of Timbo's. He had secured three meetings with some major playas. That was enough for the night. He had a nigga on each side of town who he could supply work to. It was all part of his dad's plan, for Wink to spread his wings across the city. When he plugged him in with the real connect, he'd be able to handle the work, 'cause it was coming by the truckload. The sixty kilos were to serve as a means of Wink hooking up with niggas like JC, Gucci, and Squirt. He could supply them until Gunz put his other plan together.

Chapter Thirty-two

Wink paced the floor of Broadway's men clothing store while constantly checking his pager. "How much longer?" he asked Nate.

"About ten more minutes," said Nate. He was kneeling down, hemming the African cab driver's pants. Offy was smiling from ear to ear. He hadn't ever bought or worn a suit like the one Wink was putting him in. The suit alone cost twelve hundred dollars, and the loafers ran four hundred. Everything was on schedule and looking good. Wink wanted Offy looking like money when he met with JC, Gucci, and Squirt. Offy kept smiling.

"Stop smilin'," ordered Wink. The shit was starting to drive him crazy. "You remember everything?" he asked.

Offy nodded. "Yes." He fit the make of a Nigerian drug lord. His accent was thick, his black eyes were still and uncomfortable. He just had to stop fuckin' smiling, and everything should be good.

"Where the fuck is Willie?" Wink mumbled to himself. Willie was supposed to serve as Offy's runner, the nigga who would deliver the coke and pick up the money.

Just as Wink started to curse his pager for not beeping, Willie walked through the door. The bell underneath the front door jingled, causing Wink to look up.

"Where's Trey?"

"He just got on a plane. That's what took me so long, 'cause I had to drop him off," said Willie.

"A plane to where?"

"Back down to Texas, I guess. That's all he's been talkin' about is hookin' up with them Mexican mothafuckas."

Wink was furious. Trey hadn't said a word to him about going out of town, especially not to go see about no work. In a minute, they were going to have all the coke they needed.

"What he call his self doing, hookin' up with them amigos?"

"Wink, I don't know. You know how Trey is."

Yeah, I do, thought Wink. *He's hardheaded and stupid at times. How the fuck he gon' hop on a plane all by himself to go meet up with some Mexicans in the middle of the desert? Stupid mothafucka.*

"Did he take some money with him?"

Willie nodded.

"I wouldn't be surprised if they robbed his dumb ass," Wink said.

Good, Wink thought. *That fool doesn't know what he's buying no way. Them amigos fuck around and sell him some straight gank.*

Wink was fucked up that Trey would just bounce like that. He was out there putting in all that work, lining things up, but Trey obviously wanted his own connect and wanted to call his own shots. Wink smiled at the thought, 'cause he knew Trey wasn't built like that. Even if he did come back with some work, all was gon' happen was some gorilla was gon' slap him and take it or might not pay his ass.

"I think that I'm about finished," said Nate. He stood up, and his old bones cracked from being bent over for so long. "Step down and let me take a look at you," he told Offy.

"Take that stupid smile off ya face," said Wink.

"This mothafucka always smilin'," Wink told Willie.

Nate fixed the suit jacket on Offy's shoulders, then buttoned him up. "That's it. You're in there, my man."

"Good, 'cause we're runnin' late. How much I owe you, Nate?" Wink pulled out a bankroll and followed Nate around to the register.

"That'll be sixteen hundred dollars with no tax."

Wink paid for the suit and shoes, then rushed Offy and Willie out the store. "Follow us over to the Pontchartrain Hotel on Jefferson," Wink told Willie. He and Offy climbed in his El Dogg.

"Just remember everything I told you, and don't try adding anything." Wink looked over at Offy as he nodded. "And whatever you do, don't smile."

Wink had went all out to paint the picture like Offy was the man. He rented a presidential suite on the top floor of the Pontchartrain, along with a regular suite two doors down where the sixty bricks sat stashed. All Offy had to do was play big, like he was a kingpin, and everything would go smoothly.

At the hotel, Wink slammed down the phone and walked over to the table where Offy sat smoking a cigar.

"That was just JC. He's on his way up now, so get ready." Wink turned to Willie, who was slumped on the chaise lounge. "Be on point, my nigga."

"I got you." Willie nodded.

Wink paced the floor while waiting on JC. A few minutes later, there was a knock on the door. Wink turned and snapped his fingers at Offy and Willie. Wink walked over to the door and peeked out the peephole. JC was standing beside some bear-lookin' nigga, both dressed in all black. JC had a duffle bag in his hand. Wink snatched the door open and stepped aside, letting them in.

"JC, my man. Glad you made it," said Wink. He gave JC a play and then proceeded to walk over to the table. "This here is my man."

"Woo." Offy stood up, interrupting Wink. He set his cigar in the ashtray, then walked around the table with a mean-mug on his face. "Who's this?" he asked, waving to JC's cohort.

JC looked back at his partner, then said, "He's my gun. You know it's our first time doing business, and he's here to make sure everything's on the up and up."

"From now on, when you come to see my men, you are to come alone. Are we understood?" asked Offy.

"Yeah, we're good."

"Have a seat. And you, take a seat over there where I can keep my eyes on you," Offy told JD's henchman.

Wink excused himself over to the sofa so that they could talk. So far, Offy was handling his. He sounded like the real McCoy.

JC took his seat directly across from Offy and waited as he relit is cigar, then took a long puff.

"What can I do for you in terms of cocaine?"

"Ghost was telling me you could give me a key for twenty-two. If the coke is good, I'll grab five right now and keep in touch."

"I am glad that you plan to keep in touch, because you know this is a very generous price, and not just in these times. I am looking for us to establish a relationship, long term, of course."

"I'm with that."

Offy played it cool. He waited for a few minutes, just studying JC as he puffed his stogey. Offy snapped his fingers for Willie.

"Bring me five." Offy waited for Willie to leave the room before speaking. "I personally will not be dealing with you in the future. You will be dealing through my worker, who just left the room. I just wanted to meet with you. The product will always be the same, and so will the price. I will always have eyes on you. This is a marriage. The only way out is death. Jail can't even save you if you were to cooperate with the government. I will stop at nothing to get you. Are we understood?"

JC really thought he was sitting there with the African Godfather himself. "I understand, and I will not cross you."

Willie walked back into the room. He carried a duffle bag over to the table and removed the five kilos. Wink had rewrapped the bricks using black tape and some African symbol as the stamp. He didn't want to chance anybody recognizing the bricks as being from Fatts, plus the black tape gave them that real African look.

Offy stood up and pulled a switchblade from the inside of his suit jacket, then split one of the keys down the middle. He pulled up a nice-size chunk of coke on the tip of his knife and held it out to JC.

"You see that? Fish scale." Offy didn't know what the hell he just said. He was just reciting what Wink had drilled into his brain a thousand times.

JC could see all the oils and crystal flakes embedded within the coke. He nodded his approval.

"Money," said Offy.

JC reached down between his feet for the bag of money. He unzipped it, then dumped a bunch of rubber-banded rolls of money onto the table.

"Each one is a thousand. Altogether, it's a hundred and ten G's," said JC.

"I'll count it later. Here you are. I believe these belong to you." Offy waved at the kilos.

JC stood up and began packing the bricks into his duffle bag. Wink walked over like he hadn't been ear-hustlin'.

"Y'all straight?" he asked.

"Yeah, we're good," said Offy. He kept his eye on ole bear, who was not standing.

"I should be done in a couple days. I'ma call you," said JC, zipping the bag shut and grabbing its handle.

"Just remember what I said." Offy nodded at JC.

"Come on. I'll walk you to the elevator," said Wink. He was trying to hurry up and get JC out of there in case Gucci showed up early.

Once they got out into the hallway, JC dug in his pocket and gave Wink a large stack of money. "That's for pluggin' me in. That was some real nigga shit. If you ever need anything, just holla."

Wink gave JC a pound and watched them get onto the elevator. He was cool with niggas thinking he was the middleman. He'd last a lot longer that way.

Fifteen minutes later, Wink's pager went off. *Beep! Beep! Beep!* It was Gucci. He was downstairs in the lobby, on his way up. Wink hoped that Gucci hadn't run into JC. If so, there could be problems. They would operate as if that didn't happen. Offy just had to put it down exactly as he did with JC, and Gucci, then Squirt, would be on the team too.

Chapter Thirty-three

Wink was putting the finishing touches on his dad's plan. Everything worked out smoothly with Gucci and Squirt. They each bought ten bricks and promised to be back within a week to snatch ten more. Meanwhile, the old heads in the city were still holding fast to their drought scheme. Little did they know the only thing there was a drought on was the amount of money they'd be making once Gunz plugged Wink in with this Cuban connect he kept talking about. Wink couldn't hardly wait, neither. He had plans to lock down the city and beyond.

Willie was driving Wink around, making last-minute stops before he jumped on the plane to go see his father.

"Pull over behind that Jag," ordered Wink. He pointed to an empty spot out front of Mr. Walls' Arcade.

"I'll be right back," said Wink. He got out the car and looked at the pearl-blue Jag that belonged to Mr. Walls. That was all the old nigga pushed since back in the day. With the exception of the pearl-blue Jaguar, 7 Mile Rd. was deserted on that early Sunday morning. Every day at the same time for the past thirty-five years, Mr. Walls broke down the doors to his ole arcade. No matter if it were rain, sleet, or snow, his old ass was there, and often he was the only one there. He still had all the vintage arcade machines, nothing really too up to date, which was why hardly no one ever frequented the spot.

But Mr. Walls didn't care about customers unless they were buying kilos of cocaine. Mr. Walls used the arcade as a front. For the past thirty-five years, he'd been selling keys out the place, and his old ass showed no signs of retiring. He owned casino boats and real estate all over the world, but he wanted to sit inside the dingy arcade and sell his coke. Old bastard was far beyond stubborn. He refused to pass the torch.

Wink had been meaning to pay Mr. Walls a visit since he got back from seeing his dad, but things got hectic, and so time was on the old nigga's side. Today, however, was a different story. He was going to hang up his jersey and retire whether he liked it or not.

Wink played two games of Ms. Pac Man. He hadn't played that game since he was a kid, but it was still fun.

"Ah, man," he said, tapping the side of the machine. He turned and walked over to the counter where Mr. Walls sat watching him suspiciously. Wink hadn't spoken a word since he walked in the door, and Mr. Walls knew he wasn't there to play no damn game.

"My mother used to bring me in here when I was little, and I would always play Ms. Pac Man. Is that the same machine?"

"It is." Mr. Walls was real dry. He didn't trust this young thug draped in gold, standing before him.

"My father says that he used to come in here before he got locked up."

"Oh, and who's your father?" Mr. Walls was now curious.

"You oughta remember him well. He used to work for you. He's named after one of these." Wink pulled a beaming chrome Taurus 9 mm from his waist and pointed at Mr. Walls forehead. "You don't remember Gunz? You just the fuck oughta. Your rat ass told on him about some bodies you paid him to hit for you."

"I never took the stand on Gunz," said Mr. Walls. His voice trembled along with his old brown, wrinkled hands. He was giving Wink exactly what he craved to see in a man's eyes right before he killed 'em: fear.

"Gunz was like a son to me. I would never—"

Mr. Walls' words were cut short by gunfire, ripping his face apart. *Boom! Boom! Boom!*

Wink walked around the counter after Mr. Walls staggered back and fell to the ground. He stood over Mr. Walls and let the clip ride out on his old ass. When the shots ceased, Mr. Walls was dead, with his eyes locked to the ceiling and his mouth wide open. That was the look of death and high Wink had come for.

He was getting more like his dad with every kill. It was almost addictive. The sight of blood and a stretched-out dead body gave Wink a rush and a sense of power. Just knowing that he could take a life with the simple squeeze of the trigger infatuated him.

He wiped the gun clean and used his shirt to lay it across Mr. Walls' chest. He figured, *Fuck it, just leave it. Long as it doesn't have my prints on it. Plus, the homicide won't have far to look for their murder weapon.* He had killed two birds with one clip. He had avenged his father, and Mr. Walls was now one less old stubborn bastard he'd eventually have to kill.

Wink came walking out of the arcade, eating some Chewy penny candy he lifted from behind the counter. He climbed in the passenger seat and offered Willie some candy.

"What were you in there doing all that time?" asked Willie as he took the wrapper off a candy.

"You know I had to play me some Ms. Pac Man. That's still my shit. Come on. We gon' be late," said Wink. He tapped the dashboard, then popped another Chewy into his mouth.

A while later, Willie pulled around to the front entrance of the Detroit City Airport and parked. He leaned back in his seat and faced Wink, awaiting his orders for while he was away.

"You got the keys to the storage, right?"

"Yeah, I got 'em." Willie nodded.

"A'ight, hold it down until I get back. Only fuck with JC, Gucci, and Squirt for right now. And no shorts."

"What about Ball? He called me this morning and said he was outta work."

Wink thought about it for a moment. He wasn't ready to give Willie the game on how to mail it.

"Just tell his big ass I said to take a week off and I'ma hit 'im when I get back."

"A'ight. I'ma see you when you get back." Willie gave Wink a pound, then reached over to pop the trunk.

"No shorts, no losses," said Wink as he climbed out the car. He walked around back to the trunk and grabbed his two carry-on bags. Willie honked the horn and chunked the deuces as he pulled off, looking through the rearview mirror.

Wink heard them call his flight number as he walked inside the terminal. He scanned the numbers mounted at each loading ramp, then stepped to the back of the line, set to board his plane. After handing the woman stationed at the wooden podium his ticket stub, Wink boarded the plane and quickly settled into his comfortable nook up in first class. He declined the steak and potatoes being offered. He just wanted to close his eyes and wake up in that small hick town, Leavenworth, Kansas.

When Wink woke up, the back tires of the plane were screeching against the runway. Wink sat up in his seat and looked out his window. He hated the landscape of this state. If it weren't for his dad, Wink would have never been within a hundred miles of Kansas, let alone Leavenworth.

Wink took a private cab up to the prison. It seemed like the Green Mile driving them long, farm-invested roads. All you saw was horses and cows, horses and cows. Every so often, you'd see some old cracker tending to his farm.

Wink made it inside the prison, and to his surprise, he was permitted to the visiting hall almost immediately. He sat with his arm stretched around the back of the seat next to him, watching visitors while he waited on his dad to show up. Three men were escorted into the visiting hall by a C.O., one of them being Wayne, Sr. Wink pulled back a huge grin and stood up while he waited on his dad to check in with the C.O. stationed at the front desk. Wink reached his hand out for his dad's.

"What's that? Give me a hug," said Wayne, Sr.

He pulled Wink to him. They embraced all of ten seconds, and for every moment, Wink could feel the love his dad had for him.

"Let's sit down," said Wayne Sr.

"It's all done. Everything." Wink began to name names, but his dad stopped him.

"Son, what's understood need not be said." He paused for a moment and studied Wink's eyes. They were starting to turn cold. There was still a hint of youth and innocence, but Wayne, Sr. could tell it wouldn't be there much longer. Soon, he'd be staring into his own eyes, the eyes of a cold-blooded killer.

"What's wrong? Why you lookin' at me like that?"

"Wayne, I don't want you to ever believe that I don't care about you. The only reason I'm even showing you all these things, and Allah will still punish me for doing so, it's because you're my son. I don't want some other bum nigga teachin' you, because he's only gonna teach you what he wants you to know, and that's nothing. You see where I'm coming from?"

"I think so." Wink was a little confused. He didn't understand how much it tore his father up inside to watch his only son travel down that same one-way road he'd taken.

"Wayne, I should be teaching you how to avoid the streets, but comin' from me, an old washed-up nigga serving two life sentences, you wouldn't listen. I know you're going to chase your desires, 'cause I did. All I'm saying is, I don't ever want you to lose sight of the fact that I'm still your father, and our relationship doesn't just have to consist of what we're doing. You can holla at me about anything."

"I got you, pops." Wink broke back a smile. "You okay? You always gettin' serious on me."

Wayne, Sr. managed to smile. "Nah, I just be wanting to make sure I let you know that I'm here for you. You don't know how many nights I laid in my bunk, wondering how you were doing, what you were doing, wishing I could shoot some ball with you. All the stuff kids do with their old man."

"I feel you, Dad, and it's not your fault."

Wink's dad nodded while looking down at the floor. He knew deep down it was his fault, even though Gary, Fatts, and Mr. Walls ratted him out. He was too far in the game, and eventually, jail or death was coming.

Wink knew something that would lift his dad's spirit. "I met this girl the other day. She's Muslim too."

"Is that right? What's her name?"

"Armeeah. She's Arabic."

"That's all right, Wayne. Maybe she'll rub some Islam off on you. How'd you meet her?"

"Up at this Coney Island. Her parents own it. They don't let her date or nothing, so we be having to sneak around, but other than that, I like her."

"One of Allah's greatest gifts he bestowed upon man is woman, especially if she's Muslimah. So, son, be patient with her, because I know she's not like all the other girls runnin' around out there."

"I got you." Wink nodded. All that was cool, but it was time to get down to business. Wink watched his father's eyes as they traveled around the visiting hall.

"Don't turn just yet, but there's a Cuban guy who just walked in. He's who I been tellin' you about. His name's Franko, biggest thing to ever come out of Cuba besides cigars."

Wink saw the old, shriveled-up, gray-haired man his dad praised as he walked away from the C.O. station past their seats. He might have been old, but he reeked of money. One sight of Franko, and you automatically knew you were dealing with real choo-choo long-train money.

Franko smiled from ear to ear as he crossed the floor. He opened his arms wide and said something in Spanish.

"Who's the woman?" asked Wink. He hadn't taken his eyes off Franko.

"I believe that's his wife," said Wayne Sr.

"Damn, she's right." Wink knew the old fart really had to be holding now. His wife was no more than twenty-five, exotic, with long black hair, ass together.

She could have any man she wanted, and yet she was up on visit with a yard of ancient tongue down her throat.

Franko finally finished greeting his wifey and took a seat beside her, facing Wink and his dad. Franko nodded, then smiled, to which Wink's dad did the same. He could see Franko's lips moving. Then his wife looked their way and flashed a smile.

"All right, now try not to stare," said Wayne Sr.

"When is everything gon' be straight?" asked Wink.

"We're ready now. I just needed to see you face to face before we got started. Son, listen to me. I've known Franko for a long time now, and he's a good man. He'd do anything for me, which is why he's agreed to give you a shot. Usually, it would take years and thousands of keys later before you'd ever meet Franko. He's the man. No one sits above him except God. So, what I'm saying to you, son, is to always deal straight up, because I really value Franko's friendship, and I value your life. Your entering deep waters, Wayne, and you have to man up in the event something goes wrong. Remember what I told you. This is what awaits us at the end of the road. I'ma do everything in my power to steer you clear of this place, but son, you gotta know this thang is real."

Wink nodded and continued to listen as his father gave him the game in its rawest form, straight with no cut-card. If Wink was going to lay the game, he had to play by its rules, and any violations would not be forgiven. Wink got his dad's point: no snitchin'. He had his dad's blood running through his veins, so tellin' wasn't an option. Wink was just wishing he was Franko, over there all hugged up with Ms. Cuba.

When the C.O. called for the visitors to leave, Franko nodded at Wink's dad for him to give Wink his instructions.

Wink and his dad stood up and began saying their goodbyes. This would be a short visit, unlike the last one. Wink was to only stay for that day. His father and Franko had his next few days already mapped out for him.

"I don't know when I'ma get the chance to see you again, so you be careful out there and just remember everything we talked about."

"I got you," said Wink.

"When you leave here, you'll be leaving with Franko's wife. She's got everything lined up. That's what Franko's been drilling her about this whole time. Follow her instruction, and everything will be fine."

Wink gave his dad a hug as the C.O. called again for the visitors to leave.

"I'll be out to see you soon as everything's set up and in place," said Wink.

"Don't worry about me. Just take your time. I'll give you a call sometime next week."

Wink hit rocks with his father, then stepped to the back of the line of visitors. He nodded at ole Franko, who joined his father.

"Hello."

Wink turned around, and it was Franko's wife standing behind him. Wink returned the gesture. He waited until they were out of the visiting hall to introduce himself.

"I know who you are, Wink," the woman said. "My people have done a check on you, and I know all there is to know about you."

Wink followed the woman out of the prison into the parking lot, where a triple-black stretch Lincoln limo awaited them at the curb. He opened the door for her, then climbed in behind her.

"Take us to the airport," she said. She took out a pack of Virginia Slims from her purse. She stuck one of the long, skinny cigarettes in her mouth, then handed Wink her gold lighter. She was most definitely on her mad diva trip. She took a long pull on her square, then crossed her thick, tan legs.

"You still haven't told me your name," said Wink.

"My name is not important at this point in time."

Wink knew what he had to do before baby girl got too comfortable, thinking she could treat him like a lame. Wink tossed the lighter hard into her lap, then looked her dead in the eyes.

"I don't care if you're Pablo Escobar's wife. You ain't gon' be treating me like I'm some insignificant nigga. Now, if we're going to be dealing with each other, I'd at least like to know your name; otherwise, we can go our separate ways when we get to the airport." Wink held his poker face while he watched the woman exhale a cloud of smoke high above her head. Wink hoped he didn't just blow his pipeline connect with the Cuban Godfather, Franko. But one thing Wink had never done before in his life was kiss ass, and he didn't have a taste for it today, no matter what it might cost him.

"I like you," said the woman, pulling back a wide grin. "A lot of people who work for me are spineless, so that is how I treat them. But I'm glad to see you're not easily bought. That goes a long way, because if I expect you to be loyal to my family, I must first expect you to be loyal to yourself."

"So, what's your name?"

"Susana, but you are to call me Nina."

There was a brief silence. Wink let his eyes touch every molecule of Nina's frame. She was perfect, definitely wife material. But what was she doing heading a drug cartel? The way she talked, the only person above her was Franko.

Nina reached forward and fixed herself a dry Scotch. "Can I fix you one?" she asked. Her accent was so sexy, and her eyes were so demanding.

"No, I'm okay." He wanted to be on his toes around this bitch at all times, 'cause he had a feeling she had a lot of shit with her. Nina sat back in her seat and promptly re-crossed her killer legs, this time even higher than the last. Her skirt hiked up to mid-thigh, where Wink's eyes rested. When he finally looked up, Nina was looking at him with this devilish grin on her face. She unbuttoned the top two buttons on her blouse, then cracked the sunroof a little.

"It's warm in here, isn't it?" she asked, using her freshly manicured hands to fan her chest.

"Yeah, a little bit," said Wink, enjoying the view.

"So, tell me about this operation of yours. How many kilos can I expect for you to move in a month?" Nina liked to play hot and cold games. She'd use her beauty to get men to open up to her, then she'd get down to business, because while they were open, she was more likely to get the truth out of them. Franko had taught her well in the art of seduction, which was why she was running the operation and not one of his sons.

"Right now, I'm set up to move no less than a hundred keys a month, but with the ticket you're letting 'em go for, I can be on a thousand in no time."

"You have high aspiration. A thousand kilos is a lot to move in a month."

"I got my end. You just keep 'em wrapped and at the same ticket."

"We'll see," said Nina.

They arrived at the airport, and instead of pulling into the terminal, the limo drove out onto the tarmac and parked beside a white private jet. Four large Cuban men stood outside the jet, wearing black suits and killa masks on their faces. Wink knew it was real at that moment. He was actually hooked up with the Mob, and all from some old nigga sitting in prison still calling the shots.

One of the Cuban men opened the door and helped Nina out the limo. She said something in Spanish to all the men, who in turn all acknowledged Wink with a cold stare and nothing more.

Wink followed Nina up the stairs onto the plush jet. He'd never flown in a private jet. His excitement and eagerness had to be held in check. He wanted to look at everything and gawk, but if he were to be taken seriously, he had to act cool, like flying private was nothing new to him.

He took a seat in the back beside Nina and sank into the butter-leather. This definitely beat flying first class. The seat was one of the softest, most comfortable he'd ever sat in. The plane's interior was shiny and clean.

Wink watched as the four men took their seats at the front of the plane. Everybody was speaking Spanish, and Wink didn't know what the fuck they were saying. He didn't like not knowing what they were talking about. It made him nervous. Wink wanted to control every situation he was in, and because he didn't know Spanish, he couldn't control this situation.

He asked Nina, "Where are we going?"

"It's a surprise. Just lay back and relax. Here," she said, handing Wink the remote to the TV mounted above them.

Nina kicked off her shoes, then curled up under Wink and closed her eyes. Within minutes, the plane was up in the air and on its way to wherever Nina had them going. Wink watched her sleep and wondered how long she'd been doing this. Was she setting him up? Would this be the last flight he ever took? If so, she seemed awfully relaxed. Wink was getting to the point of feeling the same relaxation before murdering someone. He got paranoid thinking this might be a setup.

Chapter Thirty-four

When the jet touched down, Wink could tell they were somewhere down south, because the weather was a beautiful sunny day, and the plane ride was too short for them to be on the West Coast. As the plane skidded across the tarmac and slowed down, Wink could see palm trees swishing in the breeze out in front of the terminal. He squinted at the license plate of a parked truck. *Florida.*

"Hmm," Nina moaned. She wiped her eyes, then sat up and leaned over Wink's lap to look out the window. "We're here," she said while sliding into her heels. She began barking orders in Spanish to her workers.

Nina wasted no time turning into the Cuban Don Diva. Wink watched her take charge of the group of men as they prepared to exit the jet, which was pulling alongside a small convoy consisting of two tinted-out Chevy Suburbans and a triple-black stretch Lincoln limo.

Nina looked back at Wink and waved him to come on. They got off the jet, looking like some foreign embassy, with the exception of Wink. He climbed in the limo behind Nina and watched as her men loaded into their trucks and led them out of the airport. One truck rode in front of the limo, while the second tailed from behind. He'd grown up with niggas on the street who had money and would flaunt with their gold and diamonds, but this was another level. This wasn't just rich; this was power.

Wink looked at the airport sign. "Why are we in Miami?" he asked.

Nina had lit one of her Virginia Slims and was fixing herself a drink from the mini bar. She took her sweet time in answering Wink. She lay back and kicked her shoes off and sighed. "We are here to relax. There will be much work ahead of us, so enjoy this time."

"But I need to get back to Detroit. I've got some people waiting on me, you know, so they can buy some more coke."

"Relax, Wink," said Nina. She slid over to the bench seat across from Wink. "Here, massage my feet. I've been needing the attention of some strong hands." Nina propped her feet in Wink's lap and closed her eyes.

Wink looked down at her pretty little feet and was tempted to do more than massage them. He had to shake the thought, stop thinking with his little head and start thinking with his big head.

What if it's a test from Franko? She's setting me up to test my loyalty. Wink shoved Nina's feet out of his lap and slid all the way over to the door, far away from her.

"What's the matter, Wink? Is it my feet? They don't smell, do they?"

"Nah, that's not it."

"Then what's the problem?" Nina set her drink down, then slid next to Wink. She got as close as close gets. "What's wrong? You don't like me, Wink?" Nina was now probing Wink's entire physique. She let her hand rest on his dick and began massaging it.

"I'm not with this, so stop," ordered Wink. He had to remove Nina's hands, but they kept coming back for more.

Nina was starting to get bold. She was kissing at Wink's neck like they were avid lovers.

"Stop!" yelled Wink.

Nina smiled as she looked into Wink's eyes. "You don't mean what you say."

"Why are you doing this? What, you call yourself testing me? I'm as loyal as they come."

The car phone in the console started ringing. Nina snatched the phone to her ear after the third ring.

"Hey, papi." She smiled.

Wink looked at Nina while she talked on the phone. *Scandalous-ass bitch*, he thought. She was probably on the phone with one of her boy-toys. *Franko gon' kill this bitch. He got his ho on some mega-boss bitch shit, and she playing games.* Wink knew Franko would find out eventually, but he wasn't gon' be the one to tell that man about his wife, nor was he going to be caught up fucking around with her.

Nina laughed, then said, "Hold on." She held the phone out to Wink. "It's for you."

Wink looked at the phone for a second before taking it. "Hello," he said, sounding a bit confused.

"Wink, how ya doin' kid? This is Franko."

"Oh, I'm good." Wink tried pushing Nina off him. She was attacking his neck with kisses.

"I'm sorry we couldn't talk on the visit, so I'll try and touch base the best I can with you now." Franko was kicked back in his counselor's office, pretending to be conducting a legal call with his attorney. "Wink, I've known your dad for years, and we have a great deal of respect for one another, which is why I am accepting you into our family with open arms. You stick with me kid, and I'm going to make you richer than your wildest dreams. The money is the easy part. Being in here is when it counts. I trust that your father has already, should I say, explained this to you?"

"Yes, and I understand." Wink's heart was beating a million miles an hour, and his dick was harder than a mothafucka 'cause Nina was relentless.

"Good. And Wink, I am glad to know you're not an easily persuaded man when it comes to loyalty. But concerning Nina—she's my wife, but there's nothing I can do to satisfy her from in here. So, if she wants you, you have my blessing. I know Nina can be persistent, and she always gets what she wants."

At that moment, Wink relaxed and stopped shoving Nina's frisky hands away from his zipper. He allowed her to unzip his pants and free his wood-hard dick. "Yes . . . I hear . . . you," Wink stuttered as Nina inhaled the head of his dick.

"Wink, my only concern is loyalty to me, and good business. You keep those two in check, and I am going to make you very rich."

"I understand, and thanks, Franko."

"No problem, kid. Tell Nina I'll call her later. Enjoy." Franko hung up like he knew what was going down in the back of the limo. Maybe he did. Nina was his wife.

Wink found the receiver to the phone and hung it up. He couldn't believe Franko was such a real mothafucka. He really didn't care that Nina had her pretty face in his lap, making love to his long, black dick. Nina was so beautiful; flawless, to be exact.

Wink could feel his stomach churning as a nut manifested and exploded in Nina's mouth. She sucked him with her eyes closed and moaned at the taste of his hot cum skeeting violently at the back of her throat.

"Shit," sighed Wink. He couldn't take it anymore. He had to pull Nina off him, because the sensation of her sucking his tender, limp dick was enough to drive any man insane.

Nina got up and fixed herself another drink and lit another cigarette. She blew a cloud of smoke through the crack of the sunroof, then gave Wink a seductive stare as he fastened his jeans.

"Did Franko tell you?"

"Tell me what?"

"That I always get what I want, and that you can have me."

Wink finished straightening himself, then looked Nina square in the face. "Yeah, he told me." Wink could understand Franko's position, knowing that Nina was going to cheat anyway, so why not let her? That way, he still felt somewhat in control. But Wink couldn't put his finger on Nina. What was her trip?

"I know you must think I'm a whore, don't you?"

Wink held her stare. "Nah, that's not what I think," he lied.

"Good, because I'm not. I am no more of a whore than a man who cheats on his wife. It just so happens that I am a woman in a man's position. I love the money, power, and respect just as much as men do." Nina sipped her Scotch and puffed her cigarette.

Wink could respect where she was coming from. Her trip was obviously power. He really didn't give a fuck about her reasoning. She had that platinum head, and Franko just green-lighted the pussy.

Wink scooted over to the bench beside Nina and went to go for his, but she smacked his hand away and said, "You've had enough for one day." Nina left him hanging. She wanted to be the aggressor, the predator, the one in control. Nina wanted to treat men just how they treated women. That's how she got hers off.

Wink said fuck it, he'd let her have her way on everything. It seemed to be the only way he could win with her.
Wink could hear Franko's voice: *She always gets what
she wants.*

Wink was right where Nina wanted him, open as a
window on a hot summer day. What was a little head?
She'd done a lot more for a lot less in her life. She had a
lock on Wink 'cause now he was thirsty to taste the pussy.
But she'd leave something for the imagination to drive
itself crazy with.

And all the while, from behind the eighteen-foot walls
of USP Leavenworth, Franko was pulling everyone's
strings. He had four other women living across America,
each calling herself his wife and running similar opera-
tions. Wink was just Franko's latest project and addition
to his billion-dollar drug empire.

Wink spent three days at Nina's exclusive estate
located on Starr Island right next to downtown Miami.
Mainly, he was learning Franko's blueprint on how he
wanted his money shipped to him and how Wink was
to receive the kilos. It was like Wink was buying into
a franchise, and he was away at one of the company's
training facilities. Franko had everything figured down
to a science, and Nina stressed the importance of not ever
improvising. J-Bo had his game, and Wink had learned a
lot from him, but this was how real playas operated. Wink
couldn't believe he was graduating to this level so soon.

"We have been doing it this way for years, and will
continue to do so," she told Wink, as if to say, "Don't
change a thing."

It was all business for the most part. The down time that they did have, Wink spent it sweatin' Nina out by the pool. She was still playing high post on him, though, not budging with the fortune between her legs.

Wink left by himself on one of Franko's private jets, stuffed with kilos of Cuban flake. Nina waved him off from the back seat of her limo and blew him a kiss.

Damn, Wink thought. He couldn't believe he hadn't got that pussy. *Next time,* he told himself as the plane prepared for takeoff. And that's exactly what Nina wanted him to look forward to—next time.

Wink tried to clear his mind of Nina and think about how he was going to lock the city down when he got back. He stared at the wood grain panels on the walls of the plane, where the bricks were secretly hidden. Franko had fronted him a hundred kilos, and he had one month to push 'em and have a steady clientele set up. Wink had plans to be moving nothing less than a thousand kilos in a year's time. Franko was gon' need a 747 to move all the work he would be pushing.

Chapter Thirty-five

While Wink was jet-setting, Trey had plugged in with the Mexican Mafia he met in Dallas. He took a hundred thousand dollars down with him, and they blessed him with twelve kilos of some primo. His connect told him if he stayed copping from them, they'd start fronting him whatever he bought, so he could build up a lot quicker. They even provided him with transportation on moving the coke back to Detroit. His connect sent two cargo vans each holding six bricks in secret compartments underneath the frame of the vans. They were willing to do whatever it took in order to make the operation work, and for them to get a stake in Detroit's drug trade.

Trey beat Wink back to the city by a day, and he was already networking and politicking with the hustlas of Detroit. Trey didn't know what he had in his possession. He was letting bricks go for eighteen hundred dollars. That was four thousand cheaper than the regular price of a key even when it wasn't a drought. He didn't have all the game Wink picked up from Gary, Fatts, and his dad. All Trey knew was that he was making a quick flip.

By the time Wink touched down in the city, Trey was on his way back to Dallas to re-up. Willie was waiting for Wink at the Detroit City Airport. He was parked near the front entrance of the terminal in his El Dogg, watching the planes land and take off. He saw Wink step off the small Lear jet and shake hands with some Spanish guy. Wink walked through the terminal and met Willie at the curb.

"What up, doe," said Wink as he climbed in the passenger seat.

"I see you hopping off private jets and whatnot. That's how we doin' it now?" Willie looked over at the plane. Two men were climbing inside.

"My nigga, give it six months and we gon' own two of them shits," said Wink. "Come on. Let's get outta here." Wink didn't want Willie seeing too much because Franko's men were about to start unloading the kilos. Nina already had everything set up. The men were to drive the hundred kilos over to Wink's storage unit and stash them. By the time Wink got there, the keys should be there waiting on him.

"You finished pushin' the rest of them bricks?"

"I been knocked them shits out. I had to grab a couple from Trey so I could serve Squirt."

Wink frowned up at Willie. "Whoa. You did what?"

"Squirt kept hittin' me up, saying he needed more work, and I was dry, so I got two bricks off Trey. Just to keep Squirt in pocket."

"Listen, from now on, if we outta work, niggas just gon' have to wait until we get back on. I don't care how much money they spending." Wink was so pissed he couldn't even stand to be around Willie. "Drop me off at my apartment."

Wink was looking at it off principle. He found Squirt and the rest of them niggas. He wasn't about to chance Trey selling them some garbage on his name, or worse, stealing them from him.

"Where is Trey ass?"

"He went back down to Dallas to re-up."

"Re-up," repeated Wink. "How many bricks he come back with the first time?"

"I think he said twelve, something like that."

Wink had underestimated his best friend. Trey was making moves. Wink just knew for sure that he and Willie would be broke by now and back on the team. Wink didn't feel any type of jealousy, 'cause after all, Trey was his nigga and would always be. It's just that now they were grown and had to be on some grown-man shit.

I'm proud of that nigga, thought Wink. He couldn't help but smile. Still, he meant every word about not sharing clientele. If Trey wanted to be his own man, then he'd have to get his own clientele. He'd have to pay for all the tricks and trades of the game just how Wink paid. Wasn't no love lost, but none would be given neither when it came to Wink's livelihood.

Willie dropped Wink off at his apartment downtown. He parked out front near the valet so they could kick it a minute.

"So, when are we gon' be back on?" asked Willie.

"It's on now, so hit everybody up and let 'em know the store's open."

"A'ight. I got that bread for you too. When you want it?"

"I'll grab it off you later on when I finish gettin' myself together. But Willie, before I go, I gotta ask you something, my nigga."

"What's up, Wink?"

"I know that we're all crew, but this here is business. Whose team are you on?"

"What you mean?"

"Whose plate are you eating off of, mine's of Trey's?"

"Damn. My nigga, it's like you asking me to choose between my two best friends."

"This ain't got nothin' to do with friendship. This is about money!" Wink watched Willie as he gazed out the window.

Willie didn't want to be on one side versus the other. He just wanted for all of them to make money and still be a crew. "I knew this was going to happen."

"I'ma give you some time to think about it. In the meantime, it's business as usual." Wink reached over and gave Willie some dap. "Holla at me later," he said as he climbed out the car.

Wink watched as Willie pulled away from the curb. He knew Willie didn't mean no harm, but the stakes were a lot higher, and it was past due time to start playing for keeps.

When Wink got up to his apartment, he took a hot shower. While he stood under the steaming water, Wink planned on how he would take over Detroit's drug trade. With the connect he had, Wink had the potential to be the biggest thing to ever come out the city since GM made Cadillac. That was his goal from the start, back when he used to sit on the porch and idolize J-Bo. But now, not even a year into the game, he'd already surpassed anything J-Bo could have ever done, and he owed a great deal of that to his dad.

Wink could hear his dad's voice from their first visit, when he told him that Gary snitched on him. "You can live through me," Wink said as he turned the water off. He grabbed a towel and dried off while walking through the apartment.

Wink stopped in the living room and stared at the red flashing light on his answering machine. He had twenty-one messages. He pushed the message button and braced himself as his sharp-tongued grandmother's voice came across the machine

"Wayne, you need to get your ass over here and see about your mother. . . ."

Blah, blah, blah. Wink stopped listening when she mentioned his mother.

The next nineteen messages were also from his grandmother, the good churchgoing woman who cursed more than ten sailors lost at sea.

"I ain't try'na hear that shit," said Wink as he started walking away.

Message number twenty-one said: "Hi, Wink. It's me, Armeeah."

Wink stopped and turned around at the sound of her sweet voice.

"I was just calling to say hello. I see that you're not in, so I'll try and reach you some other time. Take care. Bye." *Beep.*

Damn, thought Wink. He was tight because he didn't have her number. The only way to get in touch with her was to go up to the Coney Island, where her hound dog father would be watching over her shoulder. Wink had to see her, though. He got dressed and was out the door. He figured he'd spend some time with Armeeah now because in a minute, the only free time he'd have would be to count money and go re-up with Nina.

Wink jumped in his El Dogg and drove up to the Coney Island on 8 Mile Rd. He could see Armeeah through the front glass. She was waiting on some women on the inside. Wink could also see her greasy-ass father working the grill, so he decided to take the drive-thru.

"Welcome to Coney Island. May I take your order?"

"Let me get a ten-piece wing dinner with a side of chili cheese fries."

"Okay, please drive around to the window."

Wink leaned his seat all the way back so Armeeah's dad wouldn't see him when he pulled up to the window. Armeeah's face lit up with a smile at the sight of Wink. She looked over her shoulder to make sure that her dad wasn't watching. She scribbled something onto a napkin, then quickly stuffed it inside the bag with the food.

Wink dug the napkin out and read the note aloud. "I get off in ten minutes. Wait for me. Please." Wink looked up at Armeeah and smiled. He nodded, then pulled over next to the pay phone and parked. He chowed down on his wings and chili fries while he waited for Armeeah.

She walked out the front door and crossed the lot and got in her car. Wink waited a few seconds, then pulled out behind her and followed her down to the Tubby's submarine shop on the corner of Ryan and 8 Mile Rd. Wink got out his car and got in with Armeeah.

"Hey," said Armeeah as she reached over to give Wink a hug.

"I take it you missed me," said Wink.

"I did. Where have you been?"

"I had to make a run outta town. I wish you coulda came with me. It would've been a lot more fun."

"Me too. Where'd you go?"

"Miami."

"I am so jealous. I know the weather was beautiful this time of year."

"Yeah. Maybe next time I can steal you away for a few days. We can lay on the beach and soak up some sun and drink those little fruity drinks."

"My parents would never let me go." Armeeah's mood shifted. It was like she was living in a prison.

"You can say your school or class is taking the trip."

"Wink, I can't lie to my parents. Besides, my father would probably double check behind me. He's done it in the past."

"Armeeah, how old are you?"

"Twenty-one."

"You're a grown woman, in case you didn't know it. I understand and respect your family's way of doing things, but how long are we going to have to sneak around? What if you were my girlfriend? I'd still have to sneak and see you?"

"You want to make me your girlfriend, Wink?"

"I thought about it. While I was away, you were all I could think about. I couldn't wait to get back so I could do this." Wink reached over and kissed Armeeah.

It was against her religion for her to be kissing Wink, and if her parents caught them, they'd kill her, but it felt so good and so right. Armeeah closed her eyes and enjoyed Wink's passionate kiss.

Wink wanted to go a step further, but he remembered his father telling him to be patient with her because she was worth it. Wink pulled Armeeah up for some air. It took her a minute to gather her senses. She had never been kissed like that in her life.

"Does that answer your question?" asked Wink.

Armeeah looked him in the eyes with that seductive yet innocent stare. "Yes, it does." She leaned over and pecked Wink on the lips. "As for my parents, we'll have to give them some time. I have an idea. Why don't you come to Jumah with me as a guest this Friday?"

"You mean like Muslim service?"

"Yes. It'll be good for my parents to see you there. And I think you'd like the service."

"I don't know. Let me think about it."

"Okay. I have to get ready for class. I'm actually running late," said Armeeah as she looked at the dashboard clock.

"Nah, I wanted to steal you away for the day. You can miss one day of class for me."

Armeeah thought it over for a moment. "I'll make a deal with you. I'll skip my class tonight, but only if you agree to come to Jumah with me Friday. It's like the lesser of the two evils." Armeeah smiled.

"Deal." How bad could it be? It wasn't like she was asking him to become Muslim.

"So, where are we going?"

"We're going to spend the rest of the day in Paradise." Wink pulled on the door handle and told Armeeah to follow him.

Wink took Armeeah to the Purple Garden day spa out in Orchard Lake, Michigan. He had never been there before, but he'd always see the commercial advertising its incredible services and thought it would be a good way to splurge on Armeeah. He treated her to a full body massage, manicure, pedicure, and facial.

After three hours of being pampered, Armeeah found Wink sweating it out in the spa's co-ed hot tub. Wink had his eyes closed, with his head leaned back against the edge of the tub. Armeeah took a seat on the edge of the tub. She leaned down and kissed Wink's lips softly.

"Hmm. You enjoy yourself?" Wink asked.

"Yes, I have never been to a spa before. I really enjoyed the hot stone massage, and especially the facial." Armeeah was glowing. She wore only a lavender bath towel wrapped around her chest, stopping just shy of her kitty cat. Wink let his eyes explore her every curve.

"Are you listening to me, Wink?"

"You are so beautiful. You know that?"

Armeeah blushed. "Thank you."

"Come on. Get in with me." Wink held his hand out for Armeeah's.

"But I don't have anything on under my towel."

"I'll close my eyes. Come on."

Armeeah thought about her chastity as a Muslimah. She stood up and locked the sauna's door, then stepped back over to the hot tub. Wink held out his hand again.

"No, close your eyes and no peeking." Armeeah waited for Wink to close his eyes, then she quickly dropped her towel and got in the tub, dipping her body down to where the water covered her chest.

"Can I open my eyes now?" Wink asked with a huge smile on his face. He was enjoying the fact he had a woman who still guarded herself. Any other chick would have just climbed right on in and been fucking by now.

Armeeah made sure she was situated in her corner far across from Wink. "Yes, you can open them now."

"Why you way over there?" Without waiting for an answer, Wink treaded over to Armeeah. She was all tensed up, and Wink could see the nervousness in her eyes, so he told her to close them.

Armeeah did as he said, but it didn't help her heart from racing a thousand miles per second. Her thoughts went straight to her parents and what they'd do if they knew she was naked in a hot tub with a non-Muslim man.

Wink kissed all around her neck until he felt Armeeah starting to relax. She leaned her head back and let her hands subconsciously guide Wink's head. He kissed his way down to her chest, then cupped one of her breasts, pulling it up from the water and into his mouth. Before she knew it, Armeeah was lost in sheer pleasure. She squirmed from the arousal building between her legs and dug her nails into Wink's shoulders. He silenced her moans with a wet, passionate kiss, all the while spreading her legs wide and positioning himself between them. Wink put his hand under water and found the buried treasure Armeeah had been keeping from him. He played with her clitoris until he felt it expanding, and he watched Armeeah's facial expressions. His slow, circular rotation was killing her softly. He tried to put his finger inside her, but her pussy was tighter than a nigga with his last dollar. Wink had to start with his pinky finger and work his way up to his index.

"Oh, Wink," moaned Armeeah as Wink struggled to get the head of his dick inside her.

Armeeah cried out in Arabic as Wink tore through her walls and began slow stroking her. Her pussy was so tight, Wink could only get half his dick inside. He took his time and was careful not to hurt her. But still, Armeeah cried out seductively in Arabic with every thrust, and she embedded her nails deep into Wink's back.

Wink pulled Armeeah up from the water with her legs still wrapped around his waist and half his nine-inch dick stuffed inside her. She clung to him like wet clothes as he slid her up and down on his dick. Armeeah came for the fifth time, but this time Wink joined her. His knees buckled a little bit from the sensation as he shot a load inside her.

They lay back in the tub, both exhausted and extremely satisfied. Armeeah curled up under Wink like an infant. She couldn't believe she had just given her chastity to a man who wasn't her husband.

"Wink, you're not going to leave me, are you?" she softly asked while playing in his chest hairs.

"No. Why would you say that?"

"I don't know," Armeeah said in a low tone.

Wink thought about what his dad told him about taking his time with Armeeah because she was worth the wait. Wink pulled her even closer to him and kissed her forehead. "You don't ever have to worry about me leavin' you, okay?"

"Okay."

Wink wasn't sure if that meant marrying Armeeah or what, but he meant not leaving her. And if it became an issue whether they had to marry in order to stay together, Wink wasn't ruling it out. He knew from the moment he laid eyes on Armeeah that she was the one.

Chapter Thirty-six

Wink woke up the next morning with money on his mind. He had one hundred bricks waiting to be pushed on the crack-thirsty streets of Detroit, and Willie was blowing up his pager like crazy, letting him know that niggas were trying to get on.

Wink put his grindin' gear on—Carhartt coat, skull cap, thermal pants, and Timberland boots. Oh yeah, and his 9 mm Glock. He grabbed his keys off the dresser and was out the door. He climbed in his sparkling pearl-white El Dogg and pulled out of his apartment complex, heading straight for his storage unit.

Wink backed his Caddy up to the garage door, then got out to open the sliding door. When he opened the door, two large brown boxes sat in the middle of the floor, side by side. He used his key to slit the tape on one of the boxes, then pulled its flaps open. As promised, there sat bricks of cocaine wrapped in brown wrappers with a five-point star stamped in the center of each kilo. There were fifty keys in the first box and another fifty in the second one.

Wink packed his trunk with the first fifty bricks and locked the storage unit back up. He climbed behind the wheel and put his seat belt on and carefully pulled out of the unit's parking lot. He crossed back over into Detroit and called Willie on his car phone.

"Where you at?" asked Wink.

"I'm wherever you need me to meet you," said Willie.

"Shit, uh . . . Meet me at the laundromat on Anglin and 7 Mile Rd. Bring that with you, and don't have nobody with you."

"A'ight, in a minute."

Wink shot over to the 'mat and parked near the alley with his trunk facing the building. A few minutes later, Willie pulled into the gravel parking lot in his El Dogg. He got out the car and got in with Wink.

"Here you go, my nigga," Willie said, handing Wink a duffle bag. "It's five grand short. You know I had to hit the mall up."

"I ain't trippin'." Wink put the bag in the back seat on the floor. "But what's up, though? You blowing me up like crack going outta style."

"Nah, I had hit Gucci, Squirt, and JC up and told 'em I should be straight today, so they been paging me all morning, try'na see if shit back on. Is we on?"

"Is we? I got fifty slabs in the trunk. The store back open, and this time we ain't closing."

"It's like that?" Willie asked, excited.

"My nigga, we 'bout to lock the city down. All you gotta do is keep pushing the way you been doin'. For these first couple trips, though, I'ma need you to grind it out with me so we can keep flippin'. So for right now, just take two G's off every slab you sell. Bring me back the other twenty stacks."

"Shit, that's a bet. Two G's off every brick. That's more than love. Especially when them shits is already sold. I got an order for thirty right now, all in all. Plus, once the word hit—"

"Whoa, whoa, slow down, baby. Remember the plan. We're not dealing with everybody. We gon' continue to fuck with JC, Squirt, and Gucci for right now. Let them get all the attention while we got the money. In a couple more flips, we gon' take our show on the road and find us a few niggas in other major cities who gettin' money. Take Offy's fake Nigerian Mob boss ass down there and run the same script. It's the only way we gon' last, you feel me?"

"I got you, Nino Brown." Willie laughed.

"Don't compare me to that nigga. He turned out to be a rat in the end."

"I'm just fuckin' with you. But yeah, that's a bet. Let's get this money."

Wink got quiet for a moment as he stared out the window at the snowbanks mounted toward the alley. "I take it you still haven't come up with an answer to my question."

"What's that?" asked Willie.

"Whose team are you on, mine's or Trey's?"

"You still on that, Wink?"

"Yeah, I'm still on it, 'cause it's real. My nigga, I need to know, 'cause I'm playin' for keeps 'bout this paper."

"Fuck it. I'm on yo' side. There, you happy?"

"Nah, I'll be happy when we're sittin' on millions and pushin' a thousand bricks a month. But you answered my question. Willie, don't ever cross me, you hear me?" Wink turned and looked Willie dead in the eyes with that stern killer look that lived in his father's eyes. "Let no money, bitches, fame, jail, or nothin' else ever come between us. We gon' ride till the wheels fall off. When Krazy gets out, he gon' be with us, and hopefully, Trey will come around. But for now, it's us."

Willie didn't know where all this was coming from, 'cause he had never dreamed about crossing Wink or his crew in a million years. It was almost like Wink was lightweight threatening him.

Willie didn't understand what his friend was going through with knowing that all his dad's partners had ratted him out and got him two life sentences. The shit was really fucking with Wink, and it just made him view everything and everyone around him in another light.

"I'm with you, my nigga," said Willie. He reached over and gave Wink some dap and a half hug.

Wink reached for the glove box and popped the trunk. "Leave five bricks and take the rest. I'ma send the other ones down to Ball."

"Yeah, please do, 'cause his fat ass been blowin' me up too. After I snatch this money up, I'ma shoot down there for a couple days."

"A'ight, just hit me up so we can hurry up and get rid of the rest of them shits. We try'na cop and flip."

Willie grabbed the door handle and said, "I'm on it. Just keep yo' pager on."

Wink watched as Willie unloaded forty-five kilos from his trunk into the back seat of his 'Lac. Willie climbed in his car and hit his horn, then pulled out of the parking lot. It was time to get down to business.

Wink pulled out behind Willie but went in the opposite direction on 7 Mile. He made a quick stop at African World beauty supply store and bought up a bunch of organic soaps and scented candles, then he shot over to UPS on Hoover Rd. Wink bought two mid-size boxes and packaged the five keys inside the boxes, two in one and three in the other. He lined the candles and soap around the sides of the box, then placed the kilos inside and covered the top with more bars of soap. Wink wrapped the boxes in tape right there in his trunk inside the UPS parking lot, then carried them inside the station and mailed them.

Wink called Ball on his car phone as he cruised down State Fair. "Yeah, I got something comin' yo' way, so be at the house on point."

"A'ight, my nigga. I was starting to think the worst 'cause I ain't heard from y'all," said Ball.

"Nah, everything is in place. It's two boxes instead of one. That should hold you for a minute."

"I'm on my way to the crib now. I'ma hit you up when it touches down."

"A'ight. One." Wink put the phone back on the hook and closed the arm rest. He stretched out with one hand on the wheel and began doing the math in his head. He just gave Willie forty-five bricks at twenty thousand a piece. That was nine hundred thousand, plus the five bricks Ball had coming. That was another hundred fifty thousand, 'cause he was taxing his ass like the IRS at thirty thousand a key.

That's a million and some change, Wink thought. Plus, he still had fifty slabs in the storage unit, not to mention the half ticket in the back seat.

"Two and a half million," said Wink. That was his final total with everything. He owed Franko only five hundred thousand, 'cause he fronted him the kilos at five thousand each. Wink would be left with two million to the good and off just one flip. He was already making million-dollar plans, too. The first thing he was going to do was start paying for his work up front. That way he could demand a better deal and be able to cop more.

Wink decided he'd put up a hundred thousand dollars this go-around and see if Nina would give him at least 225 kilos. He would owe Franko a dime, and he'd have enough work to start working on his second plan, which was to branch out into other major cities. Wink could see it—the top wasn't too far of a climb up. With Franko backing him, the sky was the limit.

Wink did as Nina told him. He drove out to the Sheridan Inn next to the Metro Airport in Romulus, Michigan. She had given him a room key inside the hotel before he got on the plane to go back to Detroit. Wink was to leave the five hundred thousand in the room inside the bathtub and call Nina once he made the drop. Nina would then send her goons to pick up the money and somehow, it would find its way back to Miami and eventually into one of Franko's offshore accounts.

Wink made the drop. He left the duffle bag in the tub and locked the room up. Nina had explained to him during the training process that it was best for everyone involved to do business like that, so no one would have to worry about new faces. The operation was in place and had been working, so there was no need to change it.

The one thing Wink asked himself was if Franko was so smart, what was he doing in prison? Wink chalked it up to the same reason his dad was sitting in prison: trusting the wrong people. He was determined to learn from both their mistakes, and in the meantime, he was going to get filthy rich.

Wink drove down Trey's street to find him posted on the hood of a brand-new fire engine red Benz tucked nicely on some chrome hammers. He had on a three-quarter length mink with the matching mink Dob hat and some blocks on his feet. The scene wouldn't be complete without, of course, an entourage of niggas and hood rats to shine on. Trey wouldn't have it no other way. It was dead winter, and here was this fool, out in the cold just for the sake of wanting to be seen and heard. Trey was so busy entertaining he hadn't even seen Wink pull up and park.

"Look at this nigga," Wink said to himself. He wasn't about to get out and kick it amongst all the off-brand niggas hanging from Trey's coat tail. Wink hit his horn twice, and Trey turned around with a huge grin on his face. He excused himself from his groupies and crossed the street.

"Tell Wink he ain't gotta be actin' all brand new on a bitch!" yelled Chante. "Actin' like he too good to get out the car and whatnot."

"You hear yo' baby momma, nigga," Trey teased as he climbed in the car.

"That bitch like two-week-old milk. She been expired," snapped Wink. He pulled the neck shift down to drive and slid off.

"What's up, doe? Where da fuck you been at?" Trey asked. He fired up a blunt.

"Shit, I should be asking you that. I see you dropped the new Benz. What you do with the Caddy?'

"I gave that shit to my little man, Lee-Mac."

"Who the hell is Lee-Mac?"

"You don't know him," said Trey. He tried to pass Wink the blunt, but he waved it off.

"If I don't know the nigga, then neither do you. You out there with ya fan club, Trey. You don't know none of them niggas for real. Niggas is grimy out here. I know you got ya little connect and whatnot, but that don't mean stop thinkin'."

"I got this, my nigga. What you need to do is get on the team and help me get this money."

Wink laughed like, *Yeah, right.* "I'm straight, my dude. Believe me, I'm good."

"Oh, so what? You too good to work up under me?" asked Trey. "You can't stand me having the connect, can you?"

"Trey, that has nothin' to do with it."

"Then what is it?"

"I got my own connect. That's what I was try'na tell you to hold up before you took all yo' money out the pot. You jumped the gun, but I guess you wanted to do your own thing. It's all good. All I'm saying, my nigga, is be careful out here, 'cause niggas playing for keeps."

There was a long silence between them. Trey puffed on his blunt and stared blankly out his window at the passing traffic. Truth be told, both of them wanted to be the man, but neither would ever come out and say it. Growing up, that was how it was. They were always equals. So now, neither could see themselves as anything less.

Wink reached his hand over to Trey and held it out until Trey embraced him.

"My nigga, we gotta promise each other that no matter what's out here in the streets, we can never let it come between us as family," said Wink.

"Family," said Trey.

Deep down, Wink had nothing but love for Trey, but he wasn't about to play himself on the strength of a four-letter word. He loved his mother all his life and he saw what happened with her. Wink would play it fair with Trey on the strength of their history, but he'd feed his ass, just like everybody else, with a long spoon. He was certain Trey was sittin' over there thinking the same thing and refusing to be rocked to sleep. They both wanted one thing—to be the man.

Chapter Thirty-seven

Armeeah wasn't letting Wink out of the deal they made about him attending Jumah services with her. It was Friday, and every Muslim in the city of Detroit and Dearborn were closing up their places of business, heading for the mosque.

Armeeah left work early so she could pick Wink up at his apartment. When she got there, he was still asleep, stretched out across the sofa. He passed out the night before while counting up the money Willie had been dropping off.

Wink's eyes rolled to the back of his head, and then he came to at the sound of someone knocking on the front door. He sat up and looked at the money scattered about the coffee table. He had lost count. The knocking broke his train of thought.

"Who is it?" he asked, reaching for the 9 mm next to him.

"Armeeah."

"One minute." Wink tucked the gun into his waist, and then hurriedly stuffed the money into the gym bag Willie gave him. Wink rushed over to the closet and tossed the bag inside, then made sure his gun wasn't bulging from his pants before opening the door.

"Morning, sunshine," said Wink as he let Armeeah in.

She pecked him on the lips and then stopped in the living room. "It's almost noon. Why aren't you dressed?"

Wink flopped down on the sofa and stretched out. "Dressed for what?" he asked, turning on the TV.

"Today is Friday. Remember our deal for you to come with me to Jumah?"

Wink closed his eyes. "Damn, that's right. Baby, can't we go some other time? I'm still a little tired from last night."

"No, a deal's a deal, Wink. Now, come on and get up, 'cause I don't want to be late." Armeeah walked around the sofa and pulled Wink up by the arm. "Come on. Let's take a shower. You have to be clean for the service," said Armeeah. She pulled Wink down the hall toward the bathroom.

Wink was wide awake now. He stripped down to his boxers on the way to the bathroom. He heard Armeeah say "let's take a shower" like she was getting in with him. His dick rocked up and was poking out the leg of his boxers just at the thought of seeing Armeeah naked.

Armeeah started a hot shower and set out a towel and wash cloth. "There, nice and hot. Five minutes, baby. We need to get going."

Armeeah went to walk out the bathroom, but Wink grabbed her arm. "Where you going? I thought you were going to shower with me." Wink was all geeked up, and Armeeah could see the lust in his eyes.

"If I were to get in with you, we'd definitely be late. Maybe when we get back." Armeeah teased Wink on her way out the bathroom by letting her nails trail down his chest to his six pack. "Hurry up." She smiled seductively, then closed the door.

She gon' stop playin' these games, Wink thought as he stepped out of the boxers and into the shower. He was so geeked up that he had to take a cold shower just to cool down.

When he finished his shower, he found his clothes set out on the bed. Armeeah had laid out a pair of black slacks and a crisp white button-up. Wink could hear her rummaging around in his walk-in closet. He took a seat at the edge of the bed and began rubbing lotion on his arms. Armeeah walked out the closet carrying a pair of black Gucci loafers.

"My mom stopped dressing me in grade school," said Wink.

"Very funny." She smiled. "I just want you to look nice for the service, and besides, my parents will be there."

Don't remind me, thought Wink. He had no desire to meet her father because he just seemed like an old, grumpy man who thought no man God created was good enough for his daughter.

"Here, let me do it." Armeeah took the bottle of Jergens lotion from Wink. "Lay down on your back," she ordered.

Wink stared up at the ceiling while Armeeah squirted the cold lotion across his chest, then massaged it deep into his pores. Her touch was so sensual and relaxing, Wink couldn't help but close his eyes and pretend that he was back at the spa.

Wink thought to himself, *Yeah, I can get used to this.* He had never been with a woman who only cared about taking care of her man.

That's all Armeeah wanted to do—take care of Wink and please him in any way that she could. She had him roll over to his stomach and lotioned his back, down his legs, and even hitting between his toes.

"All done," she said, rubbing Wink's back.

"Mmmm," moaned Wink. He had drifted off to sleep. The massage felt so good.

"Get up, baby, and get dressed." Armeeah kissed Wink on the neck, then stood up and left the room.

When Wink finished getting dressed, he walked out to the living room to find Armeeah in the kitchen at the stove. She had fixed him a quick cheese omelet with two link sausages and some wheat toast.

"I might as well move you on in," said Wink. He wrapped his arms around Armeeah's waist and kissed her neck while she emptied the skillet onto a plate.

"What you think about that?" he whispered in her ear. "Hmm."

"I think my father would kill the both of us. Come on and eat your breakfast."

Wink took a seat at the island on a stool. "I can't blame the old man. If I had a daughter half as beautiful as you, I wouldn't let her outta my sight neither."

Armeeah blushed. "Eat your food. We don't want to be late for the service."

The only thing Wink didn't like about their relationship was that they were still sneaking around, tippy-toeing around her garlic-breath father and whatnot. They always had to meet up somewhere, versus Wink picking Armeeah up at home like a real boyfriend. The shit was starting to irk Wink, and it had to stop soon!

Armeeah didn't want to ride in the same car to the mosque because someone might see them. Her plan was to tell her parents that Wink was her classmate and she invited him to attend Jumah as a visitor.

The Al-Amin Mosque was situated right on the county line of Dearborn, Michigan. Wink pulled into the parking lot behind Armeeah and parked near the entrance, while she parked two rows over. Wink watched the traffic while he waited on Armeeah to get out of her car. Arab men were ushering their families inside the mosque. Their wives wore full niqabs. The only thing visible were their eyes and hands. Even the little girls wore niqabs.

Just as two young boys playfully ran past the hood of Wink's Caddy, Armeeah tapped on the driver-side window. Wink didn't recognize her because she had slipped into her full black niqab while she was in the car.

"Come on. Service is about to start," said Armeeah as she opened Wink's door.

"Armeeah, am I going to be the only black man in here?" Wink asked as they approached the entrance of the mosque.

"You will be fine. If someone asks, just tell them you are visiting."

That wasn't answering Wink's question, but then again, it was. There wasn't a black face in sight but Wink's. His stomach turned as he held the door open for Armeeah and walked in behind her. Armeeah gave greetings to a group of brothers standing in the foyer.

"Alaikum As-Salaam," they all said in unison, but in a low tone. Their eyes locked on the back of Wink's head.

Wink could hear them whispering something in Arabic. He didn't speak the language, but he was certain they were talking about his black ass and what he was doing there.

How I let her talk me into this, I don't know. Wink followed Armeeah inside the masjid. She led him over to the visitor section, which was completely empty.

"I have to go take wudu. I'll see you after the service," whispered Armeeah.

"You're not going to sit with me?" Wink was already feeling extremely uncomfortable, being the only black person in the mosque. Now Armeeah was talking about leaving him all by himself.

Armeeah turned and pointed at the two rows of women seated behind the men on the prayer rug. "I have to sit amongst the community; otherwise, I would sit with you." Armeeah sat Wink down and said, "I'll explain it more later. I have to go."

She rushed off at the calling of the adhan, which is the Muslim prayer call. Everyone ceased what they were doing. Some whispered the sacred chant in unison with the caller.

"Allahu Akbar. Allahu Akbar. La ilaha illallah . . ." The caller took his seat on the prayer rug in the front row.

A few minutes later, Imam Abdul bin Baz stood up and began reciting surahs from the Quran. "Bismallah al-Rahmanir al-Raheem. All praise is to Allah alone, and may His peace and blessings be upon His Messenger and slave, our Prophet Muhammad, his family, and his companion. Alhumdulillahi rabil alamin. We are blessed with another Al-Jumu'ah…"

For the most part, Imam Abdul spoke in Arabic, so Wink missed bits and pieces. But he was still able to follow from the brief English passages Imam Abdul would recite from the Quran.

"Allah is the protector of those who have faith: From the depths of darkness, He will lead them forth into light. Of those who reject faith, the patrons are the Evil ones: from light, they will lead them forth into the depths of darkness. They will be companions of the fire, to dwell therein (forever)."

It was as if he were speaking directly to Wink, because every time he spoke in English, he would stare dead at Wink. That could have been the case, but it also could have been Wink's conscience, or lack thereof. He told himself that he ain't never killed nobody that didn't deserve it, and somehow, that made it right to him. The lesson was about the hypocrites, Al Munafiqun, the imam called them, citing Surah 63 from the Quran.

The service only lasted about forty-five minutes. Then they all stood for congregational prayer. Wink listened as Imam Abdul recited Al-Fatiha. Wink didn't understand a single word of it, but it had to be the most beautiful thing he'd ever heard before in his life. Wink thought about his father and wondered if he was at Jumah service at the prison. He couldn't wait to go and see him again. He even thought about taking Armeeah with him so she could meet his dad.

Wink's daydream was cut short as everyone stood up and Imam Abdul salaamed the congregation. In unison, they all returned the greeting, and with that, service was over.

Armeeah said a few hellos to some of her friends. They all grinned and snickered as Armeeah showed them Wink. She said her goodbyes and then found her mother so she could meet Wink. Wink stood up and pulled out his manners as Armeeah ushered her mom over to him.

"Ma, I would like you to meet Wayne. He's in my business management class."

"How are you, ma'am?" Wink extended his hand for Armeeah's mother.

"Are you Muslim?" asked Armeeah's mom.

"No, ma'am. But Armeeah has been sharing with me the teachings of Islam, and she invited me here for service."

"Alhamdulillah. Well, I hope to see you next Friday," Armeeah's mom said as if it were a question.

"Insha'Allah, mother." Armeeah grabbed a hold of her mom's hand and led her away.

"Nice meeting you, Wayne," her mom said over her shoulder.

Armeeah waved Wink out the masjid. He met her in the parking lot next to her car. Wink looked Armeeah in the eyes and waited for her to say something.

"I think my mom likes you."

"Yeah. Well, it's not her I'm worried about. What's up with your dad? I saw him in there. When am I going to meet him?"

"I think next time would be best. Let's give my mother some time to speak up for you. She always gets what she wants with my dad."

"What are you about to do now?"

"I have to open the restaurant for the evening. But I'll be off around eleven."

"Call me when you get off. I have a few things I need to do for the day, but I definitely would like to end my day with you in my arms."

Armeeah blushed, then said, "We'll see." She looked over Wink's shoulder and saw her parents coming out of the mosque. "I better get going. I'll call you," she said before climbing into her Audi.

Wink always felt at peace when he was with Armeeah. She just had this sense of purity and positiveness about her that put Wink at ease. He didn't feel like he had to have his guards up when they were together, because she didn't have any hidden agendas, unlike the niggas in them grimy streets he yearned to rule.

Wink climbed in his Caddy and pulled out of the parking lot. Imam Abdul's words had gone in one ear and out the other. It was time to hit the streets and see what he could turn up. Willie should have been about done with those other fifty bricks, and if so, it was time to go see Nina and re-up.

To Be Continued

The Good Life 2: The Re-up

Coming Soon

Maggie K. Black is an award-winning journalist and romantic suspense author with an insatiable love of traveling the world. She has lived in the American South, Europe and the Middle East. She now makes her home in Canada with her history teacher husband, their two beautiful girls and a small but mighty dog. Maggie enjoys connecting with her readers at maggiekblack.com.

Books by Maggie K. Black

Love Inspired Suspense

True North Bodyguards

Kidnapped at Christmas

Killer Assignment
Deadline
Silent Hunter
Headline: Murder
Christmas Blackout
Tactical Rescue

Visit the Author Profile page at Harlequin.com.